Whipped Cream

and

PIANO WIRE

Winnie Simpson

Readers are encouraged to go to www.MissionPointPress.com to contact the author or to find information on how to buy this book in bulk at a discounted rate.

MISSION POINT PRESS

Published by Mission Point Press
2554 Chandler Rd.
Traverse City, MI 49696
(231) 421-9513

www.MissionPointPress.com

ISBN: 978-1-954786-03-5 (softcover)
ISBN: 978-1-954786-27-1 (hardcover)

Library of Congress Control Number: 2021907438

Printed in the United States of America

Whipped Cream

and

PIANO WIRE

THE FIRST ANN AUDREY MYSTERY

WINNIE SIMPSON

MISSION POINT PRESS

For Sarah

1

July 1999
It Started Out

I n the blistering summer of 1999, I was forced to solve my first murder. At the time, I was living in peaceful seclusion, a retired lawyer hidden away after years of tasteless and tacky media attention, my notoriety achieved when I testified against my husband Charlie and his criminal enterprise. But that's a different story. This story is about my best friend Theo, her affair with the wrong man, and the secret that led to his death.

On this typical July day Atlanta simmered with nasty smog, the byproduct of summer heat and too many tailpipes. During the 1990's Atlanta became a boom town. People moved here at the rate of 360 per day, more than 650,000 to the northern suburbs; a mere 170,000 to the southside. All of those suburbanites driving into and out of town pushed Atlanta to number 1—out of all metros on Earth—for the longest average daily commute. Frustrated drivers sweated on the Downtown Connector, 42 floors below my air-conditioned condo, my private retreat from speculative news reports about me and my role in my husband's takedown.

I'd spent the last years trying to forget the embarrassment of seeing my face every time I turned on the local news, the endless depositions, trial and my husband's sentencing. I sold the home we'd shared and moved into a high-rise complete with security and a protective concierge. I left my law practice, changed my routine and ignored the few friends who hadn't already dropped me. Only Theo had refused to be ignored, pestering me and nudging me to get my life back.

I turned away from watching the creeping traffic and looked upward to the north Georgia mountains. The view through floor-to-ceiling windows was fogged with pollution, but far out, deep summer-green hills rolled on beyond the sprawl of asphalt and concrete. It was too hot for my usual run along the Chattahoochee River. Instead, I planned to stay in with the Sunday *New York Times*, now spread around the living room, on sofas, glass coffee table, part of the pale rug. Coverage of the search for John Kennedy, Jr.'s private plane eclipsed stories about Hillary Clinton's run for the Senate from New York. As I read on, a hair dryer whirred in the background. Theo Humphries, the real star of this tale, had finally started her day.

Theo was single again, after her third husband, and the love of her life, George Humphries, keeled over and died at the wheel of his golf cart, still clutching a gin and tonic. She continued to live in their house on Sea Island, but since George's death, routinely turned up at my place in Atlanta—ostensibly to spend some of the pile of money George left her, but really, to try and drag me out of my retreat.

Short and buxom, Theo wore her thick straight hair cropped, voluminous and fluffed, a Southern tribute to Princess Diana. Every strand was scrupulously washed and blown to perfection each morning, sometime after ten a.m., because, god forbid she ever rolled herself out of the guest room's queen-sized bed before nine, and then only moving at the speed of January sorghum. I'd learned to bide my time until she emerged. With the buzz of the hair dryer in the background, I settled down to read.

"You're jiggling your foot and talking to yourself again," said Theo, who'd walked out from the guest room barefoot. She critically examined her feet, then bent over and rooted around in the bottom of a huge Birkin bag. "Have you seen my nail polish?"

My brain snapped to attention at the mention of nail polish. Before marriage to George Humphries, Theo always painted her toenails when she was carrying on a love affair. The impending pedicure was a blaring signal that she was up to something.

"Oh, here it is," she said, retrieving the small jar of coral polish. She unscrewed the top and placed the opened nail polish on a Time magazine cover of George W. Bush as the front-runner for the GOP nomination. She sat down and propped her feet on the cocktail table, grunting as she bent forward to squint at her toes. She adjusted her glasses before painting all ten without a drop spilled. Capping the nail polish, Theo pushed back into the depth of the sofa cushions and sighed.

"Annie, I think I may be in love again." As she spoke, she gazed at her lurid toes. It was a neat pedicure, but her toes weren't worth the dewy attention she was giving them. She looked like a cat that had just downed an opened can of tuna behind her owner's back. Not guilty—because Theo never felt guilty about her affairs—just aware that she had gotten away with something and was fine with it. That look was a giveaway.

"Is he married?" I was curious, so I was careful not to imply any criticism that would cause Theo to clam up. "Not that I mind, unless some wife shoots you."

I suspected Theo had narrowly dodged spousal fire in the past. At the reception following George's funeral, I stood in the corner inhaling a vodka Collins to obliterate the pain of wearing high heels. To distract myself, I watched a clutch of Pilates-lean women chatting together, their backs to their husbands who clustered around the grieving widow, Theo Humphries.

Wives who disregarded Theo were taking a risk. Theo likes men, and they like her. Women often are blindsided by men's reaction to Theo, with her glasses and unfashionably full-bodied figure. Theo's technique is subtle and sincere. She can engage the shyest man in a spirited tête-à-tête, making him feel handsome and clever. I recalled the party where Theo—who cannot multiply nine times seven in her head, but can beat me at chess every game—charmed a handsome and boring CPA into believing that Theo understood his explanation of the tax treatment of offshore hedge funds. Great boobs and full attention to your conversation. What man could resist?

"It's not like that," Theo said, scooching forward on the couch. "Cutler's been separated from his wife for many, many years. In fact, they have separate homes here in Atlanta."

"Cutler?" I scratched my memory until I remembered. "You mean, that developer?"

"That's right," said Theo, "Cutler Mead."

I'd met the man a few times when I'd visited Theo and George on Sea Island. Theo's husband was a successful investor, but quiet about it. Cutler Mead, on the other hand, was always bragging about his latest project. I didn't get the attraction. On the other hand, before her marriage to George, Theo had proven her wide-ranging taste in men. There had been that charming politician, the dog trainer who could have been a model, the lanky artist who'd painted Theo au naturel, the professional football player who gave new meaning to tight end, to name just a few. And George had been dead a few years now.

"If he and his wife are really living apart," I said, "why hasn't he gotten a divorce?"

"They have a son. I guess Cutler didn't want to upset him," Theo said.

And I'm the Queen of Sheba. I was surprised that Theo, with her experience, would buy that excuse. I pressed her a bit by asking, "How old is Cutler? Is the son still at home?"

"Cutler's about the same age as George. I don't know about his son."

Theo liked older men. George had been at least a decade older than us. I'd bet that son was an adult now and long out of the house. However, that was Theo's business. "How did this get started?" I asked.

"He called me to commiserate after George's funeral. I

didn't hear from him again after that, but a few months ago he invited me to dinner. We've been seeing each other ever since."

The facts were remarkably paltry, even for Theo, who was normally discreet about her romances. However, I could tell she wasn't inclined to share more about her relationship with Cutler Mead, at least for now. She'd tell me everything, eventually, so I let it go. Theo heaved herself up from the sofa and began to unthread the tissue she'd wound between her toes. She walked out of the room with her weight rocked back onto her heels so that the fresh polish stayed above the tufts of the carpet.

In a few minutes she returned wearing a pair of Jimmy Choo sandals. She dug into her purse again, coming up with a lipstick and compact. She precisely applied the lipstick, mashed her lips together, and checked her teeth in the mirror. "Annie, when's the last time you had a date?"

"Oh, now we're going to talk about *my* love life?" I really wasn't interested in dating anyone, as Theo knew. She had wasted much conversation over many glasses of wine, trying to encourage me.

"Answer me."

"Two weeks ago."

"Oh, good. Who is he?"

"Flynn Reynolds."

"Flynn is gay."

"You asked when I'd last had a date."

"I was speaking euphemistically."

"Flynn is good company, Theo, and that's all I'm looking for these days." I hoped my answer would put an end to this interrogation, and maybe Theo would ease up on me.

Theo sat back down on the couch. "Look, Hon. I know Charlie was a louse. Forget your ex-husband. Find someone straight, someone who deserves you. Failing that, find a man you want to sleep with."

"Oh my god, Theo. You should hear yourself."

"Ann Audrey Pickering—you listen to me."

Theo's use of my three names meant she was serious. Like many Southerners, male or female, I was baptized with three names and used all of them. Casual acquaintances or business associates who were on a first name basis called me 'Ann Audrey.' Only the closest friends or family were allowed to shorten my name to Annie or Audrey.

"You have gorgeous red hair," Theo continued, "and all those curls. Why do you insist on pulling it into a pony tail and stuffing a baseball cap on your head?"

"It's easy—and I don't have to worry about whether I'm fashionable or not."

Now that I didn't have to dress for the office, I'd adopted my mama's philosophy. Leila Leigh Pickering, a.k.a. LaLa, refused to be a slave to her body. As if she were choosing liberty or death, LaLa would lift her well-bred chin and declare that she intended to skip washing her hair that day, or not wear a girdle to church, or forgo panties during the Mississippi summer. These small acts of rebellion had shocked and thrilled me, and I considered this subtle refusal to conform as my birthright—a sort of homage to LaLa and a legacy to disregard fashion for comfort whenever possible. And besides, anything more would distract from my standard outfit of baseball cap and jeans, accented with sneakers.

"It's not about fashion," Theo said. "It's about accentuating your assets. Any woman would kill for those legs of yours, but the only time you show them is when you're in running shorts. Back in college you were one of the beauties in the sorority. A classic southern belle, peaches and cream, beautifully dressed and elegant."

I snorted to let Theo know what I thought about that memory. "Don't you remember LaLa's definition of a southern belle?" I asked.

"Whipped cream on top of piano wire," Theo said with a smile. "We always laughed about it."

"My whipped cream dissolved along with my marriage. I can't be bothered anymore."

Theo's smile disappeared and she got serious. "Annie, you need to make an effort and move on with your life."

"Move on with your own life." I flapped my hands at her, spurning the attempted intervention. "When are you meeting Cutler Mead?"

"At one, but I'll be back for supper. We'll talk then."

Theo should know better than to prod me about my love life. If she insisted on bringing up the subject later, I'd remind her about Baxter Wolf, who was discovered in Theo's bed at Vanderbilt when I was pinned to him. I was furious with Baxter and crushed that Theo had seduced him, in what I saw as the ultimate betrayal. In retrospect, Theo did me a favor by exploding my naïve plans for a future with Baxter. The man was as boring as three-day-old leftovers. I would have been miserable in any marriage with him.

After a flaming argument and reconciliation, Theo never even flirted with any man I was dating. We both realized the importance of our friendship. Time and again she had shown stubborn loyalty to me, not only in the maelstrom of my ex-husband's trial, but in other times of trouble. Theo's moral compass toward me had remained at true North.

Dismissing thoughts of Theo and her affair, I stretched full length on the couch and buried myself in the Sunday paper. I chewed through all the sections, even the Business Section, reading about the new Apple personal computer, available in either blue or tangerine, with the ability to have wireless connections to other iBooks and to the Internet as long as they were within 150 feet of a small white "base station" plugged into a telephone or network connection. Steve Jobs was either crazy or a genius. I read on until the glut of information lulled me into a deep nap.

When I woke the sun had slid down toward the horizon. The haze from Atlanta's pollution made for some spectacular sunsets. To the west, beyond the Chattahoochee river and Georgia's border, Alabama was on fire. I rolled off the couch and pulled the shades to soften the glare.

"Theo?" I called out, but the place was quiet. She must still be with Cutler. I strolled barefoot into the kitchen, opened the fridge and poured myself some iced tea. I turned on the tv to waste time until Theo came home. A shrill ring interrupted an ad for Stove-Top Stuffing. I stretched across the counter to lift the handset on the kitchen wall phone.

"Annie, I need help." Theo's usual soft voice was strangely high pitched.

"What's wrong?" I asked.

"Cutler's dead. I just woke up. He wasn't in the bedroom. I found him on the floor in the study. He's dead, Annie."

"Take a breath, Honey." I couldn't take it in. Had Theo said that Cutler was dead? "Are you sure? Have you called an ambulance?"

"He's *dead*." Her voice had risen to a wail on the last word.

"Take it easy. It'll be okay." I looked around the kitchen for my car keys. I needed to get over there.

"There's blood everywhere."

Theo hated the sight of blood.

"Call 911. I'm on my way." I grabbed my keys and ran.

2

Crime Scene

Driving like a traffic terrorist, I managed to get to Cutler Mead's house before the police. There were no vehicles on the circular drive. The front door was unlocked. Calling Theo's name, I let myself in to a high-ceilinged foyer. Theo was nowhere to be seen. There was no response to my calls. Beyond a wide arch on my left was the living room, on my right a masculine study's over-sized pocket doors were opened wide, giving me a full view of the room.

A crisp blue shirt with French cuffs was an elegant look, even worn by a corpse. Eyes open, Cutler Mead sprawled across a maroon Persian carpet, one of his long arms flung haphazardly toward a wall of bookcases, the other tucked under his body. His large frame filled the space between a pair of leather club chairs. Turned halfway between his side and his back, he looked like an old dog trying to roll over for a belly scratch. I swallowed hard and looked away, trying not to inhale so I wouldn't taste the coppery smell of blood. Where the hell was Theo?

"Stay where you are, ma'am. Turn around and face me, hands where I can see them." I held my hands up while I turned and faced a hardbody Atlanta police officer with gun drawn. He talked into a two-way Motorola mounted on his shoulder as he watched me. I had been around plenty of cops during the investigation into my husband's case, but nobody had ever pulled a gun on me. I needed to reassure this guy I wasn't a threat. "There's no need for a gun, officer. I'm not armed."

He ignored my statement and kept the gun raised. "What's your name?"

"Anne Audrey Pickering," I squinted to read his badge, "Officer Johnson."

"Is this your house?"

"No. It belongs to Mr. Mead. I'm just here because my friend called me. She said she'd found Mr. Mead dead." I gestured toward the body on the floor. "There."

The officer looked over at the body, but stayed where he was. "Let me see some I.D."

I pulled my wallet from my purse and held it out to him.

"Take out the license and show me," he instructed.

I held my license up close to his face so he could see it.

"Okay, ma'am. You can put it away," he said, holstering his gun. Then he knelt at the side of the body and checked the neck for a pulse that I was pretty sure he wouldn't find.

He came to his feet and asked, "You called 911?"

"That wasn't me," I said. "I just got here. Mrs. Humphries is the one who called 911."

"Does she live here?"

"No. She's Mr. Mead's guest."

"Okay. Where *is* Mrs. Humphries?"

Good question. I was trying to figure out where Theo had gotten herself to. Running away would not endear her—or me—to the police. I needed to find her and keep this policeman friendly. "She's here somewhere. I was just starting to look for her when you came in."

He spoke into the microphone on his shoulder, reporting that he'd found one person in the house, but he was looking for a second.

I didn't like the idea of the police accosting Theo without me being with her. "Officer Johnson, Mrs. Humphries has probably locked herself in the bedroom. Please do not scare her."

He looked at me in surprise. "What do you mean?"

"I'm guessing she's afraid that whoever did this is still here. Look, let me get her to come out. She'll open the door for me."

He reported this into the walkie-talkie and nodded. "Okay. You go ahead of me."

The foyer led toward an oversized great room, its glassed wall looking over a pool and stone patio. I guessed the master suite would be in one of the two wings off the great room. The rest of the bedrooms were probably on the second floor. On a hunch, I led Officer Johnson into the left wing, away from the study where Cutler Mead lay. We followed the hallway toward a closed door. I raised my hand to the door, then turned to the policeman, and with his gesture of approval, I knocked.

"Theo, it's Annie. Are you in there? It's okay. You can come out now. The ambulance is here. Police, too." I heard the officer's radio behind me as I tried to sound reassuring.

The lock clicked, and Theo stood in the doorway wearing one of her voluminous caftans. I didn't recall seeing this one before, a wild black and white abstract print against a smeary red background. She held the sticky fabric of the caftan away from her body—the vivid red not a part of the abstract print, but blood. Her face was pale, except for black smudges of mascara smeared under her eyes. She gripped the door frame for dear life, her hands stained red.

"He's dead, isn't he? I told you."

"Yes, Hon. I think so." I wanted to hug her, but the police officer was hovering. I settled for putting my arm around her shoulders to guide her out of the bedroom.

"Are you Mrs. Humphries?" asked the policeman.

"Yes." Under my arm Theo's shoulders stiffened.

"Come with me. The detectives are on site. They'll want to talk to you."

We headed back to the living room with its elaborate crown molding, marble-painted walls, and huge silk flower arrangements—modish 1990's décor done by an expensive decorator. Officer Johnson pointed me toward a chair.

"Sit down and stay there until somebody can talk to you."

He escorted Theo to the other side of the room where a man in civilian clothes that I took to be the lead detective, huddled with other officers.

From my seat, I had a full view of the study, swarming with the ambulance EMTs, cops, and crime scene officers. I watched the chaos sort itself out. An investigator emerged from behind one of the club chairs. He had been crouched photographing

Cutler's body, especially his head—a crimson wreck exposed when the coroner's men flopped the body over to zip it into their black bag. As they lifted the body to put it on the stretcher, the photographer snapped close-ups of a shiny object that had been hidden from view. He then proceeded methodically around the room, documenting the furniture, a spectacular carved hawk on the desk, bookcases, silver-framed pictures and golf trophies, even half-full mugs of coffee on the end tables and a couple of twists of yellow paper littering the floor nearby.

From behind me, I heard Theo.

"I don't know anything else. Like I told you, I just found him like that," she said.

"Okay. Tell me again what you heard."

The authoritative voice came from the man who'd introduced himself to Theo as Detective Mike Bristol. He was tall, not as tall as Cutler Mead had been, but over six feet. Broad shoulders strained his coat jacket. His hands, encased in latex gloves, were balled into fists propped on his lean hips. He wore a fedora pushed back off his forehead, announcing he belonged to the elite Atlanta homicide squad whose members were presented a hat when they solved their first murder. No man in 1999 Atlanta wore a hat these days, except the murder squad at a crime scene or when facing the press.

He stood in front of Theo, who was hunched at one end of a silk upholstered loveseat. She sat in the blood-stained caftan, her bare toes dug into the pale carpet underneath the legs of the furniture.

"I don't know what I heard," Theo said. "The bedroom's usually so quiet—it's off the main part of the house. Something woke me up, and Cutler wasn't there so I came out here to look for him. I found him on the floor." Theo sat with her body twisted away from the detective and the room where Cutler Mead's body lay.

The detective showed no reaction to Theo's response. I was impressed, despite myself, at how confident he seemed, not in the least bit overwhelmed by the confusion of the scene or Theo's recalcitrance. His reaction to Theo was curious. Most men seeing Theo in such distress would have tried to comfort her. Although, if a man were convinced she was a murderer, he'd have been more abrasive, demanding her attention. This guy did neither. I could only hope he was withholding judgment. I waited to hear what he would ask next, expecting him to press Theo further about her relationship to Cutler Mead. Instead, at the sound of the medical examiner's men bumping down the front stairs with their rolling stretcher and body bag, he turned and took notice of me.

"Now who're you again, and what're you doing here?" he asked.

"Ann Audrey Pickering," I said. "I'm a friend of Mrs. Humphries. She called and asked me to come." He blinked at my triple name, so I didn't mention that Theo had called me *before* calling the police or ambulance.

"Did you know the deceased?"

"I'd met him a few times." I didn't mind the interrogation. I had nothing to hide. In fact, it felt like old times. I'd been asked for information by many cops.

Detective Bristol gave me his full attention as I answered, leaning toward me and watching my face. Close up he was handsome, sharp cheekbones and a straight nose, the thin upper lip of his mouth softened by a high Cupid's bow and his lower lip full and sensuous. His eyes were deep blue, not that pale Land-of-the-Midnight-Sun Scandinavian blue, but dark. No wonder he's comfortable around Theo, I thought. He's used to coaxing what he wants out of women.

"What can you tell me about Mr. Mead?" the detective asked.

"He's a businessman, in real estate development, I think. I met him down at Sea Island at the Humphries' cottage." This last was a hint about Theo, since anyone who has a place on Sea Island also has money and influence, or at least, knows people who do.

He wrinkled his brow. "The Humphries?"

"Mrs. Humphries is a widow, but her husband George Humphries was still alive 4 or 5 years ago when I met Mr. Mead—that is, the deceased—at their home. I believe George Humphries did some business with Mead."

"What kind of business?"

"Theo—Mrs. Humphries—could tell you better than me. I only know George's company invested in different kinds of things—real estate, start-up companies, pine forest that was leased for lumber—that sort of thing." I was tickling my memory for whatever I could add, spinning out my few shreds of data about the dead man in order to distract the detective from Theo, now slumped miserably against the arm of the loveseat. I recognized symptoms of imminent Theo-meltdown, rarely seen and best avoided.

"Do you know any of Mr. Mead's family? Someone we could contact?"

This was a tough one, but I didn't want to be caught out in a lie. "He's married. I think his wife has a house here in Atlanta."

"She doesn't live here?"

"So I've been told." I couldn't meet the deep blue eyes, so I stared at my feet. At the moment I could have choked Theo for putting me in this position. I rose above that thought. "May I take Mrs. Humphries home?"

"Not yet. I'd like to get statements from Mrs. Humphries and you downtown."

"There's not much more we can tell you." That might or might not have been true, but I wanted to get Theo away from those peering eyes.

"Maybe not. But let's get it on the record."

It made sense he'd want sworn statements, but I was not relishing a visit to police headquarters. I could see that Theo was in shock over what had happened. I was mulling over how to convince the detective to handle her gently, when he turned from me and spoke to Theo. "Do you have some other clothes you could change into for the trip downtown?"

"In the bedroom." Theo pushed off the loveseat and started out of the room.

Her exit was halted by Detective Bristol. "Wait a minute," he said, "a policewoman will go with you." He gestured to a female officer who'd been in the hallway with the crime scene team. "This is Officer Woodall. She'll take photographs before you change, and collect the clothes you're wearing." Theo indicated she understood, and I edged closer, hoping for an opportunity to talk before the policewoman escorted Theo from the room.

Theo retreated from me. "Shush, Annie."

Friendship, real friendship, is a delicate balance. You learn your friend's most intimate secrets. If you know the other people in your friend's life—family, lovers or husbands—you suspect what facts have been omitted, glossed over, but you let that go. Theo and I had maintained our friendship all these years by knowing how far to press each other and when to back away. Normally, Theo's comment would have closed down the conversation, but this the time I ignored our usual protocol. I had to warn her.

"Theo, don't say anything," I whispered.

Theo's only response was the coughed ironic laugh she used to avoid discussing emotional subjects, even ones I knew all about—Theo's detestable family, her loneliness without George, and, worst of all, her weight.

"Let me go with you to help you dress," I said as the police-woman joined us.

"There's no need. Just wait for me out here."

I clamped my jaws shut to keep from screaming with frustration. I wanted to be in the room with Theo, to protect her. I'd had a lot of experience with police, and I knew they didn't always play straight. Long-toughened loyalty to my friend won out, and I whispered "Okay," to let Theo know I would honor her request.

Loyalty, however, was not synonymous with blind obedience. The police photographer and the coroner's men had left. I moved across the living room and edged into the foyer to peer over the crime scene tape marking off the study. I did my best to memorize everything the photographer had recorded. Displayed within the bookshelves were silver-framed photographs, each frame set meticulously next to a golf trophy, judging from the small dimpled ball at the top of several of them. One frame sat in solitude, pushed off-center on a deep shelf.

There was no trophy next to that lonely frame. I was pretty sure I knew why.

3

The
Interview

When Theo returned to the living room, she was wearing a deep blue sheath dress, knee length and fitted at the waist. She'd once told me that when dressing for a date, you were ninety percent likely to wear his favorite color if you wore blue. I hoped Cutler had appreciated her effort. Ignoring the hovering policewoman, I crossed the room to stand almost nose to nose with Theo.

"Do you trust me?" I asked.

She furrowed her brow. "Of course."

"Okay, then. Please follow this advice. Do not answer any more questions," I said.

"You heard what I told the detective. I came out and found Cutler. That's all I know." She paused and said, "Look, Annie. I know what this looks like, but there really isn't anything else I can tell them."

I considered announcing to Detective Bristol that I was acting as Theo's attorney. That would prevent him from questioning her without me present. Unfortunately, like most big-firm lawyers with expertise in civil matters, I knew squat about criminal procedure. My last encounter with that specialty had been when I took the bar exam, years ago. My attempt to represent Theo might cause more harm than good if I aggravated the detective unnecessarily. While I was trying to decide whether to claim I was Theo's lawyer, Detective Bristol joined us to explain that he'd drive us to the police station.

I didn't like that, but I could understand that he wanted to keep an eye on us. "What about my car?" I asked.

"Give me your keys, and I'll have it brought to the station."

I handed them over and joined Theo in the back seat of Bristol's unmarked sedan. The upholstery was a slightly napped fabric that I tried not to touch, imagining what that seat might have absorbed. The bench was more comfortable than a New York taxi, which is to say that it still had some cushioning and did not bear the deep imprint of the butts that had preceded mine. The scent of stale cigarette smoke hung in the air. I didn't figure Bristol for a smoker. The smell must have been deposited by previous passengers or Bristol's chubby partner, who'd spent most of the investigation thus far overseeing a search of Cutler's mansion. I'd missed his name when we were ushered outside to

Bristol's car. My guess was confirmed when the partner stood outside the car to suck down the last of a smoke before lowering himself into the front passenger seat with a grunt.

When we arrived at the station, Bristol and his partner escorted Theo and me to separate interview rooms, leaving me alone in a grungy rectangular space, its walls a sullen taupe that had probably once been a light beige. The faint crunch when I stepped on the linoleum squares gave proof that the police department had taken the low bid for the janitorial contract. Beat up, scratched and stained, the table centered in the room seemed all too familiar. Not unlike the one I'd sat at years ago for many hours while the story of my husband's scam had unfolded.

I prowled the room, hoping I wasn't in for another round of endless questions all over again. Mostly, though, I worried about Theo—would they arrest her or detain her or would we be able to leave after making our statements? Regardless, she needed to keep her mouth shut for her own protection. In her present state, still in shock over finding Cutler's body, I wasn't sure she could do that. The faintest admission could be twisted against her.

Detective Bristol shoved open the door and walked in, holding a bulging file of paper under one arm. Gone was the trophy fedora. He had a thick head of dark hair, lightly sprinkled with gray. Either he was older than he looked or the stress of police work was making him gray early. Why was it that salt and pepper made men more attractive and made women look like they were too old to bother with? His hair was starting to creep down his neck in the back, showing a slight curl and threatening to climb over his shirt collar.

He dropped the file on the table, pulled back one of the plastic chairs and sat down.

I didn't want him to control the interview, so I jumped right in. "How is Theo?"

"Mrs. Humphries seems fine. Tired, perhaps," said the detective.

"Where is she?"

"She's in another interview room, just like this one."

That was good news. At least Theo wasn't in a cell. "Have you questioned her?"

He gave me a quizzical look, then apparently decided to answer. "Of course. But Mrs. Humphries is not exactly forthcoming. She claims not to know anything. Heard nothing, saw nothing, etc, etc, etc."

I was relieved that Theo was sticking to the same recitation of facts, and I attempted to bolster her story. "You saw Cutler's place. It's enormous. The master bedroom is in the other wing of the house. It's possible—in fact, it's probable—that someone in the bedroom couldn't hear anything going on in that study."

"Maybe." Bristol shrugged. He sat back and gave me a hard look. "Tell me again, what Mrs. Humphries said when she telephoned you."

"She said 'Cutler's dead. I woke up and he wasn't there. When I went to find him, he was dead.'" My statement had the double benefit of being true, and corroborating what Theo had told him when he interviewed her in Cutler's living room.

"Did she sound upset?"

Was he intentionally asking me a stupid question, or was he just playing dumb? "*Very* upset." I thought back to the phone call I'd received from Theo that afternoon. "I figured he'd had a heart attack, so I told her to call an ambulance."

"How well did you know the victim?"

We had already gone over this at Cutler Mead's house, but I played along so he couldn't complain that I was uncooperative. "Not well at all. Like I told you, I'd only met him a few times."

Thankfully, the detective did not ask what I knew about Theo's relationship with the dead man—although, given Theo's deshabille at the scene, he must have already figured out the nature of their relationship.

"Would you say you and Mr. Mead were friends?"

"No. Acquaintances, maybe."

"How well do you know Mrs. Humphries?"

"I've known Theo since we were sorority sisters in college. Ages."

He didn't seem to be listening. His long hands fenced in the stack of papers, squaring them precisely on the table in front of him. No wedding ring. Was he single or did he leave his ring off so he could keep his options open? I put a choke collar on my monkey brain to curb any speculation in that direction. Bristol shifted in the chair and opened the file. I had the feeling the direction of the interview was about to change.

"One of our financial crimes guys saw you coming in and got really excited, thought you were going to make his day," he said. "I didn't recognize you, but, I never worked fraud."

Oh, here we go. So much for keeping a low profile. I concentrated on maintaining a neutral expression, consciously transferring any tension from my face and hands to my feet, where he couldn't see my toes gripping the insides of my shoes.

Bristol tapped the pages. "This is you, isn't it?"

There was no need to prompt me. I could read my name

upside down. I sat silent, avoiding as long as possible reopening the misery those pages represented.

"Ms. Pickering?"

I relented. I wanted to get out of there. "If those printouts are about my adventure with the Justice Department, that was a long time ago."

"Adventure. What a word. You were the whistleblower and principal witness for the federal government against your own husband and his investment fraud. Even helped locate his off-shore accounts." He looked up from the papers and asked, "Where is your husband, by the way?"

"Leavenworth. My ex-husband."

"No surprise."

I wasn't sure which statement he meant was not a surprise. Either would be correct, but I resented him saying so. My divorce was no business of his. He couldn't understand the pain of finding out someone I'd loved—deeply—was a crook who'd duped me along with the victims of his scam.

I deliberately turned my mind away from my past to consider Mike Bristol's strategy. He was looking for leverage, using my history to get me to talk. I needed to stay cool, find out what he was thinking about Theo. It shouldn't be that difficult. I'd learned how to endure goading comments when I'd been questioned by tougher cops and god knows how many intimidating lawyers.

Those dark blue eyes had deep creases around them. Caused by what? Either he had a good sense of humor and laughed easily, or he'd weathered some pain. There was a faint five o'clock shadow on his jaw. He was definitely going to need a shave if he had to appear in front of tv cameras at a press conference today. The blue eyes were looking amused now. I hate men who are amused at women. He'd try to pat me on the head next.

"What does that file have to do with Cutler Mead's murder?" I asked.

"Probably nothing," he said. "But it is illuminating about you, Ms. Pickering."

"You can call me Ann Audrey."

"Huh?"

"My name. Ann Audrey. Two names, but that's what I'm called."

"Okay, Ann Audrey, let's forget the past and talk about the present. Why shouldn't I arrest your friend right now for the murder of Cutler Mead?"

"She's not capable of murder."

"I've heard that a lot."

"No, really. Theo can't squash a roach on her patio. Much less smash in a man's head."

"She was covered in his blood."

"Smeared with—not splattered. Your crime lab will confirm that probably happened when she found him. Theo is not an idiot. If she'd killed him and gotten splattered with blood, don't you think she'd have changed her clothes before she called the police? Get real."

His bristly jaw moved back and forth as if he were chewing over that idea. Since he wasn't arguing with me, I decided to press on.

"She had no reason to kill him," I said. "They'd just had lunch and spent the afternoon together." None of this information was news to him, but I figured repeating it wouldn't hurt.

"What about you?" Bristol asked.

"I'm sorry?"

"How do I know you didn't kill him? I only have your word that you'd arrived on the scene just before we answered the 911 call."

"Why would I kill him? I barely knew the man." I was agog to be considered a suspect. But on reflection, I had to admit Bristol was justified in asking.

"Maybe you were jealous?"

"You think I had a thing for Cutler Mead?" I laughed. "Good Lord, no. He's not my type." I regretted my flip answer, as soon as I said it.

Bristol favored me with a tight-lipped smile. "I can barely resist asking the obvious follow-up question, but under the circumstances, I'll move on. Were you jealous of the victim?"

"What are you implying? Get that out of your head right now. Theo and I are old friends—not lovers."

He was definitely amused now. I realized I'd been yanked from my carefully constructed isolation and dropped into the rat's nest of the criminal justice system. I had to regain the upper hand in this conversation.

"It's not Theo." I said. "You need to look around. Whose fingerprints are on the murder weapon? Was the security system on or off? Was there someone else in the study with Cutler Mead? Who are his associates? Was he involved in something illicit?"

Bristol pretended to search for a pen and pad of paper. "Let me write some of this down, Ms. Pickering. What else would you suggest I do?"

His mockery of me stung. I was contrite, not because of what I'd said to him, but because it might aggravate him and that wouldn't be good for Theo. To cover my embarrassment, I tried to pretend the whole conversation was a joke. "Well, I have watched a few episodes of Law & Order."

"It's hard to trump a suspect who was alone with the victim right before his death, and when we arrive, she's covered in his blood."

"She is *not* capable of it. I've known her for decades. It's impossible." I scraped my chair back from the table. "Are you finished? I'd like to take Theo home."

"Take her home?"

His tone of incredulity was well done. I would need to watch him carefully to figure out what he was truly thinking when he asked questions.

"Are you arresting her?"

He rubbed his thumbs back and forth across the tips of his fingers. He had every right to take Theo into custody and charge her, but I was gambling there were enough questions unanswered—and he was an honest enough cop—for him to hesitate. I saw him decide.

"Not right now."

I hadn't realized I was holding my breath while I waited for his answer. Now I let it out and gathered up my purse. "May we go?"

He let the question go unanswered for several beats before he said. "I'll have her sent out to you in the waiting room. You might want to leave the back way through the police garage."

As I rose the exceptional blue eyes looked up at me. "In the interview, she told me that you're her best friend."

My throat tightened and I blinked back tears. The emotional onslaught was unexpected; I could have argued with him all night about timing, motive, blood splatter—all the usual policeman's weapons. But his simple statement defeated me, reminded me of the debt I owed Theo. I was going down the rabbit hole again. Only this time, instead of fighting to prove that my husband was a thief who'd defrauded clients of their life savings, I was going to prove my best, my most-loyal friend was not a murderer.

4

Theo's Story

A uniformed officer led Theo from the interview room. She kept her head high and was gracious to the cop, thanking him for escorting her to the waiting room. I wondered how often he got that kind of polite acknowledgement. I could tell Theo was holding on to her composure with both hands, and I hoped her grip would last until we could get out of here.

We took the elevator down to the underground parking garage, and I hustled Theo into the car and drove out the exit. A clump of trucks emblazoned with TV-channel logos were parked on the street. Blow-dried reporters from the local news teams surged forward. I avoided running over any of the microphone-wielding press, although Channel 2's cameraman had a narrow escape.

Any further chance of vehicular homicide was averted when the front door of the police station opened and Detective Bristol strolled out, along with a group of stiff-backed men. They fanned out, and Atlanta's long-time chief of police, recognizable by his ruddy cheeks and thatch of silver hair, stepped to the microphone set up on the front steps. The reporters swarmed *en masse* away from the car and toward the impending press conference. I figured they must not know who we were yet, or they wouldn't have turned away.

Theo leaned her head against the passenger side window in the front seat. Her eyes were open, but I didn't think she was seeing anything. Once we were away from the police station, she closed her eyes and let her head droop.

"Hang in there, Hon," I said. "We'll be at my place in a minute." I drove home, parked, and led her to the elevator. We rode up the 42 floors in silence. When we were inside the condo, I took her purse and set it on the coffee table.

"Wine?" I asked.

"Please," said Theo, sinking into the couch.

I poured two glasses and handed her one. "What did you tell the police?"

"Please leave it, Annie."

I considered what to do. Theo does not panic in a crisis, but her preferred tactic is to ignore it or flee. Neither one of those was an option. I wanted to baby her, but I didn't think we had time for that.

"Theo, don't you understand the mess we're in?" My voice was sharper than I intended, and I saw her flinch at the question.

"We? Since when is this about you?" She clunked her glass down on the table. "I need to take a shower."

She shifted her weight to get up from the couch, but I sat down next to her and put a delaying hand on her arm. "We're in this together. You've got to tell me everything that happened so I can help." I lowered my voice to assure her I wasn't angry. She shook her head, but she settled back.

"Theo, we can't pretend this isn't happening," I said. "You had blood all over you. You were the only person at the house. The police think you killed Cutler. They're not likely to waste energy looking for someone else."

Tears stood in her eyes as she said, "Just don't yell at me. I've spent the last day being looked at as if I'm some kind of pond scum. That awful policewoman stood over me and watched me undress. Can you imagine how that made me feel?"

I could, actually. She's always had a weight problem. She's self-conscious about it. When adolescence gifted her with a generous bust and a provocative nature, she learned to use sex to feel better about herself. Now that weapon had misfired. But I couldn't get sidetracked into sympathy for Theo. Not yet. I had to find out everything so that I could plan our defense.

"I'm sorry I yelled," I said. "Let's go over what happened." I topped up her wine glass. "You two went out to lunch. After lunch you went back to his house. You went to bed." I waited for her to pick up the story.

She took a sip of her wine. "He was gone when I woke up. That's not unusual, 'cause I sleep like the dead after sex." She swallowed and said, "I didn't mean..."

"It's ok."

"I pulled on my caftan, and went looking for him. I guessed he'd be in his study." She hesitated. "And he was. He was lying on his back on the rug, and I asked him if he was okay." She paused and looked down at her wine glass. "I should have known. I should have known. I was so stupid."

"No, you weren't," I said, even though I really wasn't sure what she meant.

"I thought he was playing a game, Annie. It was only when he didn't answer, I figured something was wrong. I can't believe how stupid I was."

"You weren't stupid." My heart went out to her, blaming herself for—what? For not realizing her lover was dead when she first found him? Or was there something else? "How did you get covered in blood?"

She gave me an agonized look.

"Surely the police asked you. What did you tell them?"

"I just told them it happened when I found him. That's all." She pressed her lips together.

I suspected there was more, so I said, "Tell *me* about it."

She closed her eyes. "I didn't see any blood at first. It must have soaked into the carpet."

I thought back to the study, and the dark red oriental rug where Cutler's body had fallen. It made sense.

"I knelt down next to him. He was warm, and I reached out and stretched my arm across him and stroked his shoulder. I'm not sure, I guess I thought it would comfort him. You know how baggy that caftan is–all that fabric. That's why it's so comfortable. Anyway, the front billowed out when I leaned over."

She closed her mouth, blowing out through her nose. For a few minutes she struggled to speak, then she picked up the story.

"It got caught around his head. I stood up and got my feet tangled in the caftan. I stumbled back and almost fell. I yanked it and when I pulled free, he started to roll away from me and his head, the back of his head, and it was, it was…"

I had seen the back of Cutler's head when the coroner's men rolled him over before removing his body. I could sympathize with Theo's reaction, being wound up in that gory mess. That certainly explained all the blood on her.

She panted and wept. I hugged her and let her cry herself out. At last she was quiet, and I coaxed her into the guest bedroom to shower and try to sleep.

I left Theo alone there, carefully closing the door so she would sleep undisturbed, and went into the kitchen to turn on the television. Cutler Mead's murder was the first story on the late news. The reporter did not mention Theo's name and there was no footage of us leaving the police station. So far, so good, but it was only a matter of hours before someone leaked the information that the victim's girlfriend had been in the house when he was killed. Once the press made up its mind that Theo was the murderer, the pressure to indict and convict her would be relentless. No more reacting. I needed to make a plan.

There was a soft triple knock at my door. It was after midnight, but the three knocks told me who it was.

"I thought you might need a drink–or two," said Flynn Reynolds, cradling a large bottle of Maker's Mark.

"Flynn, thank God."

Flynn Reynolds was slim and dressed in Neiman Marcus preppy. His dark, almost black hair was cut very short, emphasizing a widow's peak that appeared almost painted at the top of his forehead. His small ears curved away from his skull, so that the overall effect was a handsome man with the look of an elf, or, a good-looking demon.

We had been friends since our childhood in Mississippi. I fell in love with him in the first grade, expecting to marry him and have beautiful babies. Then one night in junior high school, we'd stolen some of Flynn's daddy's bourbon and gotten drunk under the high school bleachers. My hopes for an evening of heavy petting were dashed when he confessed that he had no interest in me…or any girl.

I kept his secret through high school, providing cover for his interest in other boys. That wasn't difficult. Flynn was a natural athlete. Too slim to be a threat in football, he lettered in basketball, tennis, and pitched for the baseball team. Half the girls in school were in love with him. In those days, the idea of a star athlete being homosexual was beyond comprehension.

For my part, I had no intention of becoming an unwed mother, having seen the most popular girl in school become a social pariah. None of us knew anything about birth control, which decent girls didn't talk about, so when my latest teenaged conquest became too demanding, Flynn came to my rescue. I would breakup with the current boyfriend and return to the long-suffering Flynn—so categorized by high school gossips who couldn't imagine why he continued to carry a torch for me.

It seemed that Flynn was riding to my rescue again. I watched as he tore the red wax seal off the bourbon and poured each of us a large tot.

"I take it you heard about Theo?" I asked.

"Don called me. He thought you might need a friendly face. One of his lawyers was at the station when you came in. He recognized you." Flynn's partner, Don Marshall, ran a pro bono service whose lawyers often represented criminal defendants.

He pointed toward the guest bedroom. "How's Theo?"

"What you'd expect. A total mess."

"And you?"

"Not much better."

He reached over and squeezed my hand. "You'll get through it, just like before, Audrey." He had dubbed me that in first grade when my double name was too much for his stutter, long since overcome.

"I can't do this again. Last time, the story was—my husband the crook. This time, it's—my best friend the murderer."

"Is she a murderer?"

"Theo? You know better. She's not capable of it."

"What is she capable of?"

I thought of Theo's kindness to me. Her grief over George's sudden death. Her tendency to cry over the smallest thing. Those were the obvious things. But there was another side.

"She's smart, that kind of under-the-radar-smart that most men don't recognize because they're blinded by her tits."

He whistled. "Ohh-kaaaay, then. Just tell me what you think."

"Sorry. I just remembered all the times Theo got us in trouble in college."

"You're mad at her."

I shook my head, my thoughts a mixture of affection and aggravation. "Mad, sad, afraid. Pick one. I've spent years trying to lead a quiet life and that's over as of this afternoon."

"Then you'd better find the real culprit."

I cringed to hear that idea out loud. Flynn was voicing what I'd already been considering, but resisting. "Me?" I asked.

"Who else is going to help her? Look, I know she's your best girlfriend—notice the modifier—but this is your playpen. You've been here before and managed to come out unscathed."

"Hardly unscathed, but I take your point." I had already

come to the conclusion that I was the only one who could drag Theo out of this mud pile. After seeing Theo tonight, I couldn't avoid helping her, no matter how much I dreaded it. "The question is how to go about it?"

"You're a trained lawyer. You were good at it, before that mess with Charlie. You know how to gather facts and put together evidence."

"Thanks, but this is different." Flynn had always been one of my biggest supporters, but I doubted my legal skills were enough to save Theo.

"Not so much. How bad is the case against her?" asked Flynn.

"If you were a homicide detective with a dead man's lover found on the scene covered in blood, what would you think? Detective Bristol was polite, but maybe that's not a good sign."

"Bristol? Beau Blue Bristol?"

"Mike Bristol. Arrogant and full of himself." I ground my teeth recalling how the detective had teased me during the interview. "Why did you call him Beau Blue?"

"Oh my lord, Audrey. Didn't you see those eyes?"

I wasn't going to admit that I had. Flynn's imagination didn't need any encouragement. "What do you know about him? Is he any good?"

"What a loaded question," Flynn said with a mischievous look.

"Don't be obnoxious. I'm too tired for gay repartee."

"Sorry. According to Don, the defense lawyers think Bristol is smart and honest. He's been known to buck the brass when he thinks they're railroading someone. And he occasionally bends a rule to look outside the box. That might mean he's willing to look at alternatives to Theo."

"I wish I could think of some alternatives." I considered what I knew about the murdered man. "If Theo didn't kill him, who did? Who hated him enough to bash his head in? We need to find out everything we can about him. He must have made enemies, Flynn. He had a reputation as a ladies' man."

"It's not always that kind of sex. Maybe he screwed one of his business partners," said Flynn.

"Brilliant idea," I said, grabbing Flynn's arm. "Can you find out about Cutler Mead's business?"

Flynn was an investment banker with Sisson & Watkins, a long established Atlanta-based group with a solid portfolio of clients. S&W would have the databases and the contacts to find out information about any business with Atlanta connections.

"Sure. Routine sniffing around disguised as due diligence. All in a day's work."

"I'd be grateful. So will Theo."

"I'll start in the morning." He threw back the last of his bourbon and gathered me in a crushing hug. "I'm leaving, and you need to try to get some sleep. Call you tomorrow."

5

The Morning After

I was standing at the kitchen island counting scoops of coffee beans into the grinder when I heard Theo emerge from the guest room the next morning. I couldn't sleep, so I'd given up and started making coffee before the sun rose. This was not my first pot. I clicked the machine to "on" and sat down on one of the barstools, swivelling to face Theo. She was barefoot, her coral painted toes gripping the hardwood floor. Her face was haggard and her eyes barely open, the lids so swollen I guessed she'd cried even more after I'd left her.

"How 'bout some coffee?"

"Thanks."

She cradled the big mug between her hands. "What's all this stuff?" she asked, gesturing at the counter littered with pages of yellow legal paper covered with notes.

I took it as a good sign that she was making an effort to converse. "You need a criminal lawyer. Somebody to go with you who knows the ropes, when you talk to the police."

"I know you're right, but doesn't having a lawyer look like I'm guilty?"

She had a point, but I remembered my previous experience. An ambitious cop intent on an arrest could easily confuse a suspect into self-incrimination. "It's just for your protection, Hon. There are all sorts of procedural complications that you may want some advice about." I left it at that.

Theo gave a soft moan of resignation.

"Flynn came over last night after you went to bed," I said. "He asked Don to send me names of the best criminal lawyers. That's what all these notes are about."

"That was good of Flynn." She stood in her bare feet, sipping the coffee.

I waited to see if she would say more.

She shifted her weight from one foot to the other and cleared her throat. Her light soprano voice had a scratch in it. "I keep going over it, to see what I missed. I feel like I'm in a movie, watching myself and Cutler, and it just keeps repeating again and again."

I moved off the stool toward her. "Hon, you're in shock. It's going to take a while for you to absorb what happened."

"I don't think I have the luxury of waiting till it sinks in, but I don't know what I can do."

"You mean, what *we* can do. You're not alone here."

The wan smile she gave me nearly broke my heart. I saw some light there. It looked like Theo might be facing the situation. That was a victory not to be dismissed. I seized on the faint hint that her shock was beginning to recede.

"Tell me about Cutler."

She swallowed some of her coffee but didn't respond.

"Hon, I need to know about him, so that I can help. Talk to me about what he was like, what you remember about him, his business, anything you can think of."

She stared down into her coffee cup like she was looking for a message. Then she gave a little sigh and sat down on the sofa.

"I was so lonely after George died."

Not helpful, but I had to let her get to it in her own way.

"I think I slept 20 hours a day, and the rest of the time I watched TV. Went to the doctor. He gave me some anti-depressants, but they just made me gain weight. That didn't exactly help my mood, so I quit them. People were nice. They invited me to small parties, dinner, whatever. I made myself go sometimes, but I just felt like a fifth wheel. Cutler was at a few of those events, and he seemed to go out of his way to speak with me. He was easy to talk to, and before I knew it, I was laughing with him. That's big—being able to laugh with someone."

I understood. I remembered how devastated she'd been when George died. Over the last few months she had seemed more like her old self. I should have realized there was a man behind her improved moods.

"I knew he had a reputation for carrying on with women,"

Theo said, "even though he was married. You know me well enough to know that didn't bother me—or scare me off. We were well suited in many ways. He had an appetite," she broke off for a minute, then raised her chin and continued. "So do I."

I didn't move a muscle, willing her to keep going until she said something useful.

"He had a lot of confidence. He never expected to be turned down, if you know what I mean."

I kept my face neutral, even though I wanted to show the distaste I was feeling at Theo's description of the man she'd fallen for.

"I never saw anything of that sort," Theo continued, "although I heard he'd had his face slapped at a late-night reception after one of the golf tournaments at the Island Club. One of the women said he groped her."

The coffee and the conversation were making my stomach churn. Cutler must have gone beyond the smooch and tickle that were tolerated by women at these affairs. Most of them knew how to handle a drunk with roving hands, and those episodes were invariably kept quiet—except for gossip among one's own set.

"Do you think there might have been others—who weren't able to stop him?"

"I don't know." She shrugged. "I find it hard to believe."

I couldn't help but wonder. There could have been others—women he'd refused to take "no" from. Those women or their husbands would have a motive to smash Cutler's head in.

I set aside thoughts about the man's womanizing to search for any other motive. "Did he talk about what business deals he was involved in?"

"A little. He was thinking of buying some land in Cobb

County, outside the perimeter. He thought that was the direction Atlanta was growing. I don't know who was involved in that, though."

I made another mental note to pass that along to Flynn for him to investigate.

"Talk me through everything that went on after you left here yesterday. Maybe you saw or heard something that you weren't aware of."

Her eyes slid sideways. "Everything?"

"You can skip over the details in the bedroom."

She bit her lip. "Good. I met him at Marigold's, you know, the restaurant over in Atkins Park."

The Atkins Park neighborhood was an older upscale residential area with several intimate restaurants. Marigold's was quiet, with plenty of nooks where tables for two were tucked away. A good place for a rendezvous, unlike one of the faddish Buckhead bistros where Cutler Mead would have been likely to run into someone he knew. Apparently the man had some sense of discretion, or maybe he didn't want to embarrass his wife or the current mistress.

"Why didn't he pick you up?" I asked.

"He would have. I just wanted to have my car with me."

Made sense. She'd have the freedom to leave if she wanted to, and it was slightly less compromising. I needed to revise my idea that Theo was a victim of Cutler Mead's predations. This was not the first time Theo played footsie under the table with a married man. That reminded me, I needed to see if I could unearth some info about what kind of marriage Cutler had. I added that to my list.

"What happened at lunch?"

"Nothing."

I sighed. "Try again. What'd you order?"

"Oh. I had the fish special. I think it was grouper."

"Pardon me, Theo. You live on the coast and you come to Atlanta and order fish?"

"Salad can get stuck in your teeth. Most meat you need both a knife and fork. Fish is easy to eat with just a fork. You don't have to struggle with it so you can still talk. And you have your other hand free, in case you want to reach across the table for something."

Or someone. The way her mind worked was an education. "Go on."

"Cutler had a burger. We talked. Flirted. He asked me if I wanted dessert."

She stopped and wrinkled her brow. "I just remembered. I was looking at the dessert menu and Cutler sneaked a look at his Rolex. Kind of casually pulled up his French cuff and glanced down. He saw me watching him and started a full court press, telling me how sexy I was and all. I figured he was in a hurry to get back to his place and...." She colored up, her cheeks bright pink. "But now that I think about it—I think he was checking the time because he was planning to meet someone later."

I felt some excitement. Here was something to go on. "You need to tell this to the police, Theo. They should make an effort to figure out who Cutler could have been meeting."

"Why wouldn't they?"

"That's what I was trying to tell you last night. They've got you covered in blood at the scene. Why would they look for someone else?"

Theo's eyes filled with tears. "I'm sorry," she said. Her nose was running again.

"Don't, Theo. That won't help us."

I tapped the toes of my flip flops on the barstool footrest, trying to drum my brain into gear.

"There were two used coffee cups in the study, and you only drink coffee in the morning. If he poured a cup for someone on a Sunday afternoon, who would that likely have been?"

"Maybe somebody he was doing business with?"

"On a Sunday?"

"Sure. He usually drove to Atlanta for business meetings during the week, but he told me once that he'd meet people whenever it was convenient for them, if it got the deal done."

"Okay. That's good information. Who else?"

"I don't know."

"Another woman—or his wife?"

She made a moue of distaste. "Highly doubtful. That would be rude, and Cutler's manners were impeccable."

I personally doubted the flawless purity of Cutler Mead's manners, but I kept my opinion to myself. "Did his wife know about you?"

"Why're you asking that?"

"Because, Theo, 90% of the time, murder victims get done in by their spouses."

Theo sniffed. "I don't know if she'd heard about Cutler and me."

"Do you know her?"

"I met her once. She hardly ever came to Sea Island. Prefers Atlanta. She's one of those Buckhead Bettys who go out to lunch almost every day."

Buckhead Bettys was a term applied to the women living in the poshest neighborhood of Atlanta. Tennis-playing former debutantes, charity-ball-giving members of that scene were an imbedded part of Atlanta society. That didn't necessarily mean they weren't smart and accomplished. Fate had dealt them a life unfettered by financial worries—assuming their husbands hadn't become over-extended in Atlanta's late 1990's boom town atmosphere. In many ways the Bettys were a throwback to the 1950's, expected to stay home and not work—not because they were cooking meals and taking care of children. These days those tasks were left to household help and nannies. Buckhead Bettys did not work outside the home because to do so would advertise that their husband didn't make enough money.

"We need to interview her."

Theo shook her head. "Not *we*. You'll have to talk to her without me. For obvious reasons."

Of course she was right, but I wasn't ready to confront Mrs. Mead. I decided to put that one off for now. Anyway, Mrs. Mead was going to be busy planning the funeral or memorial service for her husband. "We need to be doing something," I said. "I wish we could go back to Cutler's house. If they've removed the crime scene tape, we could look around." Even as the words came out of my mouth, I had second thoughts. Mike Bristol wouldn't hesitate to arrest us for interfering with a crime scene—assuming the house was still marked off limits.

"You must be kidding. I can't go back there." Theo's voice rose higher with each word.

"You might remember something that would give us a lead, something that the police might not pay attention to." I suddenly realized there was a flaw in my plan. "But I don't know how we'd get in."

Theo looked down at her feet. There was something she wasn't telling me. "What is it?" I asked.

"I've still got a key," she said.

I couldn't believe what I was hearing. "Did you tell the police that?"

"They didn't ask."

"You want to find out who did this to Cutler, don't you?"

She looked at me like a trapped animal, but she nodded, slowly.

"All right then," I said. "Let's go tonight. I'd rather not take a chance that the neighbors or the mailman would see us and call the cops. You drive."

6

Return to Cutler's

I spent the rest of the day trying to come up with possible motives for Cutler Mead's murder, but as a practical matter, I didn't know enough to even speculate. We needed to identify people who could fill in the picture of the man. Other than his wife and whatever Flynn could dig up about Cutler's business, the only hope was to find a lead at his house.

The afternoon and early evening crawled by, until I felt it was dark enough for Theo and me to leave. I was regretting my decision to let Theo drive as she gingerly backed her Mercedes out of the parking space and crept out of the deck. Theo was a nervous driver, and she whistled when she drove. The tuneless whistling bore into my brain. I spoke to interrupt the warbling.

"Don't get on the connector. The traffic's miserable. Take Piedmont out."

We drove up Piedmont, cut over Roswell Road and made the left onto Blackland, weaving around the exclusive neighborhood in silence until we turned onto Cutler's street. She passed his house and took a right at the corner, then another right before she pulled over to park the Mercedes in a narrow lane that acted as a service alley behind the upscale homes.

She clearly knew this way in. Maybe all of Cutler's mistresses used the back door. We walked toward a pair of handsome iron gates set into a brick wall surrounding the backyard. To encourage Theo, I acted like I sneaked into dead men's houses every day. The truth was the hair on my neck was standing up and saying, *What the heck are you doing, Ann Audrey Pickering?* It was too late to turn back now, but I was so nervous the band of my bra was soaked through.

We slipped through the unlocked gates and followed the flagstone walk past azaleas banked around the swimming pool. Its underwater lights glowed. The effect was either inviting or creepy. I couldn't decide. The pool's surface was immaculate, not a leaf or blossom floated on the water, despite the overgrown foliage crowding the pool deck.

We tiptoed across the patio and up the terrace to the back door. We were on the other side of the big windows in the great room at the center of the house. Theo produced her key, and we were inside the dark house in seconds. I pulled out my flashlight and lit her way down the hall and the wing that led to the study. There had been no sign of the police outside the house, and the yellow crime scene tape was gone from the double doors of the room where Cutler died.

Theo stalled at the threshold of her former lover's study.

I walked around her and circled Cutler's desk in order to reach the frames arranged in the bookshelves. I avoided stepping on the rug where his body had lain, the way old people won't walk on top of a grave.

"What're you looking for?" Theo said.

"I don't know. Something to give us a line of investigation—identify people we could talk to. We've got to start somewhere." When I'd started snooping on my husband, I'd known some of his clients, and they'd told me things. I was hoping we could get some information about Cutler from people who knew him—maybe the people in the photos that decorated the bookshelves.

Theo tiptoed into the room.

"See if you recognize anyone," I ordered, handing her an eight by ten picture. I was deliberately brusque, to shock her into action. She took the picture, and we began to work our way around the room, scrutinizing the photos under the flashlight until Theo halted to pick up one of the silver frames.

"These guys are familiar," she said, pointing at the group. "That's Drew Littlefield, Cutler's lawyer. And that guy in the madras pants — can you believe they wear those in public?— is Tom Boxer. He's a veterinarian and owns one of those doggy day spas."

I put in my two cents. "The guy holding the beer is Scot Raybourn. I've seen him in the Atlanta Journal. His tech company sponsored one of the charity runs for something this year. But who's the fifth guy, the shifty looking one?"

"That'd be me, I 'magine." The overhead lights in the study were flicked on.

I whirled around, heart pounding. The man's voice had been amused, but his eyes weren't. Theo dropped the frame, and it bounced on the thick carpet, landing face down. She and I backed against the bookcases as he advanced on bare feet. That explained why we hadn't heard him behind us. He loomed over us so that I had to tilt my head to look into his eyes. They were an unusual shade, almost yellow, and high cheekbones stood out above the bristly chin. His body was runner lean, but plenty of muscle showed under the white tee shirt. An odor of paint thinner, or maybe years of booze, hung around him.

My tongue was stuck to the roof of my mouth as I scrambled to come up with an excuse for our presence.

Then Theo said, "Freddie. What are you doing here?"

"I live here, Miz Humphries. In the pool house. Remember? You've seen me here often enough." His exaggerated drawl mocked her.

"Still?"

Freddie smirked at the question. "I keep an eye on the place. Good thing I saw the red lights on the silent alarm start flashing. There's no telling who might break in and take something before the cops respond."

I had frozen in place at Freddie's sudden appearance, but Theo did not seem to be fazed. She put her hands on her hips. "Does Mrs. Mead know that you're still hanging around?" she asked.

He shifted his weight more toward Theo. "Does she know you're here?"

I decided I'd better break this up.

"No, she doesn't," I said.

"Who're you?"

"I'm a friend of Theo's. She asked me to come with her."

Fortunately Freddie had turned away from Theo when I spoke up, so he didn't observe Theo rolling her eyes at this blatant lie.

"Come here? What for?" Freddie asked.

"Theo is deeply upset that Mr. Mead is gone. She's mourning him. She wanted to be here where he lived. To feel his presence again, I guess you'd say."

This was over the top, but in my experience, men who don't spend much time around women are susceptible to such baloney. I was gambling that Freddie was such a man.

"Uh." He shook his head. "If you say so, lady."

I bent over and picked up the framed photo that Theo had dropped. I held it in front of Freddie's face. "So, this is you."

He took the photo and studied it. "Yeah. Me, Cutler, Scotty, Drew and Tom."

"Y'all were friends." I made it a statement and waited to see if he'd deny it.

"You could say that. We saw each other almost every Sunday."

"You played golf together?"

"I don't much play golf. Usually just came to have a beer."

"How'd y'all meet?"

"We served together."

"In Vietnam." It was a safe bet, given his age and that of the other men in the photo.

"Right."

The Baby Boomers' miserable war. Thirty years or so ago,

and little was heard about it now. I probably knew men who'd been there, but none of them talked about it. I said the only thing I could think of. "Y'all must have been awfully young."

"Young and stupid." Freddie gripped the framed picture, staring down at it. His thumbs rubbed the glass over the picture of the men. I had the feeling he'd forgotten we were there.

While he stared at the photo, I caught Theo's attention and looked toward the hall, signalling for an exit.

"I'm sorry we bothered you. We'll see ourselves out." Without waiting for him to respond, I hurried out of the study and into the hall, heading for the great room and the outside door leading to the patio. Theo scooted ahead of me and was across the patio and through the back gate in no time. In my hurry to catch up, I stumbled against a webbed chair on the edge of the pool deck. When I paused to rub my shin, Freddie stepped out of the bushes to block my way.

"Stop there," said Freddie.

How had he gotten ahead of me? My question must have showed on my face.

"Ran around you," he said. "I know the terrain, and I can see real good in the dark."

I took a step back. "What do you want?"

"I want you to stay away—from here, from me."

"We didn't come here to bother you," I said. I was glad Theo had already gone through the back gate. I hoped she had started the car.

"You're looking to help Mrs. Humphries." he said. "I 'magine the cops think she killed Cutler, but you don't believe it."

"That's right."

Freddie gave a whoof of disgust. "Finally, something honest out of your mouth. Was that so hard?"

"Now just a minute," I said. "We haven't done you any harm by coming here. I'm sorry if we surprised you, but…"

"You didn't surprise me." As he opened his mouth to continue, a shrill ring from a telephone interrupted him.

I started to move away, but he grabbed my arm above the elbow. "You and I aren't finished." He waited for the phone to go quiet.

For a brief moment there was silence. Then the ringing began again. "Ah fuck," Freddie said, "Come on."

With me spluttering, he half-dragged, half-led me back toward the house. An extension phone on the patio kept up its loud ring. Freddie reached for the handset, but stopped midair, before punching the speaker button.

"Where've you been?" The high tenor voice had an edge to it that carried easily in the warm night air.

"Outside. We've had visitors." Freddie put a finger to his lips to warn me to stay silent, still holding me in place with his other hand. The caution wasn't necessary. I was dying to know who was on the phone.

"Police?" the voice asked.

"No. Cutler's latest girlfriend and a buddy of hers."

"Latest girlfriend? You mean Theo Humphries? Dammit, I told you this morning to expect something."

"You told me to expect the cops would be asking around about Cutler." Freddie shifted his weight, but seemed more amused than concerned by the caller's anxiety.

"Yeah, okay. But, what were they doing there? My instinct is that Theo Humphries would stay away from Cutler's place. My contacts told me the policeman in charge has her figured as Cutler's killer."

"Your instincts are obviously wrong, Drew. And your contacts may be wrong, too." Freddie glanced over at me, smiling like a hunter who's just watched an animal fall into a trap. He was enjoying the other man's case of nerves, and letting me know the man's name.

I couldn't help but wonder why Freddie was letting me listen in to the conversation. Did he want me to know that he wasn't the only one protecting Cutler's interests—and opposing Theo's? Was he trying to tell me something about Cutler's friends? Or was Freddie leading me into a trap by letting me hear what Drew was saying?

"Okay, say you're right and I'm wrong," the voice went on. "Even so, what was she doing there? Wait, you said there were two of them. Who was she with?"

"We never got around to formal introductions. I surprised them in the study, looking at all those framed pictures Cutler kept in the bookshelves. They said..." at this, Freddie looked directly at me, "they *said* they were visiting because Mrs. Humphries was mourning Cutler and needed to feel his presence. Once I showed up they skedaddled."

"That's crazy. I'm coming over there."

"No. Stay away. We can talk about this on Sunday when we get together."

With this instruction, Freddie dropped his voice to a deep purr. The sound raised the hair on my neck. Whatever that voice meant to the man on the other end of the line, it worked.

"Maybe you're right." I could almost hear the man swallow. "Somebody could be watching the house. I'll see you at the funeral. You going down to Cutler's Sea Island place afterwards?"

"Yeah."

"Ok. But call me if anything else happens. I don't like to be surprised."

Freddie hung up the phone and shook his head.

"What a pussy."

"Was that Drew Littlefield?" I asked, remembering Theo's identification of the man in the photo.

"Yep. Imagine following that bundle of nerves into a fire fight."

"What's he got to be nervous about?"

"Who knows with Drew. He needs to be reassured all the time." Freddie sighed. "Cutler used to do that."

"And now he's asking you for reassurance."

Freddie huffed a laugh. "He's gonna wait a long time."

I searched for something that would keep Freddie talking. "I take it Drew wasn't a natural soldier?"

"When Drew was walking point, he thrashed around so much every VC in 20 miles must of known we were there." Freddie looked down and shook his head. "That was a long time ago. I try to forget that time."

"Sorry. I didn't mean to stir up unhappy memories."

At my comment, Freddie straightened up and his face hardened.

"Stir up unhappy memories. You don't know shit. What do you think was stirred up when I saw Cutler being zipped up in that body bag. Any idea how many guys I've seen zipped up in a black bag?"

I swallowed hard. "I apologize." It sounded feeble, but I couldn't think what else to say.

He shook his head, refusing my apology. "Don't come

back here. There's too much at stake for you to mess things up poking your nose in where it don't belong."

I started to speak, but he shushed me, his yellow eyes staring into mine. "I'm telling you to stay out of this. I learned some useful things in the war. I learned a dozen ways to...protect myself."

If he intended to scare me it worked. I wanted to run away, but I was afraid to turn my back on him. "And don't think you can sneak in," he said. "I heard you tonight. Knew you were here even before the alarm lit up. Next time I'll know you, even in the dark, by your walk—and your smell." He leaned slightly toward me and sniffed, moving his head from the crown of my head to my chin.

I jerked backward and pulled my arm from his grip. Ignoring the flagstones, I bolted across the grass to the back gate and ran for the car, grabbing the door handle and falling into the front seat. One look at me and Theo wasted no time starting the engine.

"What took you so long?" she asked. "I was just about to go back and look for you."

"I ran into Freddie."

"He's a weirdo. Freddie....Somerset, I think. I should have remembered he'd be there. Let's get out of here." Theo put her foot down and accelerated out of the neighborhood. "You okay?"

"Yeah. But I'll admit he spooked me."

"He's spooky, all right," said Theo. "I think I peed in my pants when he snuck up on us."

"Good thing we're in your car then," I said, in a half-hearted attempt at humor. My pulse was returning to normal. "How come this Freddie dude is living at Cutler's?"

"He sort of follows—followed—Cutler around. He lives in the pool house here, but I've seen him down on Sea Island at Cutler's other house, too."

"He doesn't seem like the Sea Island type. Why did Cutler put up with him?"

"Cutler had a soft spot for him. Freddie came back from Vietnam with a lot of problems. He's better now, but sometime he freaks out. Thinks he's back there. Scary."

"Scary enough to kill somebody?"

Theo considered the question while she drove. "I don't know. Maybe some of the other guys in that picture would know."

"If we can get them to talk to us. That'll be our next problem."

7

Funeral

Cutler Mead's obituary appeared in the Atlanta Journal that Friday. He had been awarded several medals for his service as a First Lieutenant in Vietnam. It was impressive that he'd managed to come home at all, much less in one piece. Lieutenants in Vietnam had a short life expectancy. If the other golfers had been with him, perhaps they credited him with bringing them back alive. Was that the glue that held them together?

Now that the police had released the body, a funeral service was planned. I read the announcement over my coffee and tried to decide if it was too ghoulish to attend. I couldn't pass up this chance to get a look at alternative suspects, but I didn't want to go alone.

Flynn answered the phone on the first ring. "What's up?"

"I need you to go to Cutler Mead's funeral with me."

"Ugh. I hate those things. Why would we go?"

"I want to get a look at who shows up. Especially the golfing buddies. Remember I told you about that guy Freddie spooking Theo and me when we were at Cutler's house?"

"You two goofballs were lucky he didn't call the cops." Flynn had been appalled by our nighttime exploration of the Mead residence.

"I know, Flynn. But listen. Freddie told us that all of those golfers served with Cutler in Vietnam."

"Do you expect one of them to confess to the murder in front of God and everyone?"

"Humor me. Let's go and just watch."

Flynn grudgingly agreed to drive with me to the rites. Now I had to tell Theo we were going. I suspected she would not react well. I was right.

"I feel like I should be there for him," Theo wailed.

"Are you out of your mind? This is an event where Sissy Mead—*Mrs. Mead*—will be justifiably center stage. It would be awful, just awful for you to show up. Can you imagine the press coverage?"

Theo sank back into the couch cushions. "You're right, I know, but it seems unfair. I can't wait for this to be over."

Theo's misery was obvious in her puffy eyes and splotchy complexion. Maybe I could encourage her to do a spa day, have a massage and a facial. On second thought, Theo would infer grooming criticism from that suggestion. Better to let it go than add to her suffering.

Despite my sympathy for her, I was annoyed by Theo's seeming naïveté. After all, it had been only a few days since

Cutler died under circumstances that implicated her. She had no idea of the scrutiny to come from the cops and the public. Theo's reaction was perfectly in character. She expected things to work out, until—like George's unexpected death—they didn't. By contrast, I was routinely cynical—justifiably so, on occasion. The real miracle was that we had remained friends after all this time.

"Honey, I'm sorry," I said "but I'm working on it. Let me and Flynn go to the funeral, check out who's there. We'll come back and tell you everything. It's best if you stay away."

On the way to the service, I told Flynn about Theo's reaction.

"Maybe she should be here, so that the cops can see how distressed she is. Could someone who is that distraught be guilty of killing him?" Flynn asked.

"I don't think that will convince them of anything. There must have been lots of murderers who cried at the graveside of the dearly departed."

"There's a chilling thought," he said.

We waited for the parking valet amidst a line of idling Mercedes, Lexus, Audis and Jaguars that advertised the prestige of the funeral home's clientele. Patterson's has been known since 1882 for handling the final obsequies of Atlanta's wealthy or well connected. Its prestige was so secure that, although the funeral home and its garden now sit surrounded by high rise office buildings in midtown, it was still the preferred venue for Atlanta society's memorial services.

"I don't think I've ever seen valet parking at a funeral," I said.

"I'm sure that Sissy Mead's sorority sisters are here in force, and none of them could be expected to walk all the way from the parking lot in stilettos." The comment was unusually cynical for Flynn.

"Are you ok?"

"I've been here a lot." He had a white-knuckle grip on the steering wheel of his BMW.

I was confused at first, then I realized what he meant. Atlanta had been the South's destination of choice and party central for gay men. Backstreet, a gay bar, was such an institution that no Atlanta politician would miss a campaign event held there. A decade ago, the entire scene had been upended by AIDS. Flynn had several friends who'd succumbed to the disease.

"I'm sorry, Flynn. I shouldn't have asked you to come. I don't mean to dredge up unhappy memories."

"Forget it—life must go on." He relaxed his hands, but wouldn't turn his head to look at me. The lines of cars moved up a space and he eased our way forward. "Let's talk about you. When are you going back to work?"

"I'm not thinking about that now." I wished Flynn hadn't brought it up. I had not decided whether I wanted to return to the practice of law. With the money Daddy had left me and some investments that weren't connected to my ex-husband, I was financially okay for the time being. Theo's situation gave me an excuse to do something useful and, in the meantime, avoid making any decisions about my own future.

"You should, Audrey. You were a good lawyer. There weren't many who could have figured out what Charlie was up to."

I guessed Flynn wanted a distraction from his memories of this funeral home. I owed it to him to talk. "I don't think there are many Atlanta law firms who'd hire me after all that publicity."

"Don't you still have your license?"

"Sure. Thought it might come in handy."

"You could always move somewhere else."

"Are you insane? And take another state's bar exam?"

"You can't sit around and do nothing for the rest of your life, Audrey. You'll go nuts."

"Right now you and I are trying to help Theo. I'll think about what I'm going to do after this is over. Correction—after Theo is cleared of any suspicion and the real killer is locked up."

We both fell silent as the end of the line grew near. Flynn guided his BMW to the valet stand, and we left the car with the attendant. I had bowed to Theo's opinion of what was appropriate for a Buckhead resident's funeral and wore my sole designer outfit, an Armani sheath and jacket. I was stylish enough to blend in with the couture-clad mourners shuffling respectfully toward a palladium window that floated above the double doors leading to the chapel.

Built in the 1930's, Patterson's funeral home was designed to mimic an old English manor, complete with 18th-century-style furniture. The entrance hall's black and white tile set off the creamy paint on the chair rail and elaborate moldings over the windows. Silk draperies puddled on the floor, complementing the pale yellow walls. The effect was luxurious, elegant, and soothing.

Flynn and I followed the crowd into the chapel and took seats midway back on the aisle. We were aiming to be inconspicuous, but able to see guests, especially the players who would be seated in front to mark their status as family familiars. On our left, off a side aisle, a gate separated the congregation from a smaller chapel. The crowd was still settling into their seats when a dignified staff member opened the gate for a portly man who gripped a slim middle-aged blond by the elbow and maneuvered the two of them into the sanctuary. They were trailed by a young man with over-long hair, who walked with his eyes downcast.

"Look. There's Sissy," whispered a woman's voice behind us. I nudged Flynn. Our first glimpse of the widow.

"Who's that older man?" asked another voice.

"I think that's Martin Frye, her older brother," said the first voice.

The third member of the group had to be Cutler's son, the one Theo had told me was the reason the Meads had remained married, despite Cutler's infidelities.

Mrs. Cutler Mead wore her hair in a smooth chin-length bob. She was dressed in black and walked rigidly erect, her face frozen. If she stumbled and fell she'd shatter on the marble floor. Once through the gate, her son moved alongside her, turning his back on the crowd to insulate his mother from the eyes of the congregation. The three sat alone on the front pew.

The boy appeared concerned about his mother, putting his arm behind her on the back of the pew. Where had he been on the day his father was bludgeoned to death? The kind of beating given to Cutler Mead could have exploded from a son's lifetime of seeing his mother repeatedly shamed by his father's infidelities.

I squirmed, seeking a less uncomfortable position on the oak pew. Why didn't Patterson's upholster these benches? My Calvinist/Presbyterian upbringing answered the question—funerals were *supposed* to be an uncomfortable reminder of our mortality.

"Quit fidgeting, will you?" Flynn said.

"Sorry. I'm trying to look around to see who's here."

"Take a look at the back row. On the aisle."

I swiveled around and locked eyes with Mike Bristol, looking remarkably relaxed in a dark navy suit. He had the nerve to nod, so I nodded back. Was it my imagination, or did he wink at me?

"Did he just...?"

"Yep. Winked," Flynn answered. "I can't wait to get home and tell Don." Flynn was barely smothering a laugh.

That smug son-of-a-...Mike Bristol's ego was completely unchecked. "What's he doing here?" I hissed in Flynn's ear.

"The same thing you're doing. Checking out the suspects. Probably standard procedure." Flynn hesitated and added, "He does wear that suit well."

"Stop it."

I was embarrassed that Detective Bristol had seen us. I had assumed that no one at the funeral, except Freddie, would have any idea who I was. It had been years since I'd ventured out into a large gathering. In the past I'd gotten dirty looks from more than one person who'd lost money from my husband's stock manipulation. *Stop thinking about yourself and focus on learning something to help Theo,* I scolded myself.

I craned my neck to view the front of the room. Four men sat stiffly across the aisle from Sissy Mead. I had no trouble identifying the quartet in the picture from Cutler's study. There was Freddie, clean shaven and uncomfortable in his black suit and white shirt. Dr. Tom Boxer, the veterinarian, was slim to the point of skinny, dressed in an Italian designer suit. Scot Raybourn loomed over them, broad shouldered and handsome and occasionally looking at his heavy gold wristwatch. A small man I guessed to be Drew Littlefield, occasionally sniffed and used his handkerchief. He was crying, the only one of the four who showed any emotion. The other three were stone-faced, eyes front and completely ignoring each other.

I bowed my head and read the program setting out the service and the speakers who were to eulogize Cutler Mead. "That's interesting," I said, pointing to the program, "none of the golfing buddies are listed."

"The choice of speakers would be up to the widow. Maybe she didn't want them to speak."

"Wonder why."

I watched them for the duration of the memorial service. There appeared to be little interaction among the four, but nothing suspicious.

When the minister indicated the close of the ceremony, the four golfing buddies exited their pew and, joined by two funeral parlor employees, managed to hoist the casket. To my surprise, Freddie was the one who directed the pallbearers. He stood at the back right corner of the procession and gave commands to the others, inaudible to the congregation, but when his lips moved the others responded. What else might Freddie have been in charge of without others realizing it? The widow watched the men as the casket passed down the aisle. She stared at Scot Raybourn, finally catching the big man's eye. She raised an eyebrow and he nodded an acknowledgement, before she stepped into the aisle to follow the bier, trailed by her son and brother.

Outside the chapel, I watched the pallbearers slide the casket into the hearse for the trip to the cemetery. When the doors were closed, Cutler's friends broke away from the other two pallbearers. Scot Raybourn put his hand on Drew Littlefield's shoulder, only to have it roughly brushed away. Shrugging, Raybourn leaned down and said something with a laugh, before he turned and joined Tom Boxer who'd stepped back and was watching them. Freddie had disappeared.

Flynn joined me outside and we waited for the valet to retrieve Flynn's BMW. Once we were inside the car and away from any listeners, I asked, "Did you see that exchange between Mrs. Mead and the big guy—Scot Raybourn?"

"Saw him nod at her," Flynn said. "What do you think that was about?"

"I'd say those two have some unfinished business," I said.

"You got all that from a nod?" Flynn said, looking over at me with exasperation.

"Just a guess," I said. "She waited until she could catch his attention. Has to be a reason for that. Otherwise, what did you think about Cutler's buddies?"

"It's pretty obvious—not all of the golfers are sorry they've lost one of their foursome." said Flynn.

I had to agree. The chemistry among the men was telling

"Not only his friends," I said. "Mrs. Mead appears as cold as ice—not what I'd expect from a grieving widow."

"People grieve in their own way," said Flynn. "Appearances can be deceiving."

8

Shoe Shopping at Neiman Marcus

After the funeral I returned home, kicked off my shoes and dug my toes into the soft plush of white carpet. Sanctuary—forty-two floors above the push and pull of Atlanta. I was grateful for it. I cut through the living room and headed toward the kitchen, intent on pouring a glass of wine to ease back into the pleasure of living. I hadn't expected to see Theo, who was perched on my sofa like a jungle cat waiting for prey.

"Oh, hey. I didn't see you there."

"We need to talk, Annie."

"Okay. Do you want a glass of wine?" I reached into the fridge for a chilled bottle. I was stalling for time while I rehearsed what I could say about the funeral for her dead lover. I poured us both a glass and walked back to the sofa to hand hers over.

"Do you want me to tell you about the funeral?" I began.

"Later. That's not what I wanted to talk about."

"What, then?" I asked.

"I went to Lenox Mall this afternoon."

In spite of my disapproval, Theo had insisted she would go shopping while Flynn and I went to Cutler's funeral. Her clothes announced that she hadn't gone to Walmart. She wore a dark teal dress tailored to fit, along with a thick gold choker and earrings to match. A pair of low-heeled Ferragamos were an unusually solemn fashion choice for Theo, perhaps in deference to the funeral taking place without her. Any observant salesperson would have understood that Theo could afford to buy anything in their department.

"I went to Neiman's to browse for shoes."

I grinned at her. I couldn't help myself.

"You don't understand," Theo said.

Actually, I did. I'd been to Neiman Marcus with her often enough. I knew the soft background music, plush carpet and rows of pumps, mules, boots and delicate sandals in the shoe salon comforted Theo like a warm hug from grandmama.

"I needed to take my mind off Cutler's murder, police

questions, trying to think of people who'd want to kill him," Theo said.

"Did it help? Buying shoes?"

"At first. I spotted some slingbacks. Very pretty. A kind of taupe color."

That spoke worlds. Theo loved bright colors. The fact that she considered putting her feet into brown/beige/gray was akin to donning sack cloth.

"I asked Alton to get my size and sat down on the banquette to try them on."

It was no surprise that Theo knew the shoe salesman's name. She'd told me that he earned the store's top bonus last year, partially due to Theo's fondness for designer labels. I murmured my understanding to encourage her to go on.

"That's when I saw Mitzi Huntington and Sue Beth Wharton. They had their backs turned, pretending to look at some Kate Spade wedges. They acted like they hadn't seen me, though they must have passed right by where I was sitting."

I recognized the names of the two casual acquaintances from Sea Island. Not close friends, but members of Theo's social set. Suspicion of criminal contagion is the smallpox of our time. People are quick to cut you in public when they think your troubles might infect them. I should have warned Theo to be prepared for that. "Theo, I'm so sorry," I said.

"I'm okay. Well, not okay. They were *rude*, Annie." She paused, bending her neck sideways as if to shake the memory out of her head. "I've been ignored by thinner blonds in my life. I bluffed it out, chatted with Alton while I paid for the shoes—although I'm not sure I'll ever wear them—until Mitzi and Sue Beth had gone."

That pair of blond bitches. I ground my teeth at their

treatment of Theo. If I ever see those two again, they'll be lucky if those peroxided locks don't burst into flame. While I fumed, Theo kept talking, reliving her afternoon.

"I went downstairs to the Neiman's Bistro and ordered the popovers with strawberry butter. I was licking the strawberry butter off the top of the popovers. It was the same color as a pair of hot pink stilettos I'd bought years ago to wear to a cocktail party on Sea Island."

Where was she going with this story? Only Theo would make a leap from gourmet pastry to high heels.

"I loved those shoes," Theo said. "I remember how George laughed when I told him I'd bought them because they reminded me of sour watermelon candies. I was wearing them at the party when George and his lawyer, Drew Littlefield, got into an argument."

"Wait, Theo. Stop right there. You never told me Drew Littlefield was George's lawyer." I was flabbergasted that Theo hadn't mentioned that fact when we were looking at the photos in Cutler's study.

"Sorry. Someone else was handling George's affairs when he died, and I'd forgotten that Drew used to do George's legal work. That's what I remembered when I was at Neiman's. I'm trying to tell you now."

"Okay. Go ahead with the story," I said.

"They were outside near the bar out on the patio. I was sitting with some girls in the living room, but I could hear George's voice. He was swearing. I slipped out of the room and went to see why he was yelling so."

"I don't think I ever heard your husband raise his voice," I said. "He was the most easy-going man I ever met."

"He was usually such a sweetie. That's why I remember this

party. I went out to the patio and asked him what was going on. I put my hand on his shoulder to try to get him to come inside. He looked like he was going to punch Drew.

I said, 'Honey, we can hear you hollering inside the house.' I thought he'd realize he was making a scene. But no. He pulled away from me and dropped his voice. Got right in Drew's face. He told Drew he intended to have *nothing to do with it*, and Drew would make it right, or George was going to make sure he did."

"What was it that George was refusing to have anything to do with?" I asked.

"He wouldn't tell me."

"What did Drew say when George made that threat?"

"He said there was nothing he could do."

"What happened then?"

"I finally got George to go back into the house. We left. George drove home in a rage. Passed other cars, even blew his horn at someone trying to back out of his driveway onto Frederica Road. That scared me more than anything, 'cause he was usually such a polite driver."

She was right, I thought, recalling many times George had driven us home after we'd all had one too many salty dogs along with our seafood dinner.

"For a while after that, either Drew or Cutler kept phoning the house—interrupted our dinner a couple of times. George would leave the table to talk to them. I'd hear him pacing back and forth in the den. He was arguing with whichever was on the line. After a week or so the calls stopped, and George told me that he'd changed to another law firm."

"Did you ever figure out what the squabble was about?"

"No. But I'm willing to bet it involved one of Cutler's real estate schemes. There were all kinds of developments just start-ing on St. Simons then, and it would be the kind of thing George would invest in. It was all in the past, more than five years ago now, but you said we needed to find a lead to investigate."

"We do, but we'll have to figure out if George and Cutler were doing some kind of deal together."

"Annie, I think I know somebody on the island who could tell us what George and Cutler were arguing about. If he fell out with someone as easygoing as George, he must have had blow-ups with other people. Do you think it's worth follow-ing up?"

She looked at me with those big, soft brown eyes, the ones men had drowned in. Theo was an unabashed hedonist, reveled in sex and accoutrements of wealth. She cried easily at the most appalling sentimental claptrap. Her heart should have been mush, but in fact, was as tough as over-cooked pot roast. She'd proven that when she'd opened herself up to love after suffering through George's death. That showed courage. Middle-aged love is terrifying. You know too well what pain it could inflict.

I shook my head in admiration. Life had kicked Theo in the gut, and she'd gotten dressed and gone to face the world with her gold credit card. As a result, she'd come up with a theory, and maybe, some hope.

"It's a great idea," I said. "The other golfers live on the coast, too. We need to be there if we're going to talk to them, find out about who could have a grudge against Cutler. Other than Mrs. Mead, and nothing points to her right now, I don't know any leads here in Atlanta. We should move our investigation to your place on Sea Island."

"Let's go first thing in the morning."

"Wait, Theo. We have to inform the police. Detective

Bristol said you weren't supposed to leave Atlanta, remember? I'll call him and clear it." I crossed my fingers behind my back, hoping that Bristol would agree to let us go.

"Fine. You talk to him. And call Flynn and ask if he wants to come down and stay at my place. Bring enough clothes for a week, and Annie, remember the Cloister dining room won't admit anyone in jeans. No need to tell Flynn that. He's always well dressed."

She swirled out of the room to pack for the return home.

I should have been insulted, but she was right. I headed to my closet to see if I could dredge up a clean skirt and some nice sandals to throw in my bag.

9

Deal at the OK Cafe

I called the Atlanta police the next morning and asked for Detective Bristol. When he came on the line, I made my pitch.

"It's Ann Audrey Pickering, Detective. I'm calling because Theo is anxious to go home to Sea Island. I'm going to drive down with her. I hope that won't be a problem."

There was silence on the other end of the line. I waited.

"Miss Pickering…"

"Ann Audrey."

"Right. Just so I'm clear, you're asking if it's ok by me for a suspect in a violent murder to leave the Atlanta PD's jurisdiction."

"She'd still be in Georgia," I said.

"What if she decides to jump on a plane and head out of the country?"

He wasn't going to make this easy. "I said I was going with her. You have nothing to worry about."

"Yeah, sure."

Sarcasm dripped through the phone. I wasn't liking the way he was taking this, so I decided to change tack. "Theo only wants to go home and get away from the Atlanta circus."

"You can't seriously expect that she won't be in the news down there?" He chuckled.

"No. There might be gossip, but it'll be harder for someone to camp outside Theo's doorway and ambush her. There's private neighborhood security, and non-residents stick out on Sea Island."

"*Might* be gossip. What an understatement. Theo Humphries killing her married lover has got to be the juiciest tidbit on the coast. If she wants to hide, she'd be better off in an Atlanta high-rise with lots of security to keep out the riff-raff."

That put me in my place, all right. But my task still hadn't changed. If I couldn't get Bristol to approve our leaving Atlanta, Theo would bolt without me, and be brought back in handcuffs. "I'll be there to keep an eye on her," I said, "and you can ask the local police to keep an eye on us." When he didn't respond, I asked, "How can I convince you to let us drive to Sea Island?"

"Meet me."

"What?"

"I want to talk to you—informally. There's some background you may be able to help me with."

Informally—what the hey did that mean? Flynn had said that Bristol was known to occasionally bend the rules and think outside the box. I was uneasy about Bristol's motives, but I started this conversation. I couldn't back down.

"Fine," I said. "What about the OK Cafe in an hour? It shouldn't be too crowded then, and we can get a table."

"See you there."

* * *

I didn't bother to dress up to meet Bristol, but went straight to the restaurant in my jeans and tee shirt. The OK Cafe sounds like it belongs in Wyoming or Texas, but is a popular spot for a power breakfast in Buckhead—the heart of Atlanta's business community. It sits in a free-standing building next to a 1950's era strip mall that would have been turned into a big box store or condominiums in any other Atlanta neighborhood. However, the location at the corner of West Paces Ferry Road in Buckhead insured the businesses in the mall were gold mines. The parking lot was so busy that on the slowest retail day of the year, you still had to keep circling to find a spot.

The cafe's pine-paneled interior is lined with uncomfortable wooden booths accented by gingham half curtains at the windows. In addition to breakfast, the restaurant has a 'meat and three' menu served by waitresses in crisp mid-century white and blue uniforms and overdone Southern accents. I think they get those girls from Michigan. I normally avoid the cafe's dining room and the faux waitresses and head to the separate entrance on the back side of the restaurant. Here is the OK Takeaway, where you hang a red basket over your arm while you heap takeout containers full of meatloaf or fried chicken or pot pie accompanied by fried okra, mashed potatoes and corn bread muffins.

The OK Takeaway is a panorama of Buckhead—bankers in suit and tie, car salesmen, construction workers who are ubiquitous as they build/rebuild commercial and upscale residential neighborhoods that surround the OK Cafe. Later come the soccer moms buying supper after the game at one of the three private schools within two miles. And then there are the little ol' ladies. The OK Takeaway might be the last place in Atlanta where you see an elderly white lady trying to decide whether the collards are going to be too tough to chew, accompanied by the (invariably African American) nurse/housekeeper who with one hand is holding the old lady's elbow so that she doesn't do a header into the overcooked greens, and with the other hand balancing the loaded basket for checkout.

I eyed the Takeaway entrance with regret, and entered the main room of the cafe, asking the hostess for a booth toward the back. From there I could watch the door. I contemplated ordering a chocolate malt, but decided I might need my wits about me so I settled for coffee. The waitress had refilled my cup twice before I saw Bristol walk in. He gave the hostess a big grin and said something that lit up her face. She led him to my booth with a hip-swinging sashay.

"Sorry I'm late," he apologized.

He didn't look sorry. The brief interchange with the hostess had confirmed my opinion. Mike Bristol was a player. I couldn't deny his attraction—handsome, muscled and self-confident—but I had no intention of becoming another notch on his belt. I quelled my instinctive reaction to be gracious and forgive his tardiness. "Sit down," I said, "Do you want some coffee?"

"No thanks, I'm over my limit already." He slid into the booth and sat, putting his elbows on the table and leaning forward.

He seemed to be searching for an opening, so I jump-started the conversation. "You said I might be able to help with some background."

"Yeah. Tell me, how long have you and Mrs. Humphries known each other?"

"Too long, Theo would probably say. We met in college, the first day. We were standing in line for registration, and we struck up a conversation. After college we went separate ways, but we kept in touch." It was a minimalist description of our friendship, but I was wary of telling him too much.

"You seem closer than just 'in touch'."

"We've become closer the last few years. She's been a good friend to me, and I try to reciprocate."

His answer was a noncommittal, "Un hunh," his fingers tapping the table.

I struck back with the most reliable conversational gambit in Atlanta. "Where are you from, originally, Detective?"

"Ohio. School in New Jersey. Rutgers." He anticipated my next question. "I came to Atlanta with my ex-wife. She works for Turner Broadcasting."

"So you're one of the 50%?" It was well known that at least 50% of Atlantans were not Southerners.

"Right."

"You've managed to fit in."

"Not too hard if you learn to ignore some customs."

"Such as?" He was treading on dangerous ground.

"Anne Audrey Pickering, for instance. What is it about Southerners that causes them to string three or more names together and hang them on babies?" He appeared dead serious.

I was preparing a scorching reply when I saw the slight quirk at the corner of his mouth. "It is a burden, but we learn to live with it. And it can give you a lot of flexibility."

He threw back his head and laughed. He had very fine white teeth.

"About Mrs. Humphries. Did she tell you about her relationship with Cutler Mead?"

He was fishing for information. Thankfully, I didn't have much to tell, so I didn't feel like I was betraying Theo. "She told me they were seeing each other."

"When did she start dating him?"

"He took her out to dinner after her husband George died. According to Theo, Cutler was *commiserating* with her over George's death." I couldn't help myself. I deliberately drawled out the word *commiserating*.

"You seem skeptical."

"I'll admit I was surprised, but they were acquaintances. I believe George and Cutler had done some business together. Theo grieved George Humphries for a long time—years. He was probably the love of her life."

"Probably?"

"That's my opinion, I don't know about hers. I don't think you can ever know for sure who people love most. People love a person as much as they can, and when that ends, they try to love someone else just as deeply. Maybe it works—maybe it doesn't." I regretted saying that as soon as it was out of my mouth. I didn't mean to give this man any insight into my thoughts. I hoped he'd ignore it. No such luck.

"Are we talking about Theo Humphries here?"

"That's who you asked about."

"Sorry."

The atmosphere in the booth became chilly. He shifted on the hard seat. Those pine benches are brutal on people with no padding on their backside.

"How did you and Mrs. Humphries become such close friends?" Bristol asked.

"I told you we'd known each other a long time."

"I've known guys I went to college with that I wouldn't invite for a beer."

His blue eyes were looking right into mine. He seemed to be waiting for me. I looked down at the table top and reconsidered that chocolate malt. What the hell, I thought. I need to play this out for Theo's sake.

"When my husband…" I swallowed, "was indicted, and the police revealed that I would be testifying against him, there was a lot of publicity. People I thought were my friends made it clear that they were not. A lot of nasty phone calls. From family. People I didn't even know. I finally changed my number, but they still found me."

"But Mrs. Humphries wasn't one of those people?"

"No. Not Theo. She never wavered. She was in my corner the whole time."

He shifted again. He must really be uncomfortable.

I hadn't intended this meeting to be so one-sided. It was time I got some information out of him. "What did the medical examiner's report say?" I asked.

"Death from blunt force trauma."

"One of the golf trophies in the study?" I hoped he wouldn't realize that I'd slipped into the foyer to get a closer look when the scene was off limits.

He sat back and didn't answer. What was he thinking? Had I overplayed my hand? After a minute, he said, "Right."

"Then it couldn't be Theo," I said, in a manner that brooked no room for disagreement.

"Why not? She was right there. She was covered in his blood when we arrived." He didn't seem angry that I'd been so definite. It was more like he was enjoying the give and take, as alert as any sports competitor, watching for his opponent's next move.

"That happened when she found him—as she already told you. And anyhow, how would Theo, who's barely 5 foot 2, strike Cutler Mead in the head? He was a very tall man."

"He could have been seated. She could have gotten up and grabbed the trophy while they were arguing."

"You can't be serious. That's a stretch even if they'd been arguing—which they weren't. I know when Theo's happy, and she was happy with Cutler Mead."

That drew a soft chuckle from him. "I forgot—you didn't know. Cutler Mead was going back to his wife."

"What? I don't believe it," I said. Bristol was starting to aggravate me, maybe intentionally.

"When I interviewed Mrs. Mead she told me they were reconciling. How do you think your friend would have reacted when he told her that?"

I thought back to the icy widow I'd watched at the funeral. Could she have really seduced Cutler away from Theo? I didn't think it was likely. "Did anybody else know that the Meads were getting back together?"

The detective blinked at my question. "We're trying to find any witnesses who might corroborate Mrs. Mead's statement. But in the meantime, there's no question your friend remains the most likely suspect."

"Most likely," I repeated. "Are you at least *looking* for other suspects?" I was angry that he still couldn't see that Theo wasn't capable of this.

"We're following other leads," he said.

I played a hunch. "When we spoke on the phone, you said I could help you with background. What did you mean? Something other than these questions about Theo?"

For the first time in the conversation, Bristol looked uncertain. "I think the crux of this case is out of the APD's jurisdiction—on the coast—either St. Simons or Sea Island."

I put my own elbows on the table and leaned toward him. He smelled like some kind of spicy soap. "Go on."

"Mrs. Humphries is well ensconced in society down there. She probably knows most of the people that Cutler Mead knew or did business with."

"Probably." I wasn't about to let on that he was telling me precisely why Theo and I wanted to go to the coast.

He seemed to be searching for how to continue. He unwound the napkin on the paper placemat and played with the silverware. "I'm not encouraging you to do anything dangerous," he began.

"Thanks. I'm familiar with the standard trope to leave everything to the police." Not that I had abided by that rule when I decided to go after my husband. Charlie would still be swindling people if I'd left it up to the cops to stop him.

"If you talk to people on the coast, and you discover something I should know about this murder, I want you to tell me."

"Of course." Easy enough. Why wouldn't I tell him anything that might exonerate Theo?

Bristol didn't look convinced by my statement. "Tell me—Ann Audrey—and let me handle it. Don't put yourself or Mrs. Humphries in danger."

Let's not kid ourselves. I would have said anything just to get his permission for us to leave Atlanta. "Of course," I said. "So Theo and I can go to Sea Island—with your blessing?"

10

Drive to Sea Island

"That's ridiculous. I don't believe it for one minute," Theo said, clenching the wheel of her Mercedes so tightly that her knuckles were white. I wasn't sure whether her death grip was because I had just told her that Sissy and Cutler Mead were reconciling or because of the traffic flowing around us. We were moving fast on I-75 out of Atlanta, so fast that switching lanes required total concentration. South-bound lanes five across sped wheel to wheel far above the posted speed limit. You had to keep up or be run over. This kind of driving was not Theo's forte, and I regretted distracting her.

"I'm just reporting what Detective Bristol told me," I said. "Maybe Cutler didn't say anything to you because he didn't want to upset you."

"I promise you, Annie, if Cutler Mead were planning to go back to his wife, he would not have had to tell me. I would have known." She flung one arm out, her palm open, dismissing the possibility.

"Keep both hands on the wheel."

There would be plenty of time to hash over my conversation with Mike Bristol during this drive. The trip from Atlanta to St. Simons and Sea Island is almost five hours, even taking the interstate the whole way to avoid speed traps in small towns. At one time the town of Ludowici, outside of Brunswick, was so notorious that then-Governor Maddox erected billboards warning drivers to take another route. No, we would stay on the interstates. South from Atlanta to Macon on I-75. Turning east on I-16 toward Savannah. Diving south again on I-95, until we exited on the Golden Isles Parkway toward the city of Brunswick and the barrier islands that protect the coast from the Atlantic Ocean.

I leaned my seat back and closed my eyes to hint I was taking a break from the conversation and to avoid watching Theo drive. I took the opportunity to consider what Sissy Mead had told Detective Bristol. Did Sissy know the effect that information would have on the case against Theo? If the Meads were reconciling, a prosecutor would relish painting Theo as a woman scorned. She would have a motive to murder the man who had been leading her on. I could imagine the opening statement at the trial now.

Could Theo have read the signs wrong? Cutler was a dealmaker. Theo and Sissy were competitors, so to speak. He was used to keeping secrets from competitors. He might have told his wife he wanted to return to her, while he was still carrying on with Theo. Whether he was a businessman or not, he was a man, so deception came naturally.

We drove in silence until signs began to appear for Macon, where we would pick up eastbound I-16. If I were alone I would pull off and stop into the Waffle House for pecan waffles and a side of bacon, but Theo was determined to drive straight to the coast. As she negotiated the Macon bypass, she restarted the conversation.

"I still don't believe Cutler was going back to his wife."

"Yeah, you said that."

"Annie, there're a thousand signs that a man is losing interest, and Cutler wasn't showing a single one. In fact, if anything, he was getting serious."

"What about him looking at his watch at lunch? You told me you wondered if he was meeting someone."

"Not his wife!" Theo kneaded the wheel.

We wrangled amicably about the perfidy of men (me) or their loving natures (Theo) while she drove. This part of the route, the 150 miles or so between Macon and Savannah, is tedious: low-land, sometimes forested, occasional standing water edging up to the highway. The terrain dropped slowly, scrub pine, Palmettos, and sandy patches indicating we were approaching the Georgia coast.

"How do you want to do this?" Theo asked.

"You mean, how do we investigate Cutler to find out if

anyone had a motive to kill him?" I saw Theo wince at my bald statement. "We start with people you know, like the guy you think was aware of why George and Cutler had a falling out," I said.

"That would be Rob Prescott. He was George's business partner."

"Okay. That's a good place to start. Then we can try to interview the guys Cutler played golf with, the ones who were pallbearers at his funeral. The problem is that some of them might not want to talk to us."

"Can't we just casually chat with people and see what anyone knows?" said Theo.

"We need a bit more organization."

"Not my strong suit." Theo wrinkled her nose.

"You forget I was there when you planned your wedding to the last toothpick—in colors that matched the bridesmaids' dresses." Theo could be organized when she wanted to. I wasn't fooled when she put on that helpless act.

"That was different. That was fashion and interior design. I can do all that."

"You made lots of lists and kept up with expenses and deliveries. This is similar. We need to work our way through anybody we can think of who might give us information about Cutler. When do you think you can get an appointment with Rob Prescott?"

"Don't worry about Rob," Theo said. "He'll meet us anytime that's convenient for me."

I turned in my seat and widened my eyes. She had the decency to blush.

"It's not what you're thinking. I own half of the company—Humphries Enterprises—Rob and George's company. George left his shares to me when he died. Rob offered to buy me out, but it didn't make sense to me when the company was doing so well. I guess you could say I'm a silent partner now."

Once again I remembered not to underestimate Theo. There was more to her than designer clothes. If anybody could figure out a way to learn more about Cutler Mead, it'd be Theo. I turned my thoughts from the murder victim to our suspects. "When we looked at the pictures of the golfers you said you didn't know Scot Raybourn. His office is on St. Simons in the Village. I'll make a call and see if he'll meet me. But first I want to talk to Flynn and see what he's been able to find out.

"Fine." Theo put on the blinker as she moved into the left lane to pass an overloaded truck carrying logs to the area paper-mills. "I'm going to my tai chi class while you do that. I might pick up some information at the spa. Everybody on Sea Island goes there."

"Good idea. We now have a plan." I reclined the passenger seat and squirmed deeper into it so that I could nap for the remainder of the drive.

* * *

I woke when I felt us climbing for the first time in 300 or so miles. Theo had turned the car onto the Torras causeway, which connects the mainland to St. Simons Island. The highway rises onto a bridge stretching four miles over salt water marshes that hide where the land stops and the water flows. A green sweep of cord grass makes up the marsh, a few crevices in its velvety surface revealing a gleam of water and the true nature of what from the bridge looks like a dry prairie.

Low tide had exposed a border of grey mud where the marsh meets creeks that meander between the grasses and the Frederica River. A turkey buzzard swooped over a clump of trees that had managed to grow up from a hummock in the middle of the waving bog. I was glad I wasn't driving so that I could enjoy the view. The sight was hypnotic, as many drivers on the causeway bridge learned to their detriment. Until a center divider was installed, marsh-gazing tourists had often drifted over the center line to smash head-on into oncoming traffic.

Theo guided the car down the other side of the bridge's span onto St. Simons Island and bore left onto Sea Island Road, a two-lane blacktop that circles through St. Simons before leading onto the much smaller—and private—Sea Island. The two islands are separated by only the narrow Black Banks River and a wide swath of money. Spanish moss-draped live oaks line the road, their branches stretching from the road's shoulder as far as the center yellow line, curtaining the road from the late afternoon sun.

In a day or so, we'd start working our way through meeting Cutler's golfing buddies. I don't play golf, but I pay attention to the Masters Tournament each spring, if only to see pictures of the spectacular azaleas blooming on the course. I had researched the tournament for this year. The 1999 green jacket had been won by a Spaniard named Olazabal, chased by Greg Norman and Davis Love II in the final round. Golf was important to the men we were planning to interview. I needed to educate myself, and besides, I was tired of sitting in the car. "Theo, which golf course did Cutler prefer to play?" I asked.

"Seaside." Her answer was firm. Clearly she knew what he'd liked.

"Could we swing by the course before we go to your place?" I asked.

"Now?" she asked. "We're almost at the cottage."

"It can't be very far," I said. "St. Simons is only twelve miles long, and a lot of that is marsh."

"All right," she said, turning the car around. "Just tell me why."

"I need to get a feel for where these guys spent their Sundays together before I interview them."

Theo turned south and headed for the Sea Island Golf Club, a golfer's paradise of three courses, including Cutler Mead's favorite. Once into the club grounds, we followed Retreat Avenue alongside the Avenue of Oaks, a spectacular double row of 160 year-old live oak trees, constantly babied and fussed over by the maintenance crew. Theo drove toward the main clubhouse, weaving around to park on the verge of one of the narrow lanes bordering the course. "Most of what you can see closest to the clubhouse is the Plantation Course," Theo said. "Seaside is over there," she waved toward the west. "We can't get onto the course," she said, "but you can see some of it from here."

The undulating fairways were smooth, emerald. Even the rough was carefully manicured to rise away from the fairway to a punishing scrub. The course weaved through marsh grass, around sandy dunes, and beneath towering oaks, nudging the shoreline. Around and in the water hazards snowy egrets stretched out their long necks. A heron stood on one leg, ruffled feathers blending in with the foliage, only the occasional flash of a beady eye giving him away. The course overlooked the Atlantic Ocean and offered spectacular views from several vantage points. I began to understand why Cutler Mead wanted to spend his Sunday mornings here.

"Let's get out and watch for a while," I said.

"In this heat?" Theo had left the car motor running with the air conditioning on.

"I want to get out of the car and stand up," I said. "There's a good breeze. Look at those palms swaying."

The heat smacked me when I opened the car door, but the wind was strong enough to dry off the perspiration before I got sticky. I held my hair up off my neck, and Theo flapped her blouse away from her body to take advantage of the cooling air current. We leaned against the car to watch a couple of golf carts carrying a foursome of middle-aged men approach the hole. The wind from the Atlantic was rattling the fronds of the Palmetto palms. Each hole on the Seaside course is marked with a pole topped by a red basket, instead of the usual green flag. With each gust, the black-and-white poles swayed and bent.

By the time the carts were parked and the men stepped on the green, the wind was whipping the golfers' pants around their legs, but the golfers seemed determined to finish their round. One jammed his cap down to his ears as he bent over his shot, trying to chip into the wind and avoid seeing his ball gust off the green. The other three crouched, backs to the wind, hunkered down until it was their turn. No one would make par in this weather, but the foursome fought the gale and their own wild shots to clinch the hole, laughing and slapping each other on the back before heading to the locker room.

When the last of the foursome had disappeared, Theo turned to me. "Seen enough?" she asked.

"Yeah," I said. "I'm ready to go home."

We climbed back in the car and Theo started the engine, cranking the air conditioning to high. We reversed our route and before long were pulling into the half-circle driveway in front of Theo's three-bedroom cottage.

Hers is one of the smaller so-called cottages on Sea Island, built by her grandparents before the years of McMansions. Flanked by tall Palmetto palms and lush foliage, the single-story house had a red-tiled roof above pale yellow stucco walls. I loved the portico, situated to the east of the front door and offering covered access to a side door of the house or to a high wooden gate that blocked Theo's back yard from public view. You couldn't see much of the house from the street, but the relatively narrow frontage hid wings that jutted back from the entrance to wrap around an ancient live oak and a decent sized swimming pool. Theo's sunroom was glass on three sides, over-looking the tree and the decking that paralleled the encircling wings of the home. Inside the sunroom Theo had set opposing couches upholstered in bright florals. The effect was comfort-able and relaxed, perfect for putting my feet up to plan the next stage of our investigation.

I thought back to the scene we had just witnessed at the golf course. Those men looked like they were fighting a war. Is that what Cutler and his foursome did every Sunday—re-live their time in Vietnam? Why would they do that? On the other hand, on most days playing the Seaside course, the blue skies and the ocean would have been soothing. My imagination was run-ning away with me since I couldn't do anything until I heard back from Flynn about Scot Raybourn. I looked up to see Theo watching me. She had a glass of wine in each hand.

"Can we call it a day?" she asked.

"Let's do that."

11

Scot Raybourn

We spent the next day keeping a low profile. Other than some annoying phone calls from reporters hoping to get an interview, things were quiet on the island. I went for a long run on the beach. I was anxious to get started, to feel that I was moving toward a real investigation, something that would prove Theo wasn't a murderer. I got back just in time for the call from Flynn reporting on what he'd been able to find out about Scot Raybourn.

"Whatever you may think about the guy, Audrey, you got to admire his ability to survive and prosper. New Century Tech is his fourth or fifth business. His previous ventures either went bankrupt or were sold for a profit."

"Is he lucky or crooked?"

"Hard to say. Maybe he's got good lawyers."

"And now?"

"New Century Tech seems to be doing well, but I'm reading tea leaves here. It's a private company."

I understood. Flynn was telling me the company didn't have to make the kind of public filings with the SEC that someone with Flynn's knowledge could parse to discover the real financial picture.

"What do they do?" I asked.

"Have you heard of the Y2K issue?"

"Sure. At the turn of the century the world is coming to an end, planes will fall out of the sky, etc. because every computer in the world will stop working on Jan. 1, 2000."

"Uh, yeah. That's the mass media hysteria version."

"It must be true. It was on the cover of Time magazine." I waited to see if Flynn would pick up on my sarcasm and banter with me, but he stayed serious.

"It's actually a fairly banal software glitch," he said. "Seems that most computers were programmed to recognize only the last two digits of the year—97, 98, etc."

"Okay, so?"

"Well, when the calendar turns to the year 2000, that's going to mess up all the calculations based on dates. The computers will read 2000 like 1900—see?"

"What does that have to do with Century Tech?"

"Most private companies and the U.S. Government are

working on patching the problem—rewriting the software to recognize 4-digit years. I'm seeing estimates that the government alone will spend over $100 billion for the fix. That's a pretty good incentive."

"So they're working on reprogramming computers."

"Essentially. If this Y2K thing doesn't happen, a lot of money will be spent for nothing."

"And one way or another, a chunk of it will be paid to New Century Tech."

"Right."

The next morning, I called and got an appointment to see Scot Raybourn. After dropping Theo at her tai chi class, I headed to Century Tech's office in the Village of St. Simons at the southernmost end of the island. I drove down Frederica Road, watching the sun flash between the twisted branches of overhanging trees. I tapped the brakes just long enough to salute the 4-way stop and turned left onto Kingsway. I had reached the corner where Kingsway intersected Mallery, the heart of the Village and tourist central. To my right small shops and restaurants on both sides of Mallery led to a pier that jutted out into the Atlantic. As usual the tourists and some locals were hanging out, staring into the ocean or just sunning themselves on the benches.

The New Century Tech sign came into view, and I looked for a shady spot to park. I swung up a side street and parked half on the cracked asphalt and half on the sandy ground, the car snugged under a moss-dripped live oak. As I walked out of the shadowy gloom, the sun's glare blinded me. I put my hand up to shield my eyes. Squinting, I managed to pull open the heavy doors and stepped with relief into the cool interior.

New Century's plush executive suite was a mix of cool aqua

and grey, almost spa-like, an ethereal atmosphere that might have been decorated to lower the thermostat for the benefit of Scot Raybourn's female audiences. He emerged from his office into the waiting area, Hollywood handsome, a thick head of dark hair greying at the temple. His green eyes were intent on me as he approached.

"You're that friend of George Humphries' widow, aren't you?"

"Ann Audrey Pickering. Thanks for meeting me."

He shook my hand with warm, gentle pressure. Still holding my hand, he gestured toward the open door of his office and an oversized sofa lounging against one wall.

Once in his office, he released my hand and invited me to sit at one end of the sofa. He joined me on the adjacent cushion and sat turned toward me. I wondered if I should have opted for the Barcelona reproduction placed at a right angle nearby, to keep some space between us. The chair's backward tilt would be difficult to scramble out of. I decided to stay put.

"I heard you were on the island," he said.

He saw my surprise. "Tommy Boxer told me he'd seen a pretty woman with Mrs. Humphries at the Cloister bar last night. Tommy's a sucker for long-legged redheads." He grinned, a brilliant gleam of teeth set off by a tan permanently baked in by rounds of golf in the Georgia sun.

"Tommy Boxer?" I ignored the heavy-handed compliment. I wondered if that kind of approach was how Raybourn typically interacted with women.

"He's a close friend from way back."

"Did you and he grow up on the island?"

"No, I grew up on the mainland in Brunswick. Wrong side of the tracks. Tommy's family is old St. Simons."

"Does 'Old St. Simons' mean old money?"

"Not really. St. Simons was always more downscale, casual. I knew Tommy because the kids on St. Simons went to school in Brunswick. There was a lot of mixing in those days between the Islands and town. Nowadays the big money stays on Sea Island. It's become quite exclusive."

He straightened, turning away from me, and sat back, indicating that the preliminaries were finished.

"I'd imagine Mrs. Humphries is well versed in the history of this area," he said. "So, what can I do for you, Miss Pickering?"

"I've come down from Atlanta to help Theo. She's been very upset by Cutler Mead's death." I wondered if the man sitting next to me was gullible enough to buy my pitch.

"I'm sure." His expression was interested, but noncommittal.

I plunged in with the script I'd devised for explaining why I was asking questions about a dead man. "Theo wants to know as much as she can about Cutler. His death makes no sense to her, at least she can't envision the man she knew as a homicide victim. I think she wants to understand what happened to him, and that means she wants to know his friends. She feels she owes him that, somehow."

He looked doubtful, his mouth in a tight smile one muscle shy of a smirk. "Women. I'll never understand them." He raised his hands in mock surrender. "No offense."

"None taken."

"Mrs. Humphries doesn't owe Cutler Mead a thing. Between you and me, I'm sure he was no more faithful to Mrs. Humphries than he was to his long-suffering wife. Cutler was not a man you'd rely on for your happiness."

He'd confirmed my suspicions about Theo's boyfriend, and

I wondered if there was more bad news to come about Cutler Mead. "Nevertheless, she's curious."

"I don't believe curiosity is the right word. I knew her husband, by the way. In fact, I was playing golf at the same club when George died. Wasn't Mrs. Humphries at Cutler's house when he was killed? She must be the prime suspect." Raybourn's attitude was matter-of-fact. We could have been discussing what to order for lunch.

"Theo did not murder Cutler Mead." I should start keeping a count of how many times I'd said those words.

He shrugged, the most masculine shimmy I had ever seen. I couldn't help but imagine his broad shoulders without that silk sport coat and pale shirt. It was a good thing I was conducting this interview and not Theo.

"Weren't you one of Mr. Mead's best friends?" I said.

"Not really."

"I understood that you were a pallbearer at his funeral." I deliberately phrased the question so that I didn't have to admit that I'd been there in person. I didn't want him to guess the extent of my interest—at least, not yet.

"We had known each other a long time, so Sissy asked me and some buddies to do the honors."

"How long had you known each other?" My question related to his relationship with Cutler, but I remembered the exchange I'd witnessed between Raybourn and Sissy Mead at the funeral. He'd casually used her first name. How close was *their* relationship?

"He was our lieutenant in Nam," Raybourn said. "We all ended up in the same squad. A bunch of us were from this area originally, so we kept in touch after we got back—did business together, played golf." His tone was offhand, as if the information were no big deal.

"You and Tommy Boxer, you mean?"

"And Drew Littlefield, too. He's from here." Raybourn leaned closer and spoke softly. "Comes from money. Mommy issues, in my opinion. Cutler was kind of a father figure to him."

"What about Freddie?"

"Freddie, oh my god. He may be the best one of us."

That was a surprise. Freddie hadn't struck me as the best kind of anything. I pressed for an explanation of Raybourn's opinion of that weirdo. "He's from this area, too?"

"No. Somewhere in the West, I think."

"What does he do? I thought he was some kind of handyman."

"You could call him that. Freddie can do pretty much anything, but I was thinking about during the war. He didn't have any nerves. That's a valuable man. Someone who doesn't panic, stays cool."

The goon who threatened me at Cutler's house had certainly not panicked when he'd discovered Theo and me. Sure, he'd taken control of the situation, but he was intense. I hesitated before saying. "He doesn't appear that cool."

"I only ever saw him unsettled once. When one of our guys..." Raybourn trailed off. "Long time ago, sorry."

"And after you guys came back from Vietnam?" I asked.

"He's had some issues," Raybourn said. "But he seems to be doing pretty well these days. Stays in the present, when I've been around him."

"Does Freddie play golf, too?"

Raybourn chortled, head thrown back and mouth open. "Are you kidding? No way. Freddie thinks golf is for wimps."

"Then why did he meet you at the golf course every Sunday?"

He closed his mouth and tilted his head to one side. "Now how did you know that?"

"Freddie told me." I offered no explanation and waited to see what Scot Raybourn would do. I thought he'd follow up to find out more, but he didn't seem interested in discovering how I'd met Freddie.

"Cutler wanted him there." He shrugged again. "Cutler would call Freddie when we were on the back nine and he'd meet us at the clubhouse for a beer."

"It all sounds like a feel-good buddy movie."

"Appearances can be deceiving." His expression changed. No more charm and easy gossiping about his buddies. He moved away from me toward the other end of the sofa.

"You said you did business together," I said, "those of you who had served in Vietnam together and came back here. What business did you do with Cutler Mead?"

"Cutler owns shares in New Century Tech."

"What percentage?"

He shifted his weight on the sofa. "New Century Tech is a private company. That information isn't for public consumption."

"I'm just trying to understand all of Cutler's business interests." I tilted my head and attempted to look, if not innocent, at least harmless.

"Not that it's anyone's business, either yours or Mrs. Humphries, but he owned 25%."

"A big chunk," I said. "What happens to those shares now that Cutler is dead?"

"According to the agreement, I have the right to repurchase them—at cost." The green eyes gleamed with satisfaction.

"Were you in Atlanta when he was killed?" I asked.

"I was, as a matter of fact." He didn't seem the least bit uneasy about answering the question. "I drove up there with my lawyer for a meeting."

"Is your lawyer Drew Littlefield?"

"That's right." Raybourn rose to his feet. "Sorry to end this conversation, but I need to get moving. Please give Mrs. Humphries my condolences." He extended his hand to help me up from the low sofa.

"Thanks for talking to me," I said, when I was on my feet. "If you think of anything that might be helpful to Theo, please let me know." I retrieved a card from my purse and gave it to him.

He looked at the card, which showed only my name and a phone number.

"I can't help but wonder," I said. "Why did you continue to play golf with a man you obviously despised?"

Raybourn gave an old-fashioned bow as he took my hand.

"Miss Pickering, sometimes in life, we have to do things just to get on."

That statement left open a lot of possibilities.

12

Arzy

When I left New Century Tech's office, it was too early to pick up Theo, so I decided to wait for her at the only place on Sea Island where I don't feel out of place. The Beach Club is the most casual spot in the cluster of venues that make up the resort. It sits across the road from The Cloister Hotel, an elegant three-story Spanish colonial built in 1928. The hotel grounds of manicured Bermuda grass are dotted with trees planted by U.S. Presidents, royalty and celebrities during their visits. The heavy weight of protocol squats on the Cloister's red-tile roof. Oriental carpets, massive chandeliers, gothic stained glass windows, stuffy restaurants adhering to strict dress codes.

In contrast, the Beach Club serves buffet breakfast and lunch from steam tables sitting on vinyl flooring, in deference to the sand tracked in by the hungry patrons. Standing in line for waffles, omelettes, or grits, sun worshippers in bathing suits and shorts rub shoulders while they help themselves. Smells of bacon and coconut oil fight for supremacy. Diners carry their own trays out to the patio overlooking the Atlantic Ocean, where they chew and gossip.

Beach Club habitués are mostly female—golf widows watching the kids play while their husbands spend the day on the links. Coppertone basted sunbathers bake poolside, only occasionally venturing from the tiled pool area to the nearby beach when their children scream loudly enough to cause embarrassment. I snagged a table to myself under the shady porch that encircled the pool area, which kept me out of the sun and mostly out of the direct view of the cluster of women around the pool. The temperature was creeping toward 90 degrees, and despite the faint offshore breeze, the humidity was keeping pace. I sat down to watch and wait.

Theo emerged from the spa next door just as I was settling in. She was wearing pink capri pants and a Lilly Pulitzer blouse. Her sunglasses—Jackie O dark—completely obscured her eyes. Four-inch platform sandals accessorized the look, the combination of the capris and sandals showing off her trim ankles. I waved and she cut across the pool area toward me, moving effortlessly on the high platforms. A few women beckoned to her, and I stared hard, in case anyone was rude enough to directly snub her. Theo waved to them but didn't pause as she zigzagged between the chaise lounges to reach me on the porch.

"You okay?" I asked.

"Why?"

"Normally it would take you 15 minutes to get through that crowd, what with laughing and gossiping along the way."

"Hmph. The ones who want to chat only want the awful details about Cutler's death."

"Right." I eyed her behind my own sunglasses. She was wound up, humming with some emotion that she was suppressing for now. "What's going on?" I asked.

"You first. What did you think about Scot Raybourn?"

"He's handsome and knows it. Sexy. Probably conscience-free where women are concerned." I'll admit I was embellishing a bit, but probably only a bit.

"Sorry I missed it."

"You won't be when I'm finished telling you about him. He didn't like Cutler very much."

"I see." Theo leaned back in her chair. One of the Beach Club's staff came by cleaning up leftover plates and silverware. Theo took the opportunity to order two glasses of iced tea. She did not specify, nor did the server ask, whether the tea would be sweet. That was a given. While we waited for the server to return, I filled Theo in on my interview of Scot Raybourn.

"We probably shouldn't read too much into what Raybourn told me," I said. "He might have a grudge against Cutler for some stupid guy thing—cheating at golf or some such."

"I don't think so," Theo said. She took a swallow of her tea. The dark lenses of her glasses wouldn't turn my way. Her lips pursed in sour distaste, though the tea was excellent—sweet but not tooth rattling.

"What do you mean?"

"Well…I had a manicure after my tai chi class." She waggled her fingers so I could see the glossy sheen of the new lacquer.

"Nice. How is Arzy?"

"She doesn't seem to have aged a day. It's unreal," Theo answered.

Arzeleen Montgomery, a tiny bent figure, had been tending to the hands of Sea Island matrons for more than 40 years. Behind thick bifocals, her brown eyes loomed huge. A tight helmet of salt and pepper hair framed her small face. Despite her age—she must be close to seventy by now—her café-au-lait complexion was unlined.

"She's always been fond of you," I said. On the few occasions I managed to get an appointment with Arzy, she'd made it clear that she was only willing to tackle my ragged nails as a favor to "my sweetest girl," her nickname for Theo. Because Theo lived in a cottage built by her grandfather, my friend qualified as "old" Sea Island. That appealed to Arzy, an intractable snob whose standards were high. She disdained the nouveau riche women who wore artificial nails. None of Arzy's clients—whose Sea Island cottages hid million-dollar art collections behind low tabby walls—would be so trashy.

Arzy had filed and smoothed Theo's nails through three marriages, two divorces and George's untimely death, even coming in on her day off to give Theo a manicure before George's funeral. Theo once told me that Arzy could deduce the state of her clients' marriage or finances from the condition of their cuticles. It occurred to me that Arzy probably knew a lot about what was happening behind the scenes at Sea Island. The manicure table is an intimate space. Many of Arzy's clients sat across from her, their hands in hers, every week. They felt safe confiding their personal business, knowing that she would keep a confidence for her regulars.

"She'd heard about Cutler," Theo said.

"No surprise." Undoubtedly Arzy had heard the whole sordid tale before Theo and I had even driven out of Atlanta.

"No," Theo said, "but she was so kind and sympathetic."

I was glad to hear that Arzy'd been kind to Theo, unlike the blonds who'd given her the cold shoulder when she tried to go shopping. Times like this you find out who your real friends are. "What else had she heard?" I asked.

"Most of Arzy's client's husbands did business with Cutler, but Linda Littlefield's reaction to his murder was the strangest."

"Who's Linda Littlefield?" I asked.

Theo rolled her eyes. "She's Drew Littlefield's wife, Annie."

"Oh. I thought Arzy was tight-lipped about her regulars."

"She is. Arzy made it clear she rarely saw Linda."

You really do need to know the rules of the game to keep score. I supposed that by indicating that she only occasionally saw Linda Littlefield, Arzy was telling Theo it was okay to gossip.

"So what?" I said. "You and I know Drew Littlefield not only played golf with Cutler, but was his lawyer. She's probably worried about losing those legal fees."

"You'd have thought. But Arzy says, it's the opposite. She was surprised that Linda seemed relieved."

"Did Arzy know why?"

"Not really. Only Linda was glad her husband would no longer be doing business with Cutler—said he was a bad influence on Drew." Theo hesitated, then continued. "Arzy also told me Cutler wasn't a nice man, and I was better off without him."

I was reaching the same conclusion, but I was surprised that the manicurist had come right out and said it to Theo's face. I was a tad ashamed that I hadn't had the courage to tell Theo myself. "Wow. Did she give you any reason other than what Linda Littlefield says?"

"No. But Annie, she does the nails of a lot of women on this island. She knows more than she'll say. She's trying to help me."

Way back in our first conversation about Cutler, Theo had told me some woman slapped his face when he wouldn't back away. Was there another suspect out there? A woman or her husband who wanted revenge for a rape? I reminded Theo of what she'd said to me. "Did you ask Arzy about Cutler and other women?"

Theo pushed her dark glasses more firmly against her face as if to hide from me. "I did. It was awkward, but Arzy understood. He was known around the island for chasing women, but Arzy had never heard anything about him assaulting anyone. And she would have heard, Annie."

"Can't you get more out of her?" I was frustrated that these women were going to close ranks, and we'd never be able to learn what we needed to help Theo.

"I wouldn't try."

"Why? Theo, this is important."

Theo gave me an incredulous stare. "It's her livelihood, Annie. If word got around she'd been revealing people's private information, she'd lose her position. I can't do that to Arzy. We'll have to find another way."

There really was no rebuttal to that. Theo's sense of loyalty had worked in my favor in the past. I wasn't cruel enough to deprive Arzy of that kind of support.

13

Three Friends

Theo and I were sitting in the sunroom in Theo's cottage when we heard the *thunk* of an expensive car door closing. We went outside to welcome Flynn and his two miniature Italian greyhounds, Porgi and Amor, sitting side by side in their doggy seat on the passenger side. While Flynn pulled his suitcase from the trunk, the dogs hung their front paws out the window, quivering with excitement. Their owner lifted them down and the two ran around his legs, swerving occasionally into Theo's azaleas to investigate seductive smells and mark their territory.

We settled amongst the exuberant floral upholstery of couches and chairs in the sunroom. Theo and I took turns bringing Flynn up to date on the interview with Scot Raybourn and the gossipy tidbits we'd learned. Theo was an active participant in the reporting. Maybe Arzy's advice about Cutler had changed Theo's attitude, encouraging her to fight for herself against a murder charge.

"It doesn't sound like Cutler was any different from any other real estate developer," said Flynn, bending over to scratch Porgi behind his pointed ears. "You've got to have a tough hide to be in that business. Those guys are either loved or hated by people around their latest development."

"That's true," said Theo. "The locals are furious about all the new development on the island.

"Might be a motive," Flynn said. "While we mull that over, can we reconvene this meeting somewhere else? I could use a drink and some fresh seafood."

We adjourned to a back booth at Frankie's, known for stiff drinks and shrimp fresh off the boat every morning. Frankie's is an upscale version of a fish shack, the primitive beach restaurants where shrimp boats and anglers brought their catch to be cooked and eaten, dockside. The old shacks are gone, smothered by the condos now lining the coast. Frankie's, pine-paneled and dim, is the perfect place to occupy a booth, peel shrimp, and talk about suspects.

"Other than people who were unhappy about one of Cutler's developments, who else could have had a beef with him?" Flynn asked.

"The guys who played golf with him every week can probably give us those names," I said.

Flynn gripped a shrimp between his teeth, struggling to yank off the tail. "Don't forget his wife, Sissy," he said, tossing the shell into the discard bowl.

Theo looked down at her pile of shrimp and reached for the coleslaw.

"Let's leave her for later," I said, giving Flynn a dark look. "Anyway, she's in Atlanta, and the other suspects are here on the coast." As a good friend of Cutler's mistress, I was uncomfortable at the thought of interviewing his widow. The idea seemed tacky. Maybe I could leave her to Detective Bristol. Then I remembered Sissy's claim she was reconciling with her now-dead husband. Bristol seemed to be buying Sissy's story. I gave a mental sigh. I'd have to talk to her myself to get some sense of whether to credit her story.

"Cocktail sauce too hot?" asked Flynn. "You aren't eating." He drew his brows together as he watched me from across the booth.

"It's fine," I said. "I'm just slowing down."

"Okay," said Flynn. "So, who else could provide information, besides Raybourn?"

"There's Tom Boxer," I said. "He's a veterinarian here on St. Simons island. And Drew Littlefield, Cutler's lawyer."

"I think Drew might be helpful," Theo said. "George had some falling out with him. I'm sure it had something to do with Cutler."

"Since you know him, Theo, see if he'll talk to you," Flynn said.

"Um. Okay. I'll try," she said. "I'll have to figure out some excuse to meet him."

"What about this vet, Tom Boxer?" Flynn asked.

"I don't know him," said Theo.

"Want me to try and approach him?" asked Flynn.

"Yes," Theo and I chorused.

"Come to think of it, might be a good idea if you came with me, Audrey," said Flynn. "I'll make an appointment to take the dogs in for a checkup. While I'm there, we can see if Boxer will tell us anything useful."

With this decision, we'd exhausted our ideas. We demolished an extra-large platter of shrimp, then ordered bread pudding with bourbon pecan sauce to finish.

On the drive home, Flynn slowed as we passed the village and pier on St. Simons. "How about a nightcap?" he asked.

"Not for me," said Theo. "I just want to get to bed."

I looked at Flynn's fingers tapping on the steering wheel and got the message. "Sure, I'm game. Just a short one."

"That's my girl," Flynn said

We dropped Theo off at the cottage and circled back to the village. Flynn parked and we walked out onto the pier.

Side by side, we leaned our elbows on the railing, watching the waves lap against the pilings. "What is it?" I asked.

"You've got something on your mind," he said. "Having second thoughts about taking this on?"

"Not second thoughts. Fourteenth and fifteenth thoughts. All our talk about interviewing these friends of Cutler's. What for? I didn't get anything out of Scot Raybourn." It was a relief to voice this out loud. Theo needed me to be confident that she was going to emerge unscathed from this. Not unscathed, but free of suspicion of murder. But only if we—I—found the real culprit. I wasn't sure I could carry that burden.

"You found out that Cutler Mead wasn't a nice guy, and

that his friends didn't like him." Flynn pressed his shoulder against mine as he spoke.

"Big deal. Long way from that to finding the murderer."

"Stop it. You're panicking."

"I think I have that right."

"Think again," said Flynn.

I turned my back to the water, gripping the pier railing with each hand. "I hate you when you're practicing tough love."

He laughed quietly. "Somebody has to. Most people are too afraid of you to call you out when you have an attack of nerves."

"If telling me I scare people is supposed to encourage me, it isn't working."

He turned around and put his arm over my shoulders. For a while we just stood there, leaning back against the pier railing.

"We can do this, Audrey. I'm in it, too. And Theo. You're not alone."

"There really isn't any choice, is there?"

"Nope," Flynn said. "Not one you can live with." He squeezed my shoulder. "C'mon, let's walk over to the Sea Grill and have a drink."

"It'll be mobbed. They only have about 20 tables and they're always full."

"It's late enough. I'll bet the dinner crowd is gone," Flynn said, taking my hand and leading me off the pier.

We strolled hand in hand down the block and turned into the alley toward the restaurant. Flynn was right, the dining room, usually buzzing with conversation and the clatter of servers, was half empty and quiet. When Flynn told the maître d' that we only wanted a nightcap, he waved us to a table.

Once seated, I looked around out of habit, to make sure none of Charlie's victims who might recognize me were in the restaurant. Seeing no one I knew, I relaxed and sipped my bourbon. Flynn raised his own glass in a salute, but, as he was about to drink, his eyes widened.

"What?" I asked.

"Sissy Mead is here," he whispered. "She just sat down at the table behind us with her back to you. She must have been in the ladies' room when we came in."

"Is she alone?"

Flynn shook his head. "There's a lady with her."

"What's she doing here?" I hissed to him. "I thought she was in Atlanta."

Before Flynn could respond, the maître d' walked past us and approached Sissy's table.

"Mrs. Mead," he said, "I just wanted to say I'm sorry about your husband."

"Thank you, Don," she said.

"I hope we'll see you back on the island more often."

"I'm just here to check on things at the house. Try to decide what to do, you know."

"Of course. Let me know if we can help in any way. Please enjoy your evening." His duty done, the maître d' returned to his station.

Flynn and I focused an unnatural amount of attention on the swizzle sticks in our drinks, neither of us speaking. After a pause long enough for me to wet my lips with bourbon twice, the conversation behind me started again.

"Sissy," a woman's voice said, "why don't you stay with Bill and me while you're here? You're very welcome."

"Thank you, Anne," said Sissy. "But I'm at the Cloister."

"The Cloister? Aren't you staying at the house?"

"No. I just couldn't. Freddie is there, you know."

"That odd fellow? I know he's been with you a long time, but, really... Are you concerned he might overstep?"

"Ugh. No. Not for a minute. That's not the issue. It was Cutler who always wanted Freddie around. Cutler felt some obligation to him. I intend to tell Freddie to move out as soon as I see him."

"What do you plan to do about the house? You've never spent much time there. You could sell it in a New York minute."

"I'm not sure what will happen to the house," Sissy said.

"Drew will have some good advice about that, I'd imagine. He's still your lawyer, isn't he?"

"For some things."

There was silence, then the other woman spoke. "How are you doing, really? I know this all happened so suddenly."

"Naturally I miss him, Anne." Her voice was matter-of-fact.

"I understand it's a shock, but, Honey, you two haven't lived together in years. And if even half the rumors about him are true..." Anne's voice trailed off.

Someone's knife and fork clanged against a plate.

"I haven't heard those rumors," said Sissy. "They're obviously floated by someone who is not my friend."

"Oh, but..."

"Did you know, the Governor and his wife accepted our invitation to the gala," Sissy said. "I had hoped my closest friends would join me at the head table."

"I see. That would be an honor." The tone of the answer was placating. Apparently the dinner companion understood the implied threat from Sissy.

Flynn and I nursed our drinks, but the rest of their

conversation seemed to be about the vendors and budget for the gala Sissy had mentioned. I was reduced to licking the bottom of my glass before the screech of chair legs warned they were departing.

The two passed our table without a glance. Sissy looked good, beachy chic. She wore a sleeveless white sheath that ended above her knees, her arms and legs nicely tanned. A cloying scent of gardenia with a spicy undertone drifted in her wake.

"What a nasty perfume," said Flynn, waving his hand in front of his face.

"Yes," I agreed. "She probably paid a fortune for it, but money can't overcome that smell."

14

Theo Goes to Church

By Sunday, despite Flynn's determined efforts to keep our spirits up, I was frustrated and beginning to think we were never going to get anywhere. Flynn took himself off to play golf, hoping to pick up some scuttlebutt about Cutler's friends on the course. I was lounging in the sunroom when I heard the clatter of Theo's heels. I looked over to see her headed for the front door of the cottage.

"Where are you going?" I called.

"Church."

I eyed her outfit. "Since when do you go to church?"

"I go occasionally."

I swung my feet off the sofa and sat up. Theo turned around and faced me. She was dressed in a maroon two-piece suit that did nothing to hide her figure. The bows on her Ferragamos looked like butterflies had landed on her feet.

"You never go to church when you visit Atlanta." I said.

"Drew Littlefield goes to the early service by himself every Sunday," Theo said. "George used to joke that Drew was the only Christian he knew who went to confession *before* he played golf."

"I'm guessing you're headed to Christ Church," I said. Moneyed islanders worshiped, married, and mingled at Christ Church Episcopal.

"It's a good place to corner him," Theo said.

"You're right," I said. "Let me get dressed, and I'll tag along."

"No."

I was surprised at her uncompromising tone. "Theo, one of these duffers might be a murderer. You're not going by yourself."

"Oh, come on Annie. I'm not in any danger. It's a church. Besides, do you remember the last time we went to church together?"

"Not really."

"Well, I do. You talked nonstop and not quietly. You mocked the sermon, organized religion, and the hypocrisy of the people around us. As it is, I can barely endure the snubs I get from people who think I'm a murderer. I don't need more freezing looks because you're so rude."

I was moderately ashamed of myself for making her uncomfortable. "Sorry. I react badly to the odor of sanctified money."

The glare she gave me would have wilted a feebler woman.

"Look, tell you what—let me ride with you," I offered. "You go into the service. I'll hang out at the back of the church where nobody will notice. I promise not to make a sound. I can keep an eye on you, and I'll stay out of sight."

"As long as you let me talk to Drew by myself," Theo said, heading towards the door. "He'll need some sympathetic coaxing—that's not your strong suit."

* * *

The white clapboard church sat toward the back of an emerald lawn, circled by moss-trailing live oaks. Built before the church had been air conditioned, the deep grey roof was steeply pitched above tall windows to provide maximum ventilation in the muggy climate. A walled cemetery stood next to the church.

We had arrived in plenty of time in order to keep an eye out for Drew Littlefield. The tires of Theo's Mercedes crunched over the crushed shell driveway that led to the church parking lot. Nudging the car close to a magnolia tree, Theo parked the Mercedes so it'd be in the shade by the time the service was over. I scooted out and hung around the magnolias while Theo picked her way through the treacherous shells up to the church portico. I now understood why she had chosen the low-heeled Ferragamos instead of her usual stilettos.

Once Theo entered the church, I followed her inside. The warm chestnut walls and pews had been rebuilt after the Civil War, when a fire had destroyed the original building. Only the center aisle was carpeted, a dark red runner that reflected the dark crimson and golds of the stained glass windows, one of them fabricated by Tiffany and touted by local guides as a "must see" for tourists. The carpet's burgundy hue echoed the costume chosen by Theo, which I suspected was no coincidence.

The early service at Christ Church drew a surprisingly good crowd, elderly ladies who couldn't sleep late, kids and families who wanted to get out to the beach before the sun got too high, and middle aged men in golfing attire who wanted to get church over with before they teed off. Drew Littlefield was seated alone about a third of the way back from the altar, on the end of a pew. Theo strolled down the aisle and stood next to where he sat. He glanced up and moved over far enough for her to gain a seat. The plush cushions were velvet and almost impossible to slide on, so she was able to sit down elbow to elbow with her quarry.

She settled herself, and I found a place in the back row, expecting to suffer through the service before Theo would be able to talk to him. Instead, when the soft music of the organ prelude began, I saw Drew lean over and whisper to her. She gave a start and turned to look at him.

He leaned closer and said something else. Without waiting for an answer, Drew stood up. He spoke politely to the octogenarian seated at the other end of the row, slipped past her and tiptoed up the side aisle. His movements were so quick and furtive that I would've sworn that only me and the old lady noticed him go.

Damn. He must have heard that we were asking questions and is bolting.

Theo scrambled out of the pew, and I trailed the two of them. Drew had disappeared by the time I got outside, but

I caught a glimpse of Theo going around the building. I followed her to a gate in the walled cemetery. There was Drew, with Theo close behind, headed toward a stone bench in the northeast corner. I stayed back so that I could watch through the opening in the wall. Theo caught up with him, and they sat down with their backs to me, Drew leaning forward with his elbows on his knees.

The two of them sat in the midst of weathered headstones that narrate the history of the island. In 1820 yellow fever struck the low country. Two angels spread their wings over a young mother and infant who died three days apart. An extended family with seven sons slept in a walled enclosure of tabby, a concrete made on the island since the eighteenth century with lime from oyster shells, sand and water. Nearby, an unusual black headstone honored the island founder who had managed to thrive—or at least survive—despite fevers, poor crops and hurricanes.

Whether it was the pathos of the cemetery or a ploy to encourage Drew, Theo started to sniffle. She dug into her purse for a tissue, and Drew put his arm around her shoulders. I crept closer, wishing Episcopalians were more like Baptists, singing loudly enough to drown out my steps on the mossy brick walk, but Theo and Drew showed no sign that they heard me. I kept moving nearer, trying to find a listening post. I finally squatted behind a large double headstone that loomed behind the bench where they sat. I was close enough to see Drew was clean shaven and wore a crisp white shirt, but his eyes were bloodshot and his sport coat was rumpled as if he'd slept in it.

"I miss him," Drew said.

"I know. Me, too," answered Theo.

"I'd never have survived Vietnam if Cutler hadn't been my

lieutenant." Drew sighed. "I don't know what I'd have done. When we got back he damn near forced me to go to law school, take the bar. He introduced me to Linda, told me to marry her."

I couldn't tell from Drew's voice whether he was grateful or bitter over Cutler's role as matchmaker. Theo handled him well, murmuring sympathies as they sat shoulder to shoulder.

"What am I going to do?" Drew said.

"You've got friends here. Cutler's friends," said Theo. "You should get together with them. That might make you feel better."

He pulled away from the cozy huddle and gave her a hard look. I didn't like his body language. I didn't know how, or even if, this guy was involved with Cutler's murder, but he could be a lot more dangerous than he looked. I gathered my feet under me, preparing to stand up, when he spoke.

"They hated him. I was the only one who cared about him."

"But you all golfed together every week," Theo said.

"They were afraid not to. They were all terrified of him, what he could do to them."

"What do you mean?"

"Oh, Theo," Drew said. "I can't tell you. I just can't. It's not my secret."

"But you know?" So Cutler's buddies *were* hiding something. I pressed myself tighter against the headstone, straining to catch every nuance of the conversation on the other side. Theo had lowered her voice, trying to seduce an answer from him.

"Yes." It came out as a whisper, barely loud enough for me to hear.

"Would it help to talk about it?" she asked.

"No. Nothing can help. It's over now. Cutler's dead. That ended it for all of us." Drew stood up. "I'm sorry, Theo."

She sat there and watched him walk out of the cemetery. I kept my head down below the top of the headstone, but I needn't have worried. Whatever Drew Littlefield saw as he trudged away, it wasn't me.

15

Flynn Meets an Old Friend

After the emotional scene with Drew, Theo and I returned to her place. By late afternoon Flynn hadn't returned from his golf game at Seaside. I'd checked my watch several times, wondering why it was taking so long to play eighteen holes. Maybe Flynn was slow-playing the round while he tried to squeeze information out of his fellow golfers. Theo had started to doze off when we finally heard the front door open and Flynn dumping his golf bag in the hall. He stuck his head into the sunroom.

"Hey, what're you guys doing?" he asked.

"Drinking tea and chewing over Theo's conversation with Drew Littlefield," I said. "We'll fill you in over dinner."

"Sounds good," Flynn said as he reached for the tall pitcher of iced tea.

"In the meantime, how was your golf game?" I asked, watching him. He was a little too quiet, simmering with something. I expected him to boil over with complaints about the heat, fashion faux-pas amongst male golfers and other silliness that Flynn is a master of turning into conversation.

"Not too bad," he said. Flynn poured himself a glass, added lemon and sat down. You'd never know he'd spent hours outside in the sun. Not a drop of sweat darkened his lavender golf shirt, embroidered with the Brooks Brothers sheep logo. He'd left his golf shoes in the car and wore neat loafers without socks. The effect was quintessential Flynn, cool and collected, an impenetrable façade worn by a gay man in a homophobic society.

"Did you pick up anything useful at the golf course?" Theo asked.

"Yes and No. Nothing from the golfers," Flynn said. "None of the players would open up about Cutler even after I mentioned I'd heard one of their members had been murdered last week in Atlanta."

"That's pretty direct," Theo said, looking away from us and watching some birds on her lawn.

"I'd already tried more subtle approaches, to no affect," said Flynn. "They all knew him, and some of the men had invested with him. But they veered off the subject when I asked about his deals."

"I'm surprised," I said. "If he was as generally disliked as Scot Raybourn implied, you'd have thought the golf course would be the perfect place for guys to talk about him."

"So maybe Raybourn is an outlier," said Flynn.

Flynn might be right. It was possible that Raybourn held a grudge against Cutler that wasn't shared by others. "Maybe," I said.

"If you couldn't get the golfers to gossip about Cutler, at least you got in a round of golf," I said. "So it wasn't a total waste of time."

"To the contrary," Flynn said. "I had an illuminating conversation after the game."

"Illuminating?" I perked up.

"We stopped into the bar for a beer after the round," Flynn said.

Theo and I looked at each other and laughed. "You don't drink beer," she said.

"I can if the occasion warrants it," Flynn said, defending himself. "It was damn hot on the course, and it was too early to have a cocktail. I wanted something to drink when my foursome adjourned to the bar."

"Good strategy," I said.

"Yeah, but it was wasted. The guys were friendly, and we talked a little business once they found out I was an investment banker, but nothing to interest you."

"So another dead end."

"That's what I thought," said Flynn, "until I recognized the bartender."

"Who was he?"

"His name's Chad. Good looking. Very smooth. I'm not surprised he got hired at Seaside. Says he's writing a novel—bartenders are always writers—so he pays a lot of attention to how people act. He used to work at the Rooster, on Juniper in Midtown. Don and I like to sit at the bar there, and we talked to Chad all the time."

"Never heard of the place," said Theo.

"It's a gay bar, hon," I told her.

"Did he recognize you?" I asked Flynn.

"Oh yeah," said Flynn. "I stalled around until the others had left. No one else was in the bar by then. We got to talking. He wanted to know if I had a place down here. I explained I was staying with the gorgeous Theo Humphries." He grinned and winked at Theo.

"Didn't that put him off?" I asked.

"To the contrary," Flynn said. "It was a genius move. He was intrigued, because he recognized Theo's name."

"Oh great," Theo said.

"Not to worry," said Flynn. "I told him I was here to help you and ask around about Cutler. Once Chad heard that, he couldn't wait to tell me what he knew."

"Did Chad know Cutler?" I asked, starting to get more interested in Flynn's tale.

"A little. Chad's only been at the Seaside Bar a few months. He knows the other guys, though. The ones that were the pallbearers at Cutler's funeral. They were all in the bar together recently."

I could see Flynn sorting out the story in his head while he drank his tea. Flynn is a meticulous reporter of the "just the facts" school. Probably why he's so good analyzing financials and making investment decisions. After a few seconds, he put down the glass, crossed his ankle over the other knee, and settled into the club chair.

"According to Chad, Scot Raybourn and Tom Boxer were in the bar just a few days after Cutler's funeral. They were several rounds into celebrating a hole-in-one Boxer made that day. Freddie showed up, and he wasn't in a celebratory mood."

"I'm surprised Chad remembered Freddie's mood," I said.

Flynn chuckled. "I've only seen Freddie cleaned up at the funeral, but Chad described him as rough around the edges."

"That's for sure," I said, remembering my experience with Freddie with a shudder.

"Chad likes them rough," said Flynn. "That's probably why he paid attention when Freddie came in 'cruising for a fight,' in Chad's words. The other guys called Freddie, 'Sarge.' That piqued Chad's interest," said Flynn, "and made me sure it was Freddie."

"No doubt about it," I said. "What was Freddie's problem?"

"Freddie insisted on talking to all of them. There had been a third guy who'd already left the celebration for the locker room, but Freddie ordered Boxer to bring him back."

"That would be Drew," I said.

"I figured," said Flynn. "Boxer eventually left to find Drew, but not till he'd gotten the okay from Scot. Chad says Boxer pretty much follows Scot's lead. Once the whole group was together, Freddie read them the riot act."

"What about?" I asked.

"About Cutler's murder exposing stuff they want to keep buried."

"Whoa," I said. "I can't believe Freddie said that in front of the bartender."

"Didn't, exactly. Freddie waved Chad away, told him to

take a break, so he moved down to the other end of the bar. The guys grabbed a table and sat, but Chad could still hear a lot of it. He can practically lip read, working all those years taking orders in loud bars. They may not have realized Chad was still there. Anyway, it got pretty heated. There was a lot of finger pointing.

"Scot said he was sick of the whole thing. He wanted to forget about it, leave it behind him now that Cutler's dead. The rest of them jumped on him at that point, telling him he had an obligation to the rest of them to keep quiet.

"At one point, Drew claimed he wasn't involved in whatever they were on about. Scot cussed the hide right off him—said Drew knew all about it, and he'd lose his law license if stuff he'd done for Cutler was exposed."

"Whoa, that's motive," I said. "Maybe Drew killed Cutler to protect himself, if Cutler threatened to expose him." My brain was running at high gear, thinking about the possibility that we were on the verge of uncovering Cutler's murderer.

"There's more," Flynn said. "They're looking for something."

"What?" I asked. I could barely sit still with excitement.

"Don't know. Seems like Cutler hid something they want to find. Scot convinced the steward to open Cutler's locker at the club, but it—whatever *it* is—wasn't there. Drew thinks it's at one of Cutler's homes."

"That might explain why Freddie was so hostile when Theo and I snooped around in Atlanta," I said. "He thought we were looking for it."

"That reminds me," said Flynn. "Your cover is blown, Audrey."

"What?" I asked.

"Freddie said Theo had friends who were looking for other

suspects. Scot said he'd already met one of those friends—remembered your name, in fact. You should be flattered."

"Fabulous," I muttered.

"No, wait," Flynn was laughing as he talked. "Scot described you as a tight-assed redhead."

Theo put her hand over her mouth.

"Up to then, Freddie had been nursing his beer. He didn't react to your name, but when Scot came out with that description, Freddie sat up and said he knew you. Called you an interfering bitch."

Theo muffled a giggle. I glared at her to let her know I wasn't amused by Freddie's description.

"Okay, okay," I said, holding up my hand to indicate I'd had enough. "Good work, Flynn. But what exactly have we learned from all this bad boy chatter?"

"They're hiding something," said Theo.

"Something they don't want to come out," said Flynn.

"Agreed," I said. "But is it connected with who killed Cutler Mead?"

Theo and Flynn both shrugged.

"We're going to have to keep going," I said. We'll have to keep working our way through each one of these guys to see if we can figure out whether one—or more—of them is involved in Cutler's death. "We've talked to Scot Raybourn and Drew Littlefield. Dr. Boxer is next. Unless one of y'all has a better idea." I looked at each of them and waited. Neither Theo or Flynn moved from where they sat.

Flynn whistled to his dogs who came running to him. "Okay, Porgi and Amor. Get ready. We're going to interview a veterinarian tomorrow, and you two will be the main distraction.

16

Dr. Boxer

Flynn had argued it was better to interview Tom Boxer at his clinic, hoping the familiar location would put Boxer at ease and more amenable to answering questions. After my experience with Scot Raybourn, I would have opted to ambush Boxer somewhere that I was comfortable, but he was not. But I deferred to Flynn. After all, he was supplying the dogs. At any rate, now that Cutler's friends had found out who I was and my reasons for asking questions, the advantage of deception was lost. We might as well make a direct approach, even if it meant masquerading as pet owners to get in the front door.

The next afternoon four of us sat in the reception area—the

two dogs yawning, Flynn bouncing the foot he had crossed over his knee, and me.

"I wonder whether it's true that some people start to look like their dogs," said Flynn.

"We should research that," I said, smiling as I looked at Flynn's elegant dogs, sitting next to his Cole Haan loafers. Flynn's shoe wardrobe rivaled Theo's, which is saying something. The loafers he'd chosen today were a two-toned woven leather, the top of the shoe a light beige and the rest tobacco brown. Stylish, but not over the top.

As if to answer Flynn's question, a head of curly white hair entered through the clinic's outer door. An elderly lady, bent with arthritis, hobbled into the waiting room. She leaned forward, digging her cane into the tile floor to offset a scrabbling Bichon at the end of a dainty leash. Finally pulled through the door by her owner, the animal dived under a chair and snuffled at the floor. The dog's fluffy white coat was perfectly groomed, and its fuchsia vest exactly matched its leash. Both matched their owner's immaculate suit. Flynn turned to me with a look of triumph as an assistant in a blue smock approached the old lady.

"How is Tipper doing, Mrs. Williams?" the assistant asked, eyeing the dog hiding under the old lady's chair.

"She wouldn't eat anything for two whole days."

"Oh my. That's not good."

"She seems better today. I cut up some Vye-eenas and mixed them in her kibble and she ate that right up."

"Uh hunh." The vet's assistant took the leash and led Tipper and his mistress away.

I laughed in recognition. My own mother had used Vienna sausages—thumb-sized weiners, invariably pronounced "Vye-eeenas"—as a treat and cure-all. As I chuckled, another assistant ushered us into a claustrophobic exam room. Flynn asked both dogs to sit, and I stood back against the wall to give them room.

Dr. Thomas Boxer swept into the room and greeted the dogs by crouching down on the tile floor and tilting his head sideways. Porgi and Amor were polite, and maintained their dignity with a delicate sniff at the vet's hand. Like the greyhounds, the vet was lean and immaculately groomed. He wore his thick silver hair a bit long and cut in subtle layers. A jaunty turquoise bow tie perched at the throat of his white coat. On his feet were Gucci loafers. Like Flynn, the vet wore his shoes island-style, without socks.

Dr. Boxer lifted Porgi and Amor one at a time onto the table and ran his hands over them, checking their ears and eyes before looking toward Flynn.

"These pups appear to be in terrific shape. What brings you here?"

Before Flynn could answer, I spoke from my corner. "We wanted to ask you for some information."

Dr. Boxer straightened up from the exam table and handed Amor back to Flynn.

"I've seen you before," the doctor said to me. "Weren't you in the Cloister Bar the other night?"

"Ann Audrey Pickering." I held out my hand and he shook it.

"Scot Raybourn told me you'd been to see him. Said you were asking a lot of questions."

"We're friends of Theo Humphries, who…"

"I know who she is," Boxer interrupted. "Recognized her with you in the bar."

"Yes," Flynn broke into the conversation. "We're trying to help Theo—Mrs. Humphries. She was a close friend of Cutler

Mead, and she's very upset about his death. We were hoping to find out more about him. She's been through a lot these last few years...."

At the mention of Cutler Mead's name the veterinarian shifted his weight. "I don't know what you're up to, but I don't appreciate you coming here under false pretenses."

"I'm sorry you feel that way," Flynn said. "I thought it would be less intrusive to visit you during an exam."

"Less intrusive?" Boxer protested. "I've just wasted my time in this exam. You could have seen me in my office."

"Well, you are the best vet on the island," Flynn said. "I'm down here a lot, and I want to have the best for Porgi and Amor." He patted both dogs as he spoke. "I'm depending on you to keep my buddies healthy. As for our questions, we didn't mean to sandbag you."

I was on tenterhooks waiting to see if Flynn's diplomatic approach would work.

Flynn's charm offensive seemed to have a calming effect. "I'm not sure how I can help," Boxer said, crossing his arms.

"I was at the funeral," Flynn said. "And I noticed you were a pallbearer, so I assumed you were a close friend." It sounded incredibly lame, but if Flynn could get information using his considerable charm, who was I to interfere?

Dr. Boxer seemed to accept Flynn's explanation. "We'd known each other for ages. We both grew up around here. I was a little older than Cutler, a class ahead in school."

"You played golf every Sunday with him," Flynn said, making it a statement, not a question.

The veterinarian thrust his hands into the pockets of his white coat. "Cutler was the organizer of the foursome. I'm not sure we'll keep it together now."

"Maybe you can play as a sort of memorial." I didn't know why I said that; the words just popped out of my mouth. The reaction was not what I expected. The doctor drew his brows together and clenched his jaw. He looked more angry than sorrowful.

Flynn stepped in to defuse the suddenly hostile atmosphere, turning the conversation in another direction. "Were you involved in any of Cutler's real estate developments?" Flynn asked.

Dr. Boxer appeared to relax somewhat at the change of subject. "I invested in some of his projects when I was invited."

"Invited?" Flynn asked.

"Look, I don't know anything about real estate development. Several times Cutler said he needed capital—to show the banks that he had backers to get a project off the ground—so I'd buy in."

"How'd that turn out?"

He grimaced. "Not too well, to be honest."

"Why did you keep investing with him?" Flynn asked.

"He was a hard man to say no to."

Boxer's indication that Cutler had bullied him, gave me an opening. "I understand you served under him in Vietnam," I said. His eyes flickered. Apparently I'd hit a nerve.

"What made you mention that?"

"You played golf every Sunday with him and others who'd served together," Flynn answered for me.

"We had a bond, I guess. That was a lifetime ago. We were just kids. Didn't know whether we'd ever get home. Made us pretty crazy."

He spoke to Flynn, ignoring me. "Look, I need to get back to my patients."

I hate being ignored by bow tie wearing men. "One other thing," I said. "Where were you stationed in Vietnam?"

"We were all over the place." He looked down at the tiled floor before he turned to face me.

"I have some friends who served in that war," I said, trying to keep the subject open for conversation. "I just wondered if you were in any of the same places."

"I do my damnedest to forget every miserable inch of that godforsaken jungle. In fact, I've spent a lot of energy for a lot of years trying not to remember anything about that life." Boxer's face was flushed and the veins in his neck bulged above the bow tie. "Now get out."

He spun around, flung the door open and left Flynn, me, and the dogs in the exam room.

Porgi and Amor, made anxious by the vet's display of temper, had wound themselves around Flynn's legs. He spent a few minutes soothing them before we walked out of the clinic. In the parking lot, Flynn shifted the leashes into one hand and fumbled for the keys to his BMW. "I'm not sure that was even worth the trip," he said.

"Well, we now know Tom Boxer lost money investing in Cutler's schemes. Maybe he resented Cutler forcing him into a bad investment. Although I can't see how killing Cutler would help Dr. Boxer, unless it was sheer fury over the loss of money."

"The doc clearly has a bit of a temper," said Flynn.

"True. I wonder if that temper ever gets out of hand." I opened the front and back passenger doors and waited for the hot air to float out.

"Why did you ask him where he'd been stationed in Vietnam?" asked Flynn.

"Thought it might have something to do with whatever it is those guys are hiding. Maybe a way for us to figure out what that is."

"Good idea," said Flynn. "We have to keep snooping until we hit on something. We know Theo didn't kill Cutler Mead, so it had to be someone who knew him."

"I wonder if the Vietnam connection is even important," I said.

"The Doc bolted out of the room when you brought that up. He must have some nasty memories."

"So why did he play golf every week with the same guys who were with him during the war?" I asked. "There's gotta be some other reason he doesn't want to talk about it."

17

Rob Prescott

After the interview with Tommy Boxer, Flynn dropped me off at Theo's. I hollered to let her know I was home, and walked straight through the house to sit outside on the deck to call Mike Bristol. I wasn't sure how my call would be received, and I didn't want Theo overhearing some of my report. Bristol picked up the call on the first ring, and I identified myself. Without preliminaries, I gave him a summary of the conversations we'd had and what Flynn had learned from his bartender friend Chad. When I'd finished, there was silence on the other end of the phone.

"Detective, are you there?" I asked.

"Sorry. Someone else is at my desk trying to talk to me, and I was distracted," he said.

His lack of interest in the information I'd gathered irritated me. He was dismissing my efforts, and I don't like being treated as useless. "I apologize for wasting your time," I said in my frostiest tone.

"Ann Audrey," he said, "there's a lot going on here." He sounded tired, not as forceful as I remembered from the two times I'd been with him.

I was curious. "Are you okay?" I asked.

"Aren't you watching TV?" he said, with an edge to his voice.

"I haven't turned on the six o'clock news yet," I said, baffled as to why he seemed annoyed with me.

"We had a mass shooting in Buckhead today. Day trader lost a bunch of money and shot his family and the people in his office. Thirteen dead. Every cop in Atlanta is working full time on it."

"My God—I didn't know."

"Worst scene I've ever been at," Bristol said, "and I've seen a lot of homicides. The two children tucked up in bed...." His voice was thick with emotion and fatigue.

"I'm sorry," I said, and I meant I was sorry for him. What kind of life is that, having to look at the grisly aftermath of violence every day?

"It's the job," Bristol said, his voice brisker than before. "Keep doing what you're doing. You're getting stuff worth considering. Apologies, but I gotta go."

When he hung up, I flipped my phone closed and sat down under the massive live oak that stood in the center of the deck circling Theo's backyard. I wished the conversation had gone on longer. Hearing the sadness in Bristol's voice had connected me to him in a different way. I shook off my increasing interest in the man and reconsidered Bristol the cop. I'd get the particulars of the Atlanta mass shooting on the news later, and it would be horrible. But there was a silver lining. The Atlanta PD would have their hands full dealing with that incident, easing the pressure on Bristol to arrest Theo, and giving me more time to find Cutler Mead's killer. And the press would be distracted from Theo for a while. I was only moderately ashamed of myself for being so callous.

I went back inside the cottage to find Theo in the sunroom. She handed me a glass of wine, and took another for herself before sitting on the couch and curling her feet under her. We settled down to fill the time before supper by revisiting what we'd learned so far, going over every conversation and tidbit of information. Theo wouldn't let go of the Vietnam angle and my patience started to wear thin.

"Who cares if these guys are holding on to a secret that happened years—decades—ago in Vietnam?" I said, squirming to get deeper my chair.

"I know," said Theo. "But you can't help wondering...."

"We can't go down every rabbit hole looking for answers, Theo. And the likelihood of finding out what happened to those guys decades ago and a world away from Georgia is nil. We need to find out what's happened recently related to Cutler's death," I said.

"I know," she repeated. "But don't you think it's weird how those guys stayed in touch? They didn't like each other—didn't like Cutler?"

"Yes. It's weird. It's also a good description of daily life in a small town," I said. "Let's look at something else before this makes us crazy. What about your business partner?"

"Rob?"

"When can we talk to him?" I asked.

"Tomorrow. I'll call Mildred first thing in the morning and set it up."

"Who's Mildred?"

"Rob's secretary. She's one tough bird. You'll like her," Theo said.

"How much does her boss know about you and Cutler," I asked.

"Why?"

"I just figured you might want to consider what you're going to tell Rob, before we get there." Rob Prescott and Theo's husband George had worked together for decades. George would spot the potential in an investment and Rob managed their investments. According to Theo, it was because of Rob that Humphries Enterprises continued to thrive, even after George's death.

"I'll tell him about Cutler and me only if I have to," Theo said. "It's awkward. Rob was George's best friend."

"I get it," I said. "You don't want to make Rob uncomfortable. Let's come up with some excuse for the visit." We moved into the kitchen, and while Theo made her famous crab cakes with Remoulade sauce—she was a superb cook, along with everything else—we drafted a script for the visit with Rob Prescott.

* * *

Next morning we drove to the modern building housing Humphries Enterprises, weaved through the rotating doors into a shadowy lobby, and took the elevator to the top floor.

Mildred McIntire rose to greet Theo with a hug. Prescott's long-time secretary was a bony sixty-eight-year-old in a sleeveless dress that showed off tanned arms. The definition on her biceps and forearms supported Theo's story that Mildred routinely trounced tennis players thirty years her junior.

"Hi, Mildred." She and Theo gazed fondly at each other while Theo inquired about Mildred's latest tennis tournament and her grandchildren. Theo disentangled herself to introduce me.

"Let me stop yapping," said Mildred. "I know you want to see Rob. He's expecting you. Wait here a minute." She disappeared into her boss's office without bothering to knock.

In a few seconds the heavy door was opened by a bald middle-aged man, his doughy face smiling at us. Rob Prescott wore steel-rimmed bifocals that covered his face like goggles from above his eyebrows to his plump cheekbones. Horizontal worry lines sliced across his forehead, stopping only when his face merged into smooth bare scalp. He exuded a sense of calm competence, a feeling that everything would be okay. I understood why Theo trusted this guy to run the company she'd inherited.

We declined Mildred's offer of coffee and sat down in the quiet office. Theo launched into the story we had concocted.

"We're sorry to bother you about this, Rob. It's silly, but Annie and I are invited to the Driscoll's this weekend. After I accepted, I remembered a few years ago George got into a terrible argument there with Drew Littlefield—a real scene." She paused and I watched his reaction.

"Uh huh." Prescott leaned sideways in his tall leather chair, his right elbow on the chair's arm while he massaged his ear lobe.

"I remember the scene, but I can't recall what it was about. I don't want to go to Marjorie Driscoll's and accidently step on somebody's toes." Theo trailed off. I prayed Prescott would pick up the story and fill in the blanks.

"Theo, what are you asking me?" His voice sounded amused, but his eyes had sharpened. Rob Prescott would not be easily taken in.

"I'm asking if you know why George had a falling out with Drew. I know that he got mad at him, really mad, about something, and then George died before it got resolved. I'd like to know about that, Rob."

Prescott glanced at me. I feigned polite indifference to Theo's question.

"That's all water under the bridge, honey. You don't have to worry about it. Humphries Enterprises didn't lose a dime, even though those guys threatened to sue us for breach of contract. George walked away from the deal before we signed the final paperwork."

That was interesting. So there had been an aborted deal with Cutler. Theo had guessed right.

"I'm not worried. Just curious," Theo said. "Drew Littlefield's name has come up in connection with something else, and I'm trying to fit him in with what I remember."

Prescott hesitated, then asked, "Has this got anything to do with Cutler Mead's death?"

"I honestly don't know," Theo said. This, at least, was the truth.

"Well, it wasn't Drew Littlefield who started it. It was Cutler." Prescott quit tugging his earlobe and began to fiddle with an old fashioned fountain pen, popping the cap on and off.

I was sure he had more to say. I silently willed Theo to encourage him. She locked eyes with Prescott and raised her eyebrows.

He gave a big sigh. "It was like this." He reached forward to pull open the bottom drawer of his desk and propped his foot up, tilting back his tall leather chair, preparing to tell the story. I could almost see him rocking on his front porch and whittling while he talked.

"Cutler came to George with an idea to develop luxury homes next door to the Seaside golf course. The project sounded good. He wanted Humphries Enterprises to buy the land. Claimed he was cash poor—probably true—but he said his company could handle construction.

"We were worried about getting the zoning approved, but Cutler had Drew Littlefield working on it." He swiveled his chair in Theo's direction.

"You remember how Drew used to be the chairman of the zoning commission. He could get projects approved, one way or another."

This was news to me, and interesting. This sounded like the kind of stuff that Scot Raybourn had threatened Drew with when the men were with Freddie at the bar. My antenna was up and I was hoping that Rob would elaborate, but Theo murmured as if she was already aware of it.

"Here's the good part. George goes to play the Seaside course on Wednesday. On the number four, he clips one w-a-a-a-ay beyond the rough. The ball is so far gone it's onto that empty acreage next to the resort, the land Mead wants us to buy. Now this is the way George told it to me.

'He's pissed, pardon me, about his drive, so he stomps over there to find it, and, after he chunks his 7-iron into every clump of cane grass, he finds it alright. Sunk in an oily puddle.'"

He paused and seemed to be waiting for us to react. Theo looked sideways at me. I squinted at Prescott. I had an inkling where the story was headed, but I could tell that Theo was still in the dark. However, not for nothing had Theo learned to convince men that she understood what they were talking about. After a minute Theo formed her mouth into an "Oh," giving Rob a wide-eyed look.

"You got it." Prescott slapped his hands on his thighs, delighted at her encouragement.

"George Humphries was nobody's dummy. He scooped up some of that glop and sent samples to the environmental lab in Tampa. They confirmed what he already guessed. That land was soaked with creosote, oozing with it. Must have been a wood processing plant there at one time. This area was full of those plants as late as the 60's."

"So George was upset to find out that the land was polluted?" Theo asked.

"Upset? He was mad as hell, 'scuse me, because he knew Cutler Mead was trying to con us."

He sat up in his chair and, for the first time since he'd begun the narrative, he put both feet on the ground, leaning toward us to force our attention. "If Humphries Enterprises owned that property," Prescott said, "we would have been responsible for cleaning up the pollution, and that would have cost millions of dollars. Millions," he repeated, apparently to ensure that we heard him.

"Oh my God," Theo said.

Unlike Rob Prescott, I knew that Theo's exclamation was not about the scam. Theo had just learned she'd been sleeping with a man who'd tried to defraud the real love of her life—her late husband.

"We canceled the deal, of course," Prescott continued, oblivious to Theo's distress. "George was sure Cutler knew about it and had tried to sucker us. Drew Littlefield kept trying to convince George that Cutler didn't know about the contamination. When George wouldn't buy their B.S., Drew and Cutler tried to convince George to keep quiet about it. George thought they were going to try to sucker someone else. That's why he got so mad. That's probably what that argument you remember was about."

"It's lucky George found out." I spoke up to distract Prescott from Theo. She looked like she might throw up, head down, her face pasty and a hand over her mouth.

"Lucky? I'll tell you what was lucky." As I had hoped, Prescott turned in my direction, away from Theo. "Those rascals were lucky George had that heart attack when he did, because we were planning to turn them in to the district attorney."

I was staggered at Rob's story. Here we were looking at Cutler's death and maybe we had uncovered something else. I wondered how far George had gotten with his plan to complain to the authorities about Cutler. I wasn't a fan of coincidences, and certainly not when two men had died.

Prescott must have sensed my thoughts. He deflated, seeming to lose his enthusiasm for the story. He shook his head and sat back with his hands in his lap. "George was the one with the evidence—he had all the conversations with them. Once he passed away, I let it go. With George gone, some of our investors were threatening to pull out. I was scrambling to save the business." He paused a minute and said. "Those bastards got home scot free."

18

Complication

Leaving the Humphries Enterprises building, Theo stumbled as she reached for the car door. "Give me your keys," I ordered.

Theo fished in her purse and handed them over. She took the passenger seat and leaned her head against the window while I backed the Mercedes out of the parking spot. I drove several blocks away from before casting a glance at Theo.

"Are you okay?"

"No."

We rode in silence, cruising down Frederica Drive, until we were slowed by the lunchtime traffic backed up around Southern Soul barbeque. The hot air around Southern Soul's two outdoor barbeque drums shimmered, and the smell of sweet porky smoke billowed over the street and the idling cars. I'd often considered notifying the EPA about the pollution, but the blowback from local barbeque fans wouldn't be worth it.

When we got home, I left Theo at the cottage, changed into my running shoes and took off down the beach. I desperately needed to process the information Rob Prescott had just dumped on us, and I needed to be alone to think. Nikes scrunching on the damp sand, I followed the wiggling line of scum that marked high tide. I jogged toward the point commanded by the ugliest house on Sea Island, a 20,000 square foot behemoth that crouched seaside as if embarrassed by its own scale. The beach was smooth, its unmarked surface waiting for the tide to return and bring feeding gulls, crabs and humans.

Since the revelation that George Humphries had thwarted Cutler's real estate scam, my thoughts had pinballed from Sea Island to Vietnam to Atlanta and back. What bound those golfing bastards together? Was it something from their days in the army or was it a business deal?

I needed to talk to someone who could help me focus, but Theo was an emotional mess. Between finding Cutler's body and discovering her lover had tried to bilk her husband, Theo was unreliable just now, or worse.

Sweet-hearted Theo, who never uttered a cuss word, could have a complete come-apart when she reached her limit. But not verbally—she'd pound on a sofa arm, stomp her foot, wave her arms. What if Cutler had told Theo he was getting back with Sissy? What if Theo grabbed for that golf trophy in a fury? I didn't want to believe it, but I couldn't ignore the possibility. I'd known Theo for decades, and she had a temper. I'd seen it for myself on occasion.

There had been that time she'd tossed the drink at Mildred Sartain's creepy husband during that party—threw the highball glass at him, actually. He dodged. The crystal smashed against the wall of the Sartains' great room, just missing a sofa-sized hunt print, the muscular rear ends of the horses bunched as if to jump away from the flying cocktail. The trigger for that episode was long forgotten, but there had been a few others. What if Theo already knew about Cutler's attempt to defraud George Humphries? No. I was sure I would know about that, and Theo's reaction today was one of shock. Unless she were acting. I refused to believe she was that duplicitous.

My brain was going around in circles. The sun was intense, and I hadn't bothered to bring sunglasses or a hat, so I turned back. With the sun casting a shadow in front of me, I almost stepped into a convoy of ants dining on the corpse of a sea gull.

Cui bono? Who benefits? The ants were benefiting by the bird's death, and if they could, ants would probably kill a sea gull every morning. If Cutler Mead hadn't been killed in a temper tantrum by someone—say Theo, for the sake of argument—then who would have benefited from his death?

Head down, I almost bumped into Flynn, standing on the beach, waiting for me.

"Theo's a mess," he said, as a greeting.

"So you know what Rob Prescott told us?" I asked, as Flynn turned to walk alongside me.

"Enough. I thought you and I should talk without Theo. She's gone from weeping girlfriend to revenge-minded widow. She's calling Cutler names that even I have rarely heard. She's mad, Audrey."

"Yeah, that's not helpful to her situation. The police already think she had a motive to kill Cutler because he was going back to his wife, and when this comes out...."

"What do you want to do?" he asked.

"I want to go take a look at that land Cutler Mead planned to develop with George Humphries' money."

"Why?"

"Just a feeling."

We took Flynn's car and headed toward the Seaside Golf Course. I directed him to the byways that led to the undeveloped land on the eastern side of the course.

"That must be it," he pointed.

On a scrubby lot, a pair of elaborate iron gates stood forlorn between concrete pillars studded with shells.

"Looks like an abandoned movie set," Flynn said. "Where's Tallulah Bankhead wearing a turban?"

"You're confusing your movies. Don't you mean Gloria Swanson?"

"This is the deep South. I'm going with Tallulah."

Beyond the gates, a sign too faded to read from where we were parked had lost the battle with weeds that had grown thigh high. We exited the car and picked our way between clumps of cord grass toward the placard.

"For God's sake, Audrey," Flynn said, trying to dodge the stickers on the grass and the mounds of fire ants. "I came down here expecting to dress for the Cloister dining room, not the Everglades."

"Stop whining. We're almost there."

We stood in front of the faded announcement of the development: "Coming soon. Estate Homes starting at $1 million." There was more language touting designer finishes and top end amenities.

"Sounds like every other gated community on the island," said Flynn. "I guarantee oversized plantation shutters, bleached wood cabinets, tropical print wallpaper—no wait, make that sea shells—and ridiculous amounts of marble tile."

I was trying to put myself in Cutler Mead's shoes. Considering its prime location, this property would have netted him a fortune. How did he feel when George not only walked out of the deal, but also threatened Cutler with criminal charges? The confrontation between the two men must have been nasty. Cutler could have bashed in George's head in the heat of the moment. That wouldn't have been surprising. Instead George died an unsuspicious death from a heart attack. Maybe George's death was just that—unsuspicious. And yet....

When I didn't say anything, Flynn turned to look at me. "You think Cutler Mead was killed because of this place," he said.

I shook my head. "No," I said. "I think George Humphries was killed because of this place." The words were out of my mouth before I could stifle them. I'd just made a crossing-the-Rubicon statement, and I couldn't take it back. The feeling of being swept into something that I couldn't stop was familiar. I remembered when the FBI had talked me into wearing a wire to record my own husband's conversation. I wasn't able to back out, and the consequences followed me for years.

"Oh, fuck," said Flynn. "Audrey, how are you going to tell *that* to Theo?"

"I'm not—yet." As soon as Flynn voiced the question I had decided to keep Theo in the dark for now, but I knew it wouldn't last. Theo was no dummy. She'd figure it out eventually.

"Good. Agreed," said Flynn. "It's just speculation, for the time being. No sense in upsetting Theo further."

"Right," I said, "but we can't just drop it. It could be connected to what happened to Cutler, and Cutler's murder is where Theo is in danger." I was thinking fast. "We've got to get to the bottom of Cutler Mead's business. Did he pull this kind of fraud more than once? If so, there's a much wider pool of suspects."

We started picking our way back through the overgrown lot toward where we'd left the car, discussing how to find out more about Cutler's previous developments and possible scams as we walked.

"The cops can do that better than us," Flynn said. "You need to talk to Detective Bristol. A strategy confab. Tell Bristol everything you've found out. What you suspect. Bristol has to have all the facts if he's going to find the real killer." I didn't reply, so Flynn went on. "Come on, Audrey. How many murder mysteries have we read where the heroine keeps some vital piece of knowledge to herself only to have it bite her in the ass later in the book?"

Since the third grade Flynn and I had read murder mysteries together. One way we vicariously escaped the roles our small town imposed on us. Even mystery fiction was gender specific, according to Miss Swerington, the librarian. Under her judgmental eyes, I filled out my library card with Nancy Drew mysteries while Flynn took out the latest installments of The Hardy Boys. Naturally, we swapped them, once around the corner where we had parked our bikes. With her expensive "runabout" convertible, Nancy was too mired in the upper middle class for me. The rougher Hardy brothers were more my style.

"I agree," I said. I had already decided I wanted to talk over this new idea with Mike Bristol, but I needed more than a hunch to convince him to take me seriously. "I'll call him, but first I'll ask around. See if I can find out what happened the day George died."

"Ask around where?" said Flynn.

"The scene of the crime, of course. I'm going to snoop around the Seaside Golf Course."

"Do you want company? If Chad is working, he's more likely to open up to me."

"Chad has only been there for the last few months. I need to find somebody who was around when George died. That was several years ago. Anyway, I think it's better for you to hang out with Theo for now. She needs company."

"Fine," said Flynn. "Take the car and drop me off at the cottage."

19

Bobbie the Bartender

I wallowed in the luxury of driving Flynn's BMW. The car was quiet and powerful, smoothly accelerating through the intersection at Frederica and Demere, the interior so hermetically sealed that I couldn't even smell the smoke rolling off the grill at Southern Soul. I cruised by St. Simons' tiny airport, primarily maintained for the private planes of Sea Island landowners, arriving at all hours from wherever the rich had last partied. At the four-way stop I headed down the driveway into the golf club parking lot.

Sun-blinded by the time I'd walked from the car to the club-house, I gasped with relief at the cool darkness of the club-house bar. When I paused inside the swing doors for my eyes to adjust, the woman behind the bar looked up. I wound my way between the litter of empty tables and pulled out a stool.

"What can I get you?" She was a determinedly cheerful faux blonde with deep crow's feet at her eyes, no longer in the blush of youth, but still maintaining herself. A dark tan and her accent marked her as local. Over one shoulder a long braid rested and above it sparkly pink earrings dangled, swinging in time with the steps she took to reach where I was sitting.

"Wine spritzer," I said.

"You waiting on a tee time?"

"No. Actually, I'm looking for someone," I said.

Her friendliness cooled a bit. "Oh, yeah?"

"I'm Ann Audrey Pickering.

"Nice to meet you, Ms. Pickering."

"Call me Ann Audrey."

"Okay, Ann Audrey. I'm Bobbie."

"I'm a friend of a lady whose husband died here a few years ago. Maybe you remember him—George Humphries?"

"Oh, God, yeah. He was the sweetest man." She dropped the retail friendliness for what appeared to be real sadness.

"He was indeed. One of the nicest guys around. Were you working the day he died?"

"For sure. I served him his last drink," she said. She picked up a wet cloth and started wiping the bar in front of me. I moved my glass so she could reach all the way to the edge.

I couldn't believe my luck. What were the odds I'd run into someone who was here that day and knew George? If only Bobbie could remember some of the details. "Can you recall who else was with him?"

She screwed up her face and thought. "With Mr. Humphries? It was busy. I know Mr. Mead was here, though, 'cause he stayed after Mr. Humphries left."

It was interesting that Cutler's presence in the bar had stuck in Bobbie's memory. "Are you sure?" I said. "It's been a while."

"I remember because Mr. Mead just died too, you know. Killed. And Mr. Humphries dead, too. That day was the last time I saw them both in the bar. Weird coincidence, I think."

Bobbie was more observant than I'd given her credit for. She was proof that the standard bias against blondes—even fake ones—was wrong. To keep her talking I said, "Yeah, I heard about Mr. Mead. But he was murdered in Atlanta, wasn't he?"

Bobbie stopped wiping and leaned on the bar. "That's true. But he mostly lived on the island. He was a regular at the club. In here a lot before and after his rounds."

"Big drinker?"

"Not so much. He liked to buy drinks for other people."

Would Bobbie name names. "Other people?" I asked, coaxing her to be more forthcoming.

She winked. "Ladies. That one really liked the ladies."

"Any one in particular?" Theo was probably on Bobbie's list, but who were the others?

"Sometimes he'd bring the same lady, but they didn't usually last too long."

Just as Scot Raybourn had told me. That particular morsel of gossip didn't need to be reported to Theo. "A handsome man," I said, blatantly leading the witness. "Tall, well dressed."

"And wandering hands," she giggled, filling in the picture with facts I could have predicted.

"Did he give you any trouble?" I asked, disliking Cutler more and more with each minute of this conversation.

"Shoot, no. 'Sides, I've handled a lot worse than him. He was mostly talk—and I'll put up with talk if the guy's a good tipper."

"Was he?"

"You bet. I always liked when he was in the bar. I knew I was going home with a fat tip that night." She cocked her head. "You know, it wasn't just women. If it was business or his four-some, he'd buy for men, too."

She was defending him, but then, her livelihood depended on her ability to handle boors like Cutler. She had developed a tough hide as a result. I was careful to make my response neutral, so she'd keep talking. "That can get expensive," I said.

"You're not kidding. The manager used to say Mr. Mead's bar tab was bigger than his golf bag. None of my business, though."

"You seem to know him pretty well."

"That's why I remembered serving him right after I made that drink for Mr. Humphries."

"I see," I said, although I wasn't sure that I did.

She continued as if I hadn't interrupted her. "See, Mr. Mead always, *always*, either drank one of two drinks. A Heineken if he was golfing, or a Blanton's bourbon. But that time, right after Mr. Humphries walked away from my bar, Mr. Mead ordered a gin and tonic, the very same thing I'd just made for Mr. Humphries."

Bobbie's recall of the drinks was consistent with studies of how people on trial juries remember evidence related to their line of work. Engineers remember timing and how alibis fit into a timeline; secretaries remember whether documents were signed; chefs remember witnesses testifying about a mealtime conversation. I pressed to find out just how detailed Bobbie's memory of that day really was. "Did Mr. Mead drink the gin and tonic?" I asked.

She fiddled with the braid at her shoulder while she thought. "I can't remember. Oh, wait. I do remember. I was doing the drinks cart that day."

Maybe the axiom about ditzy blondes was right after all. Bobbie's monkey brain had apparently jumped to another subject. "Drinks cart?"

"You don't golf, do you?" She gave me a kindly smile.

"No, sorry." Humility was my only play to keep her talking, even if the conversation appeared to be nonsensical at this point.

"Well at the turn—the end of the first nine holes—lots of golfers take a break." She twirled the tail of her braid while she waited to see if I followed her explanation.

"That makes sense," I said.

"So, we have a cart at the turn—sort of a minibar on wheels—so the golfers can order a drink. And that day, I was driving the cart."

"Since you were driving the cart, you didn't see Mr. Mead drink that gin and tonic," I said.

"No. Sorry, I should have explained better." She adjusted one of the pink earrings as she thought out loud. "Back in the bar, when Mr. Mead realized I was leaving to drive the drinks cart, he told me to cancel the G and T. He'd order it from me at the turn."

"And did he?" The conversation was not so nonsensical after all. I sipped at my spritzer and waited for her answer.

"For sure. I remember because he drove his cart up in a hurry. He jumped out and ordered before the other guys had even gotten out of their carts."

"What happened then?" Had she seen what Cutler had done with that drink?

The question seemed to confuse her. "Nothing special. I got busy. A couple of other foursomes pulled up all at once. It was pretty warm, so everybody was thirsty."

"Can you remember who all was there?" If Bobbie hadn't seen what Cutler did with the gin and tonic, maybe I could track down another one of the golfers who'd been at the turn the same time.

"Mr. Humphries was there with his group," Bobbie said. "They were out of their carts and chatting away. Razzing each other, you know, like guys do. They ordered a round, and I was hopping to get everybody's order filled before they drove off for the back nine."

"Don't they stay at the turn to drink?"

"Sometimes. But mostly they just stick the drink in the cup-holder on their cart and take off."

She had nothing more to add. I tipped Bobbie out of pro-portion to my tab for the wine spritzer, but her information was worth every cent. I turned the air conditioning on high in the BMW and let the cold air from the dashboard blast my face. It was looking like my theory had merit. The bartender's story was a good lead, but she hadn't conclusively linked Cutler to George's death. There were big questions unanswered—was George poisoned, and if so, did Cutler put the poison in the gin and tonic he'd ordered from Bobbie? If we were to prove it, I would have to convince Theo to exhume George's body. That was a conversation I didn't want to even contemplate.

20

The Azalea Ball

Theo and Flynn were sitting at the kitchen island when I returned to the cottage.

"Good," she said. "You're back." Theo's eyes were no longer puffy from crying. Her mouth was set in a straight line that brooked no nonsense.

I glanced at Flynn who raised his left hand and tugged on his ear lobe, our private way of communicating something was up—angry parents, suspicious teachers, backstabbing so-called friends—since junior high.

"Yeah, it was nice to get out a bit," I said, hoping Theo wouldn't ask what I'd been doing. Her next sentence made it clear she'd rebounded from the shock of Rob Prescott's story and was moving to clear her name—and separate herself from her infatuation with Cutler.

"While you were gone, I had a phone call from Joan McKendree about Sissy Mead," Theo said. "Come into the sunroom and sit down. We need to make plans."

Joan McKendree, a hard edged brunette who flaunted layers of David Yurman silver jewelry, queened over the women lounging at the Beach Club. She was a fixture on Sea Island, and a long-time social, though not intimate, friend of Theo's. "What about Joan?" I asked as Flynn and I dutifully followed Theo into the adjoining room. I pushed aside a mound of newspapers from one of the sunroom club chairs and sat down. Flynn picked up Porgi and put him on the sofa. The dog curled up with his nose on his paws. He and his master watched me.

"Well, first of all, Joan says the night before last Sissy was at the Cloister Bar with Scot Raybourn," Theo said. "An acrimonious tête-à-tête, is what Joan tells me."

"Scot Raybourn?" I said. "That's interesting."

"Why?" said Flynn.

"When I talked to Scot, I got the message he didn't like Cutler," I said. "I'm surprised Scot's meeting Mrs. Mead. On the other hand, he's a man who likes the ladies. Maybe there was something going on there. Giving both of them a motive to get rid of Cutler."

"The description of their meeting doesn't sound like a lovers' tryst," said Flynn.

"No," agreed Theo. "But I'll ask around. If the two of them were having an affair, someone would know. I'd vote no, though. Sissy hardly ever comes to Sea Island. This is—was—Cutler's place. And Scot's business is here."

I remembered the long-haired young man at Sissy's side during the funeral. "Is her son here with her?" I asked.

"No. Joan says he's got a job in California, somewhere outside San Francisco. He just flew into Atlanta long enough for the funeral and then went back to work."

Mike Bristol would check up on that, I hoped, but it sounded like Sissy's son was not a suspect. "I wonder how long she's going to be on the island?" I asked.

"Not long at all," said Theo. "According to Joan, Sissy is headed home to Atlanta. She's throwing herself into running the Azalea Ball—full throttle."

"Azalea Ball?" I asked. I was pretending not to know what Theo was talking about, though anybody who lived in Atlanta, even one as removed from society as I was, knew about it.

Theo closed her eyes so as not to view my pretense of ignorance. "It's one of the premier charity balls in Atlanta, and Sissy is the chairwoman this year."

I shuddered. "A Disease Ball."

"That's what she was talking about the other night when we saw her at the Sea Grill," said Flynn.

"Right. A benefit to raise money for a chronic disease. And an excuse for those with money to dress up and feel right-eous about it," I said. And maybe, in Sissy Mead's case, a way to forget about her husband's death. It seemed strange that a recent widow would throw herself into such an undertaking. They say everyone grieves in their own way, but still....

"Don't be so bitchy," said Theo. "Many of these charity events raise *a lot* of money for worthy causes."

Flynn ducked his head and pretended to talk into Porgi's ears.

"Okay, okay. I'm sorry," I said. "I didn't mean to offend you."

Theo broke into my apology. "Annie, don't you see? It's the perfect opportunity for you to get a one-on-one with her. You can pretend to be interested in buying an entire table."

Buying a table meant purchasing tickets—expensive tickets— for 8 or 10 people, a substantial investment in any charity do.

Flynn was still avoiding my eye. He bent over and picked up the other dog, who'd been begging to join the group on the couch. "Ann Audrey Pickering goes to the ball. You need a fairy godmother?"

"Stop there. Both of you," I said. I hadn't dressed up for a formal ball since I'd left the law firm, where partners were expected to show up for those affairs as a matter of business. I'd always hated those evenings, and my present reclusive lifestyle allowed me to avoid such functions.

"Annie..." Theo started to argue with me.

"Theo, even if I were willing to do this, how am I going to approach her?" My voice rose to coloratura range as I scrambled to avoid this train wreck.

"Don't worry. I'll get Joan to set it up," said Theo.

Flynn turned toward Theo. "Baby girl, how are you going to pull that off?"

"My question exactly," I said. "Why would Joan do that?"

"She's furious that Sissy got the chairmanship," Theo said.

"It's very prestigious, you know. They're sorority sisters, so if Joan asks her to meet you, Sissy'll do it."

I faced the two of them—Flynn and Theo—staring at me with expectant looks. The two dogs stared at me with the identical expression.

"Theo, you'd be so much better at this kind of meeting," I said, with a weak attempt at escape.

"Probably," she said. "But Sissy's not likely to give *me* the time of day."

Her answer was so firm I was surprised. Finding out that Cutler had attempted to defraud her husband had really put steel in Theo's spine.

I sighed and gave in. "Fine. Get it set up and I'll meet her. I need to go back to Atlanta anyway." I turned to Flynn. "Can I ride back with you?"

"Sure. I'll ask Porgi and Amor if they mind sitting in the back." He gave me the lopsided grin he used in the eighth grade when we were planning to skip school together.

That settled, I walked outside to call Mike Bristol in private. "Detective, this is Ann Audrey Pickering."

"Ann Audrey," he replied, his voice low and silky. He rolled the syllables around like they were candy in his mouth.

I cleared my throat. "Yes. I'll be back in Atlanta tomorrow, and I wondered if we could get together?"

"My place or yours?" he purred.

Choosing to ignore the double entendre, I said, "I loathe cop shops." On the other hand, I'm careful about who I let in to my condo. Maybe a coffee shop? The West Coast had been downing lattes and macchiatos since the 1970's, but coffee culture was slow to migrate to Atlanta. I goggled at the first Starbucks in Atlanta when it opened on West Paces Ferry Road five years ago in 1994. Who would drink hot coffee in Atlanta in the summer? Lots of folks, apparently, as the place was packed both indoors and outside, even in July. No, not Starbucks. I didn't want anybody else listening to my theory about George's possible murder. If I was to get help from Bristol, it appeared I'd have to open the door to my sanctuary.

"Eleven o'clock. My condo. You know where it is?"

"I'll find it," he said. "I'm a detective."

* * *

Mike Bristol was right on time. I had hesitated about offering some nibbles, thinking it might seem too much like a social get-together instead of a business meeting. In the end, I put out some chocolate chip cookies, mainly because by eleven o'clock I'm usually hungry. Like the Southern hostess my mother trained, I offered him coffee. While I hovered over the pot, he prowled the living room, looking into my bookshelves and at the posters and photos of historic Atlanta that I'd hung on the walls.

"Neat," he said.

"Thanks. I love those shots of the old Atlanta Crackers stadium."

"No. I meant, this place is awfully neat. You don't strike me as a neatnik."

I wasn't sure whether to be insulted or not. I brushed his comment aside with what I thought to be humor. "You should see the rest of the place."

"I look forward to it," he said.

"That was not an invitation," I said, a bit more forcefully

than I intended. I quashed any further conversation in that direction and thrust a coffee mug toward him. We sat down, mutually sipping and munching.

"I take it you learned something new while you were at Sea Island?" he asked, not wasting any further time on pre-meeting chit chat.

I had already told him about the interviews with Scot Raybourn, Tom Boxer, and Drew Littlefield, but I filled out more details for Bristol than I'd been able to convey on the telephone. I described what Flynn had learned from Chad, the bartender at Seaside. Bristol listened intently, only occasionally changing his position to cross one leg over the other.

"Sounds like the victim's so-called buddies didn't care for him much," Bristol said. "Except for Drew Littlefield."

"From what I heard, Littlefield genuinely mourns him," I said.

"Yeah, I noticed that at the funeral," said Bristol.

"And they're hiding something," I said, emphasizing the conversation between Freddie and the golfers.

Bristol hadn't taken his eyes off me during my recital. I'd wolfed down a cookie, and I wondered if I had crumbs on my face. "Sure sounds like it," he said, sounding uninterested.

I was getting aggravated. How much information did I have to dig up before I got some kind of reaction from Bristol? "We also talked to Rob Prescott. He was George's business partner."

"Who runs the company for your friend, Theo Humphries, I understand," Bristol said.

"Well, yes," I said. Bristol had done his homework, it seemed. I summarized the story Rob had told us about Cutler Mead's attempt to defraud Theo's husband.

Bristol gave me no satisfaction. He acted as if my news wasn't news at all. "It fits," he said. "We've found a few other projects where Mead suckered people into investing in his deals, only to find out they'd been had."

I was heartened that the Atlanta cops were looking into Cutler's business deals. "Surely those people might be suspects," I said."

"They seem peripheral. We've asked for alibis, but no one at the station or the DA's office is seriously considering them. They've set their sights on Mrs. Humphries, and it's hard to persuade them there might be someone else to seriously consider."

"You haven't arrested her," I said. I hugged that thought to myself for a minute. Could he be changing his mind about Theo? Maybe all these tidbits of information were wearing him down. And I hadn't told him the rest—yet.

He shrugged. "He had a lot of enemies, it seems. I'm keeping an open mind, for now. Still running down information."

"Theo didn't know about Cutler trying to defraud George until Rob Prescott told us about the polluted land."

"How can you be sure?" he asked.

"She was almost ill when she heard the story."

"So you say." Bristol scrutinized the remaining cookies, which I read as him dismissing my opinion.

"I do say," I defended myself. "I know Theo, and she wasn't faking that reaction. Did any of Cutler's victims turn him in or sue him?" I asked.

"Oddly, no. It seems like most of these guys were too embarrassed to publicly admit they'd been scammed."

I stood up from the sofa and moved around to the kitchen island, away from him but still in his view. I needed to tell Bristol my theory about George's death, but I was too nervous about Bristol's reaction to sit opposite him while I talked. "There's something else," I said. "George Humphries caught on to Cutler before the deal closed. He was planning to go to the district attorney and press charges."

Bristol's face sharpened with interest. "Why didn't he?"

"Because he dropped dead on the golf course with a gin and tonic in his hand. Cutler Mead was playing golf at the same club when it happened." I'd dropped my bombshell and I waited to see what Bristol would do.

He stood up. In no time he crossed from the living room to the other side of the island, flattening his hands on the granite and leaning across toward me. He was close enough for me to smell that spicy soap he must shower in. "You're taking quite a leap. When you use the phrase 'dropped dead,' I assume Mr. Humphries had a heart attack."

"That's what everyone thought at the time." My pulse was racing, but I wasn't sure if it was because Bristol was so close to me or because of how quickly he'd moved. He wasn't moving now. He seemed to be frozen in place. I couldn't figure out whether my information would trigger him into action.

Finally, Bristol spoke. "I can't investigate that—even if it were Atlanta PD's jurisdiction—unless Mrs. Humphries decides to exhume the body, and that might not tell us anything. Did he have a heart condition, high blood pressure? I assume the death certificate was signed with no question."

"I don't know," I said. "But it would be a perfect cover to slip something into his drink. All those overweight guys milling around, waiting to tee off, sweating in the sun, drinking."

"Do you have any actual proof—someone was around him when it happened—not just speculation?"

"I have a witness who says Cutler was there with the same kind of drink as George. She's the bartender. She remembered because that was not Cutler's usual beverage, he ordered it after he heard George order one." I waited to see what the detective would do with that bombshell.

Bristol put his hands on his hips the way he did the first time I saw him. I was beginning to guess it was a tick, a move he made when he was thinking. "That's good. Worth following up. It's probably a wild-goose chase, but I'll pull the death certificate."

"Thank you."

"Don't thank me yet. In the very unlikely event you might be onto something, you've just given your friend an even stronger motive for murdering Cutler Mead," he paused, "even if you think she didn't know about it."

Bristol's comment reminded me of my thoughts on the beach about who benefited from Cutler's death. "One other thing. Did Cutler Mead have a will?"

"Yes."

"What's in it?" I asked.

He hesitated.

"I'll see it eventually, when it's filed for probate." I crossed my fingers behind my back.

"Most of his estate goes to his wife."

That was to be expected, but it still gave his wife a juicy reason to want him dead, assuming Cutler had anything to leave. Most developers I knew of were overextended. "And the rest of the estate?"

"A few surprises. Mead left his stock in New Century Tech to Drew Littlefield. That bequest is either worthless or could be a fortune, according to our people. They provide software for that Y2K problem. And he left his Sea Island residence to Freddie Somerset with some money, probably enough to pay the taxes for a few years. He could sell it for a pretty penny." Bristol looked at me, waiting for my reaction.

"Drew I can understand—he was the only one who sincerely liked Cutler. But Freddie?" I said. "Why him?"

Bristol's answer was a shrug.

My hair had fallen into my face as I thought about what he'd told me.

Bristol leaned further across the kitchen island, his hand brushing my face as he tucked my hair behind my ear, "Suits you," Bristol said.

My heart beat sped up with his gesture. Heat radiated off him, even after almost an hour in the frigid air of my condo, and it was all I could do not to lean my cheek into his warm palm. Instead I stepped back from the granite counter, and he lowered his hand.

"Ann Audrey," he said. "Assuming your friend isn't a murderer, one of the people around Cutler Mead probably is."

"I know," I said, but I was so heartened by the hint that Bristol was considering someone other than Theo as the murderer, I brushed his warning away.

"Stay out of it from now on. You've given me good information that would have taken the police much longer to dig up. Give me some time to run down all the leads you've found. You've done enough."

"I have to go back to Sea Island in a few days," I said. "Theo needs me." That was true, but I hoped that while I was with Theo, Bristol would find the real killer and lift the weight of responsibility off my shoulders.

His mouth tightened. "Be careful. You may have stirred something—or someone—up."

I wasn't going to lie to him, but I couldn't stop now. I decided to compromise. "I'll try."

21

Lunch with Sissy

After the tension of meeting Mike Bristol, I needed some exercise, but the trail alongside the Chattahoochee River would be hot and buggy, even in running shorts. While I waffled over starting an uncomfortable run, my phone rang.

"Annie, I've got your lunch with Sissy Mead set up. Joan called her and said you were interested in buying a table at the Azalea Ball," Theo announced.

"Yeah. Great." Theo would not let me avoid this interview, despite my evasive maneuvering. It needed to be done, but interviewing Sissy Mead under the pretense of the Azalea Ball made me uneasy.

"Can you meet her tomorrow at the Swan House about 12:30?"

"I'll be there, but give me more background, so I can pretend interest," I said. "What exactly is Sissy's role in this Azalea Ball?"

"Sissy is the overall chair for the ball. There's the social side of the event—the music, the decorations, you know—and also the budget and the fund raising," Theo said.

"How much work is involved?"

"It's huge," said Theo. "Overseeing committees full of bickering socialites, all the while trolling potential benefactors. She'll be wheedling donors for cash or in-kind donations worth tens of thousands. She has to organize dozens of different groups."

"Sounds like the Atlanta Olympic Committee could have taken lessons," I said. Three years ago the city's elite had exhausted itself volunteering and sponsoring events to raise money for the Olympics in Atlanta, only to have the city's reputation tarred by petty corruption and the chaos of a bombing in downtown Olympic Park.

"You can't even imagine. The chairwoman has to manage all that while staying perfectly groomed and poised. Everyone who counts in Sissy's crowd will be watching her to see if she's up to the task in spite of her husband's murder."

The next morning I surveyed my wardrobe for something to wear to lunch. I found a silk blouse and some slacks that I hoped would pass muster. I stuck my diamond studs in my ears to add some class. Diamond studs are routine for Buckhead women, worn with jeans to the grocery store or with sweat pants to drive the carpool. Mine were very fine one-carats, given to me by my ex-husband Charlie before he became a crook.

I drove down West Paces Ferry, relishing the parade of elaborate plantings and velvety lawns in front of one mansion after another until I turned down Andrews Drive and into the Swan House driveway. A former carriage house on the backside of an Atlanta cotton broker's 1928 mansion, the restaurant was a favorite of ladies spending old money to plan society weddings or debutante balls. The dining room nestled amid vintage pink fabric wallpaper, large floral blooms tumbling from ceiling to the molded chair rail. The clamor never rose above a soft murmur, the decibel level dampened by the insulation of the ladies' decorum and the necessity of whispering the juiciest tidbits.

Carolee "Sissy" Mead was not what I expected. At the funeral I thought she was barely holding herself together. A few days later, when Flynn and I saw her at the Sea Grill restaurant, she was wound pretty tight. By now, I anticipated Cutler Mead's estranged wife would be a delicate feminine doll frazzled around the edges by her husband's murder. Instead, Sissy Mead was no-nonsense and appeared in complete command of herself. Every strand of her highlighted blond bob lay obediently in place. Her makeup was flawless, down to the lip liner matching her peach lipstick. The impeccable fit of her St. John suit clung to—but dared not squeeze—her slim figure.

One of the Swan House's ancient waiters, stooped and shuffling, served us and bowed himself away. The conversation dwindled following our consultation over the menu. Sissy ordered a small field green salad and fish. She specified unsweet tea, which she sprinkled with yellow packets of artificial sweetener retrieved from her Chanel bag. Clearly a woman who exercised self-control. I opted for the Swan's Favorite—two scoops of viscous chicken salad inside heart-shaped cones, accompanied by cheese straws and a slice of frozen fruit salad. I picked at it, took a swallow of the Swan House's tooth-jarring sweet tea, and plunged in.

"I was sorry to hear about your husband," I said.

"Thank you. It's a difficult time." She spoke in a plummy southern accent, soft and rounded, an audible indication of class, money, and education.

I murmured sympathy. "Yes. It must be hard. Were you married long?"

"Since right after college. We met at a fraternity mixer at Auburn—Thetas and KAs. As soon as he danced with me I fell for him. We started dating and fell head over heels in love. Then came the lottery—the lottery for draft numbers to go to Vietnam. That changed everything, you know?"

I knew what she meant, even though I was too young at the time to be overly concerned about it. In 1970, CBS broadcast the proceedings of the Vietnam draft lottery live from Washington to a huge television audience. Slips of paper printed with the birthdates of American men born between 1944 and 1950 had been placed inside opaque capsules in a big plexiglass jar. Dark-suited men drew out the capsules, opened them one by one, and assigned them sequentially rising numbers. The lower your birthday's number, the more likely you would be drafted and sent to Vietnam. A nation of young men and their loved ones watched in high anxiety while their futures were cast.

"Cutler's birthday was November 22," Sissy said. "His lottery number was 9 out of 366. There was no way he could get an exemption, though his family tried. Senator Isdell was a friend of the family, and even he couldn't help. So, we married right before Cutler left for the war."

"You must have been glad when he came back okay." She must have loved him, at least in the early days. Maybe they really were planning to reconcile.

"I was ecstatic at first—but that didn't last. When he returned, Cutler was different." She must have told the story many times, maybe in therapy. Her voice was flat, no longer honeyed and soothing.

I remembered Dr. Boxer's reaction when Flynn and I brought up Vietnam. "Don't you think most men who served there were changed by the experience?"

Sissy fiddled with her silverware while she considered her answer. "Of course. But Cutler never got too far away from whatever happened over there. Even on the golf course."

She'd handed me a gift with that unexpected segue. "The golf course?" I asked, pretending a polite interest in the topic.

"Golf was like going to church for him, a worship service. He played golf almost every Sunday with a bunch of boy-men who liked island life and good times. They were all Vietnam vets. He cared more about them than anything." She sounded bitter. I didn't blame her.

"Maybe he had some good memories with those guys," I said, trying to steer the conversation toward whatever might have happened to Cutler and his crew during the war.

The look she gave me was cold enough to freeze hot coffee in July. "He suffered nightmares for years after he came back. He told me he couldn't bear to talk about some of the awful things he'd seen."

Maybe Sissy didn't know the secret the men were hiding,

or perhaps she was deliberately letting me think she didn't. At any rate, thus far in the conversation Sissy's revisionist memories of Cutler weren't giving me any leads. I decided to pressure her a bit. "Maybe he was grateful to them for something he didn't want to talk about," I said. *Let's see what she does with this.* "Didn't he leave his Sea Island house to one of those guys? And some stock to another?"

She blinked in surprise at my questions. "How did you know that?"

I shrugged. "News gets around. Did those bequests surprise you?"

"Not that it's any of your business—but, yes." Not a happy surprise, I guessed, given how her grip on her fish fork had tightened till her knuckles were white. "Since you're prying into Cutler's estate, I assume you're trying to help his latest mistress, is that it?" Sissy asked.

"Theo Humphries is a friend of mine," I said.

Sissy barked a laugh. "One of my sorority sisters works for Channel 2 News. She told me that you came and rescued your friend from the scene. Still wearing her negligée when the police arrived, wasn't she?"

"It was a caftan," I said, embarrassed that she'd guessed why I was there.

"It's pathetically obvious that your friend Theo is responsible. I can't understand why the idiot police haven't already put her in jail." Sissy autopsied the bones from her fish as she spoke. From the low tenor of her voice, no one in the restaurant would think she was urging revenge on her husband's lover.

"Don't be ridiculous," I said, matching my reply to her dulcet tones and vicious remark. If necessary I could go on all night with this verbal slapfest. "Theo Humphries couldn't hurt someone she loved as much as Cutler."

Sissy's peach mouth tightened. "He was *loved*, as you call it, by a lot of women. Theo Humphries and her fake boobs was just the latest." She put down her fork and twisted the napkin in her lap between her hands.

"I've known Theo a long time, and believe me, those boobs are real," I said.

"Hmpf," Sissy said in disbelief. Her reaction was telling. No matter how long and how often Cutler had cheated, it still rankled her.

"Usually the police take a hard look at the spouse," I said, trying for an advantage. "They have to be wondering about your marriage. If your husband was cheating on you, why didn't you divorce him?"

Sissy looked away, toward the French doors barricading the dining room from the luxuriant courtyard garden. With a sigh she pulled the napkin off her lap and wadded it up, placing it next to her plate. She was silent, apparently debating whether to answer. If she left now, I would have eaten over-mayonnaised chicken salad for nothing.

"These women usually didn't last long. I'd learned to bear it, and I knew he needed me. We were good partners. I was tied to him by golden handcuffs, if you know what that means."

"Yes. I do," I said. *You didn't want to give up your expensive lifestyle.* I refused to feel sorry for her, since she was trying to shove Theo onto the bus to the Atlanta pen. I let my answer hang in the air while I reached into the sterling basket the Swan House placed on each table, choosing a banana muffin and generously buttering it.

By the time I wiped the last greasy crumb from my mouth, Sissy's napkin was neatly folded by her plate, smoothed into place under her manicured hands. She gathered her purse and began to push her chair back from the table. I stopped her with a question.

"Were you in town the day your husband died?"

"Of course. I chaired a full committee meeting for the ball."

"On a Sunday?" I opened my eyes wide, feigning disbelief.

"We're having to work twice as hard to find donors and volunteers. People are worn out with events by this time of the year. They just want to leave town for their lake house."

"How long did the meeting last?"

Sissy gave me a cold stare. "You do have some nerve. Are you asking whether I have an alibi for my husband's murder? It was your friend who was there when he died. I suggest you remember that." She flashed an ambiguous half-sneer, then stood up and walked away. "I believe I'll skip dessert."

22

Freddie Revealed

After lunch with Sissy, I felt stuffed with calories and starved of answers. I returned to my condo and the blessed pleasure of high efficiency air conditioning whose thermostat is turned down below 70. In the cool quiet of my living room I flopped on the couch and pondered. While the Atlanta police were examining Cutler's real estate deals and checking alibis, I didn't feel like I was getting any closer to figuring out who actually killed him. Sure

I'd learned something about Sissy and found out more about Cutler's smarmy business practices, maybe even uncovered his involvement in George's death, but none of that was going to clear Theo. The pressure had to be on Mike Bristol to make an arrest soon, and Theo's name would still be the first choice, unless there was something—or someone—who had caught the attention of the Atlanta PD. I hoped they were confirming alibis and doing the necessary groundwork to either widen the scope of suspects or eliminate some. We needed to give them an option other than Theo. I thought back to Sissy and her acknowledged distaste for the men who played golf with her husband. I was sure she knew something about their past with Cutler.

"Vietnam," I said out loud to myself. I did talk to myself sometime. It was a habit that had driven my ex-husband crazy, but my friends were used to it. I told myself I needed to go back to Sea Island to see if the stint in that war was the key to Cutler Mead's death. If I left now, I'd be on the coast by sunset. Here was something that I could do while Mike Bristol worked the case in Atlanta. I threw some fresh clothes in a bag and took the elevator down to the parking garage. I turned on the radio in the car to listen to the Braves playing Montreal. Hearing the game was far better than roasting in the afternoon sun at Turner Field. The game was already underway, but being baseball, slow and drawn out, I could listen along most of the way. The Braves had won their division every year since 1995, and were headed toward a fourth consecutive title. Maybe this year we'd finally overcome the curse of the team's collapse each fall in the World Series. Unfortunately Ken Millwood was pitching. I say unfortunately, not because Millwood isn't a good pitcher, but because the poor guy has the misfortune to be on a

Braves team with fellow pitchers Greg Maddux, Tom Glavine and John Smoltz. I hoped Millwood got a win today.

With the Braves securely in the lead, I drove and considered the men who'd served with Cutler. Freddie Somerset had been seen with the rest of Cutler's foursome at the Seaside bar. I guessed Freddie was still on the island, living in Cutler Mead's house, just like he'd been living in Cutler's Atlanta house when Theo and I had encountered him. Based on the conversation Flynn's bartender friend had overheard, Freddie knew what secret those guys brought home from Vietnam. I would have to convince him to tell me.

I reached the swooping Torras causeway over the marshes just as the light was dimming over the coast. Theo had pointed out Cutler's home on one of our perambulations, and I drove straight down Sea Island Drive, pulling up across the street from his address. In contrast to Theo's more modest traditional cottage, Cutler's Italianate villa was pretty much what you'd expect of a developer—over the top and an advertisement of what a modern builder could achieve, given a budget big enough. The villa sat on the corner, surrounded by a parade of chest high columns linked by curved iron fencing. The core of the house soared to the top of the mature Palmetto palms peeking from the backyard, each of the two interior stories probably 12 feet high. Under a Mediterranean red-tiled roof, numerous arched windows faced onto Sea Island Drive and continued around to the back of the house. Single story wings projected backwards from the front of the house deep into the lot. According to Theo, a pool and guest house hid in the back, behind a tabby wall and hedges. God forbid a Sea Islander didn't have a pool, despite living a couple of minutes' walk from the beach.

I figured that knocking on the front door of the villa was a waste of time. If Freddie was here, he'd most likely be in that guest house, like he'd been in the pool house in Atlanta. I turned down the side street and parked, leaving the car to cut across thick St. Augustine grass toward the back of the house and a gate leading into the yard. I hadn't been out of the air conditioning 30 seconds, when I slapped the back of my forearm and flicked off a dead mosquito. In the sultry air my hair was beginning to frizz. I paused to reach into my pocket for a scrunchy, pulling the curly strands up off my neck and trapping the mass of hair into a thick pony tail. Standing in the tall grass to feed my hair through the elastic band, I was sure I could feel chiggers jumping onto my ankles. My hair under submission—for the time being—I moved toward Cutler's back gate. The sweet smell of star jasmine clambering up a trellis floated toward me in the humid night. I approached the gate and peered over.

Maybe it was the cloying smell of the wisteria, but something held me suspended in place, unable to make myself call out or open that gate to go into the yard. On the other side of the gate, Freddie stood barefooted with his back to me. Reflected in the shimmering light from the long rectangular swimming pool, he was crouched, his hands held out in front of him with fingers bent into claws. He jumped straight up and kicked out, landing soundlessly on the pool deck. This display of effortless martial arts wasn't reassuring. The last time I'd encountered Freddie near a swimming pool, he'd made it clear that I was to stay away from him. My heart was beating in my throat at the memory and the fear that he could—or would—act on that threat. I wondered if Detective Bristol would make the connection with Freddie if my body were to be found floating in the marsh between Brunswick and the barrier islands.

Freddie straightened his pose to stand upright. He slightly

cocked his head, but remained standing with his back to me. "Who's there?" he asked.

I forced my mouth open. "It's Ann Audrey Pickering, Freddie," I said, with a sort of gasp.

"Thought so."

"How'd you know?" My curiosity overcame my paralysis, and I had to ask.

"Recognized the way you walk on the grass. Heard it that time you and Miz Humphries were at the house in Atlanta."

I recalled that when we'd left Cutler's place in Atlanta, Theo had walked away using the step stones. In my terror after the confrontation with Freddie, I'd skipped the stones and practically run through the grass to get away from him. If Freddie was trying to spook me, he was succeeding, but I had to find out what he knew. "Do you mind if I come in?"

He turned to face me and gestured me forward. I raised the catch, opening the gate and stepping cautiously into the backyard. I held my hands open and away from my body to show him I was harmless. As I grew nearer, he sniffed the air. Was he smelling me? I fought the impulse to turn and run away.

"Shampoo," he said. "Nice."

My mouth was dry from fear, but I forced myself to speak. "I need to talk to you," I said. "For Theo's sake."

"I can't help you," he said. He bent over to pick up a towel and wiped the sweat from his face.

"I had lunch with Sissy Mead today." I watched to see if her name would provoke any reaction, but he showed no interest.

"Must've been nice." He sounded bored with the subject, tossing the towel behind his neck and patting it dry.

"She told me something that got me wondering." I let that

simmer for a minute to see if he'd respond. I saw his curiosity get the better of his need to ignore me.

"You have a bad habit of wondering about things that are none of your business."

His oblique threat actually gave me courage. I was making *him* nervous, or if not nervous, at least making him defensive. There had to be a reason for his reaction. "Sissy says Cutler cared more about the men he served with in Nam than his own family. I have to wonder why."

"Who gives a shit about that stuff now? Cutler's dead. She needs to move on." He turned and started walking away. I had to stop him.

"I'm not interested in Cutler and Sissy's personal feelings," I said. "I'm trying to find out who killed him. I think the answer might lie in Vietnam."

He turned back with a wary look. "That's quite a leap."

"Maybe so, but I won't know whether it makes sense unless you talk to me."

Freddie shook his head and walked toward the outdoor furniture grouped next to the pool. He straddled one of the webbed lounge chairs and lowered himself onto the seat. At least he had settled, and it looked like he might be willing to listen. I stayed where I was and watched while he squirmed around in the chaise until he appeared to find a comfortable arrangement for his long legs.

"Okay, what d'you want to talk about?" he asked.

I gathered my courage and made my pitch. "I think something happened while you were together in that war. Something more than just being comrades in arms. Something you and Cutler and the men he played golf with know about."

He grunted. "Of course *something happened* in Nam.

Fucking shithole we couldn't get out of. Stuff we all still dream about. Same crap as every war zone."

"Did you save his life?"

"Who, Cutler? Naw," Freddie said, shaking his head at the idea. He pulled a small knife from his shorts pocket and began to clean under his fingernails.

His casual dismissal tore my theory to shreds. If Freddie hadn't saved Cutler's life, why had the man supported Freddie all of these years, even to the extent of remembering him in his will? Maybe that was the trigger that would open up Freddie. It was worth a try. "If you didn't save his life back then, why did he leave you this house in his will?" I asked.

"Shit." He lurched to stand up from the lounge chair, and leaned toward me, tightening his hand around the knife. "What're you talking about?"

I backed up and once again opened my hands to signal that I wasn't a threat. I couldn't keep my eyes off the knife he held. "You didn't know?"

"Fuck *no*, I didn't know." The veins stood out in his neck as he spoke.

"He left you this house, some stock to Drew Littlefield, but nothing to the other guys in your squad who played golf with him." I blurted it all out, hoping the information would disarm him.

He moved closer to me. Despite my intention to stand my ground, I stepped back. He was right in my face, his yellow eyes burning into mine. My heart was hammering in my chest.

He stared at me, looking for something. I forced myself to stand still in the face of his intense gaze. The sweat was trickling between my shoulder blades before he finally said, "You're telling the truth." He folded the knife and put it back into his pocket. He stepped away from me and moved toward the lounge chair.

I sighed with relief. Now that Freddie seemed more in control of himself, I wanted to see what else he knew. "Didn't someone inform you of the contents of Cutler's will?" I asked. "Usually the lawyers would have contacted the beneficiaries."

"Haven't been answering the house phone. Don't have one of those mobile things." He seemed to be considering something. "That weasel, Littlefield. He must have written that will. Why didn't he tell me?"

"I doubt that Drew wrote it," I said. "Cutler would have gotten another lawyer, if he was leaving something to Drew."

Freddie threw his hand out in a whatever gesture. I was puzzled that he was more focused on not knowing about the bequest than on the windfall Cutler had left him. "It's a generous gift," I said. "This house must be worth a lot of money."

"Fuck Cutler. He knew how I feel about this place."

"This house, you mean?" I asked, shocked at his response.

"This town, island, whatever." Freddie waved his arms to indicate. "I asked him, when we were being discharged, 'Why the hell do you want to live on an island off the Georgia coast?' I knew it'd be as hot and muggy as Vietnam. We could've gone anywhere—a cool climate, like Michigan."

"What was his answer?" I asked. What I really wanted to know was why Freddie didn't go somewhere else by himself, but I was trying to gauge Freddie's mood before asking something so personal. I didn't want to set him off again.

"It was home to him. The beach and salt water marsh. Swarming with fucking mosquitoes. I hate the damn beach," Freddie said. "Reminds me of forced R and R. Ten days to get your shit together before another push."

"But you ended up here anyway," I said, trying to strike a neutral tone and keep the story going.

"He offered me a place to stay. I was really crazy after the war. Couldn't have taken care of myself. So I came. And stayed."

I had a surge of sympathy for Freddie, and my view of Cutler softened. In this aspect at least, the man had shown some humanity. I decided to use this opening to follow up on the relationship between Cutler and the men he served with. "Sissy told me…"

"And fuck her too," he said, spitting out the words. "She knew. When she was here at the house, she *knew*. She said she was just coming to look at the furniture. That bitch!"

"I don't understand," I said as I backed away before he lost all sense of where he was. I didn't want to become the enemy in case Freddie was having a flashback to combat.

He held his hands out, fingers spread wide. "Don't you see? She's trying to pin it on me—making it look like I killed Cutler to get this fucking house."

"Now maybe you can see what Theo is feeling like," I said. I left it there, not wanting him to feel threatened. I wasn't sure how anchored in reality Freddie was, and he was too volatile for me to predict how he might react.

He glared at me. Neither of us spoke. The air was heavy and still, the only sound the buzz of mosquitos, but I was afraid to wave my hands around to brush them away, fearing that Freddie might think I was attacking him. Finally he said, "What the hell. Maybe you can help your friend and me at the same time. You better come inside. It's too damn hot out here, and the bugs are eating me alive." He waved for me to precede him around the pool. I wasn't about to argue. He seemed to be in control of himself, but he might go off again any minute.

When I turned toward the back door of the house he called out, "Not that way."

He came around me and walked toward the guest house that sat at the narrow end of the rectangular pool. I hesitated, and he said, "For god's sake. If I wanted to kill you I could've snapped your neck or cut your throat before you got to the gate. I heard you when you parked the car."

That scared me, but I straightened my spine and followed him inside. Frigid air slapped me, the full-throated hum of the air conditioner inviting me into Freddie's world. I expected walls hung with all manner of killing implements—guns, knives, maybe even a grenade perched on a bookshelf below a dirty military banner. Instead, when I stepped inside the door my mouth fell open. The room was full of animals—racoon, muskrat, possum, tiny mice and even alligator, all carved in fine lifelike detail from wood that had been polished to a sheen. On a table stood a half-finished pelican with a gaping maw.

"You're an artist," I said, "a sculptor."

His tawny eyes softened with pleasure. "Not what you thought, is it?"

"I'm amazed," I said. That was an understatement. My brain was engaged in a 180-degree turn from my previous view of Freddie.

He gestured toward the pelican. "Feathered bastard's giving me trouble. I want that right wing to be opening up and flapping, but I can't get it right."

I wandered through the room, stroking the muskrat's smooth back and the alligator's bumpy snout. "These are exquisite." The level of detail on the animals was impressive. "How long have you been carving?"

"Started in Nam. Just small pieces. Things I could carry in

my pack. It's a bad idea to smoke in the jungle. Too many folks sniffing the air. I needed to keep my hands busy. Later, when I got back, it helped me calm down."

"You did the hawk in Cutler's study." I remembered the bird in pride of place on Cutler's desk.

"You noticed that one. Yeah, that's an early piece. I could do a better one now, but Cutler wanted to keep it."

"Do you sell many of them?" I asked. I was trying to reconcile my idea of Freddie as a deadbeat with this Freddie, who could probably support himself with his art.

His face lit up, amused at my question. "You're not kidding," he said. "Folks in big houses pay well for a fancy piece of carving on the mantle. They like native critters, as real as possible—long as they aren't moving. In fact, they tell me I'm a hot item in the art market. Crazy, ain't it?" He patted the head of a cougar rendered in a pale yellow wood. "This guy's going to a gallery in Cincinnati." His gaze wandered around the room, stopping on each member of the menagerie. "All of these are sold already, and I have commissions for the next two years. They're my ticket off the island."

"Cutler knew," I said.

"Sure. He contacted some galleries, made some good connections for me. Brought people by to see stuff when they were at the house."

If Cutler didn't leave his house to Freddie as a means to support him, then why? "Why do you think he left you his house?"

"Dunno," he shrugged.

"It's about Vietnam, isn't it." That was the only explanation for Cutler's bequest. He must have felt he owed Freddie for something.

"Maybe."

"Tell me about it."

"About Nam? Fuck no. I'm done with that. Done. Done."

"Look, I think whatever happened over there may be why Cutler Mead was killed. I need to find out to help Theo. I'm begging you." I never expected to be saying this to Freddie, of all people, but if I had to lay everything on the line with this guy to save Theo, I'd do it.

"I can't. I won't. Haven't opened my mouth 'bout that crap since we shipped home."

"That's why Cutler left you this house," I said. "To reward you for keeping your mouth shut about what happened over there, even after you got yourself together." I thought out loud. "More than that. You ignored what he was doing to the rest of the squad. He had something on Scot that forced him to give Cutler shares in the company. He pressured Tommy to invest in Cutler's deals. He used some kind of pressure on Drew to make him go along."

"It wasn't my shit. Nothing I could do about it."

"But you kept quiet."

Freddie dropped into a beat-up leather club chair. He'd picked up a carving that was so small I couldn't make out what it was. He turned the piece over and over in his hands. I was certain he was thinking it over.

"I can't tell you," he said. "But I'll tell you who can."

"Who?"

"Drew Littlefield. If anybody'll spill, it's Drew."

"Thank you." I moved toward him to shake his hand. He put his own hand out palm forward like a cop stopping traffic.

"Thank me by moving your ass out of here."

23

Drew Tells

After the revelation of my evening with Freddie, it took me several days to corner Drew Little-field. Either Drew was dodging me or he was a very busy lawyer, too busy to even answer my calls. I suspected that word had gotten out that I was asking questions about Cutler's buddies, and they were circling their wagons.

But at last, after three days of leaving messages, Drew responded, offering to meet me at his home. Mike Bristol's warning sounded in my brain. Drew's office was located in a bustling complex near the Village center. Drew lived on the far end of St. Simons island in an exclusive enclave of homes, each sitting on multi-acre lots. If I met him at home, I could be agreeing to a secluded rendezvous with a murderer. On the other hand, Drew didn't scare me one tenth as much as Freddie, and I'd entered his lair and come out unscathed. I'd chance it.

While Sea Island remained the more prestigious and exclusive place to live, over the last decades, many affluent islanders had moved to newer developments on the northern end of St. Simons. Drew and Linda Littlefield's house was a modern version of old South coastal living, a combination of white frame and stucco, wrapped by a two-story porch. Dark green wooden shutters framed each of the tall windows—upstairs and down—that let light into all sides of the house. The main entrance was on the second level, approached by a mirror image double staircase that curved up from the driveway to the porch. I climbed up the stairs and rang the doorbell mounted into the molding. Drew opened the dark oak door before the chime had faded.

"Thank you so much for seeing me," I said. This was going to be a delicate interview, so I started out with an excess of Southern charm.

Drew was no slouch in the charm department himself. Clearly, his mamma had raised him right. "It's my pleasure, Ms. Pickering. I'm glad you called by." He pulled the massive door full open and gestured me inside.

The great room could have been a cover shot for *Southern Living* magazine. Deep upholstered armchairs and two sofas were set around an impressive glass cocktail table that perched atop a twisted piece of driftwood. The matching sofas of pale aqua were buried under designer cushions that echoed the fabric on the chairs. High above, a sunlight in the cathedral ceiling encouraged luxuriant ficus and rubber plants around the edges of the room.

"What a beautiful room," I said, hoping that I didn't have to sit on the sofa and risk smothering by cushion.

"My wife designed our house. She should have been a professional."

The size of the room dwarfed him, and I wondered why his wife had built a place that made her husband appear so small. Then I remembered one of my former law partners. He was a mediocre lawyer, but brilliant at getting business. He had a similar room where he entertained clients and their spouses. Theo said that Linda Littlefield was a renowned hostess on an island full of them. She probably used this impressive room to snare Drew's clients and grease his political career—a seat on the county commission and multiple terms on the zoning board.

Drew invoked another page of *Southern Living* and insisted upon serving iced tea and cheese straws. We chatted idly, until I gauged the time was right to explain why I was there. "You may have already heard, I'm trying to help Theo by looking into Mr. Mead's death."

Drew pulled his feet under him, and started to rise. I feared he would bolt, so I launched into my appeal.

"The police are investigating a lot of avenues, but since Theo was with Cutler before his death, I'm concerned about her. And I know Theo. She's not the violent type, and she cared deeply for him." The last was a blatant attempt on my part to manipulate Drew, since, of all the men I'd met thus far, he seemed the only one who mourned Cutler.

His shoulders sagged at this statement, and he sat back down. I took that as a good sign. We sat in silence for a minute, Drew twisting his hands as he thought, until he said, "All right. What do you want?"

"I think you might be able to help find Cutler's killer." I said.

"How?"

"I've just come from talking to Freddie Somerset."

"Sarge? What did he tell you?" Drew grabbed the arms of his chair and pulled himself to the edge of the seat.

"He told me that you could explain what happened in Vietnam."

Drew shook his head. "I can't," he said. "It's not really my story." He gave me a pleading look.

I ground my teeth. I was losing patience with this excuse. Drew squirmed under my stare. "Don't you want Cutler's murderer to be caught?" I asked.

"Yes," he said, his voice agonized. "He was my friend. The others are thrilled to bits that he's gone. Even his wife is happy, though she won't let on."

"Don't you owe it to your friend for the truth to come out?" Maybe that was unkind of me, seeing his obvious misery, but I couldn't let up now. I had to get him to talk.

"I do." He swallowed. "I do. But I don't know the whole story. Wasn't there for it all."

"Just tell me what you know."

He rubbed his knees and looked away. "It all started after Paul Seller was killed." He paused, gathering his thoughts. "You could never understand the conditions."

I wasn't going to pretend that I did. Now that he had gotten started, I stayed quiet to give him space to tell it.

"We were in the bush. Seemed like we'd been humping through there for weeks. We'd just passed this village, bunch of hooches—they call it a village—and on the road this kid waved like he wanted to talk.

"Paul should've known better, we weren't rookies. Kid starts running away and Paul follows him full tilt—right into a tiger pit."

All through this Drew had been staring over my head at nothing. Now he lowered his chin and looked directly at me, his eyes black, unreadable.

"Deep hole. Sharp bamboo stakes. They cover 'em with a layer of brush. Nothing to break your fall."

My stomach knotted at the gruesome picture, but I nodded I understood. He shook his head that I didn't, but kept going.

"They lower me down on a rope 'cause I'm the lightest, but when I reach Paul, stakes are sticking into him so far—all the way through him but he's alive." Drew covered his mouth with one hand, as if he were going to be sick. He put his hand back on his knee, rubbing it. "I can't move him. Every time I touch him he screams. He's bleedin' out—nothin' we can do."

"Sarge radios back, and gets orders to sit tight. Helo on the way, but we're low priority. So we sit and listen. Paul screaming and crying." Tears were standing in Drew's eyes. "Sarge manages to pass him down some ludes. Then he goes quiet. Whole time we're looking over our shoulders for Charlie—the kid would have passed the word we were there."

I swallowed hard, imagining the terror of sitting—waiting for the enemy to pick them off—unable to move away while their friend is dying in agony.

"We'd seen a lot of our guys buy the farm. We'd killed a bunch of VC. But Paul's dying pushed everybody's buttons. Sarge takes some pills and gets stoned. Not totally out of it, but just not caring that we're spread out and slacking. He's mostly all hard ass when we're out."

"Wasn't Cutler in charge?" I asked, trying to make sense of where he fit in to the story.

"He wasn't out with us." Drew shrugged. "Wasn't unusual for Freddie to run things. When Paul's gone, we manage to get some ropes under him and pull him out, then move into the village. Shoot the old men, torch the huts. Standard operating procedure for booby traps." He stopped, looking down at his feet. "It gets out of control."

I was pretending I was watching a movie, trying to put some distance between what he was saying and my brain. I wanted to put my fingers in my ears and walk away, but I had to hear the whole story. "Go on," I said.

"I can't stop them," Drew said, not hearing me. He was talking to himself now, off in his memories. "Well, I did try."

"You tried to stop them from what?" I asked, to pull Drew back to the story. I wasn't sure I wanted to hear the rest, but I forced myself to ask.

"Scotty grabs a woman from where she's hiding behind some water-buffalo cart. There's a kid with her, real young, still squalling when Scot drags the woman into one of the hooches."

"Is that S.O.P., too?" I asked, deliberately making my voice cold, to hide the revulsion I was feeling.

Drew didn't seem to notice my tone. "Sometimes. Scot had gone there before."

"So what do you do?"

"I go to find Sarge. He's at the other end of the village, talking on the radio to the chopper. I wave to get his attention, but he's looking up—looking for the helo—doesn't see me."

"From behind me I hear Tommy's voice. 'Yow. Goddamn cunt.'"

"I turn back toward the hooch. Scotty comes out the doorway and looks around."

"'Little man,' he yells at me. 'Get the fuck over here and help us fire this up.'"

"I follow him into the hut. The woman's sprawled on the

grass mat, pajamas ripped off, legs spread. Her head's at a really weird angle. 'Shit. Oh shit, Scotty,' I say. 'Shuttup!' Scotty says. 'Help me get this dump lit up.' Tommy's over in the corner. Licking the side of his hand. Blood's oozing. 'Bit me, the bitch,' Tommy says. 'Stop whining.' Scotty tells him. 'You enjoyed it. Let's zippo this and get the fuck out of here.'

"Right then I hear the chopper coming in. I back out and run toward Freddie.

"When I reach him I point at Scotty and Tom. They're piling up dried leaves and reeds to make the fire real big so there'd be nothing left. Sarge heads back across the packed dirt, stands nose to nose with Scotty. Sarge brushes him aside and peers into the hut. He wheels around and yells at me to hurry up and finish loading Paul's body on the chopper so we can get outta there. We're about ready to take off—the cargo bay's still open, waiting for the last guys to jump on—I'm in the open bay door waiting for them to board, when I see a soldier I don't recognize. Not one of our guys. The smoke prob'ly caught his attention. He pokes his head into the hooch where Scotty and Tommy are. He goes in, but the thing is, he never comes out. Scot runs out with his personal handgun drawn. Tommy follows, both bent over and running for the 'copter. By now the hut's burning like hell."

When Drew fell silent, I asked, "What happened then?"

"We flew out. Made it back to base after a bumpy ride. Next morning I went and told Cutler. He met with them and told them to keep quiet and he'd cover for them. Nothing ever came out about it, no inquiry or anything."

So the whole thing had stayed buried all these years. But Scot and Tom were still afraid of Cutler. He must have some leverage. "What proof is there?" I asked.

"Scotty took the guy's dog tags. Cutler made him hand them over."

The dog tags. Scot Raybourn must have pawed the body, maybe unbuttoned the dead man's shirt, to get to those tags and pull the chain off over the man's head. I had a sour taste in my mouth that no mouthwash would cleanse. "Why? Why would he do such a thing?"

"They took the tags so the body wouldn't be identified, even after it was burned."

"Alright, but why *keep* them?"

"I don't know. Ask Scotty."

"So all this time Cutler had those dog tags, and he was holding that over Scot Raybourn's head," I summed up.

"Not just the dog tags," Drew said. "Cutler made Scotty give him his handgun, too."

"If Scot Raybourn still had his rifle, what good did taking his handgun do?"

Drew looked up at me, squinting to make me understand. "He didn't shoot the friendly with his rifle; he shot him with his personal weapon. The army was very careful with our guys' bodies. If they found a handgun bullet, they'd document it."

"And could match it to that gun," I said. "Where're the tags and the gun now?"

"Nobody knows."

So that's what y'all have been searching for, I thought. Now it made sense.

24

Where's Theo?

I staggered, almost falling as I made my way down the stairs from the Littlefield's porch, my feet and brain numb. In the driveway I opened the car door and fell butt first into the front seat. I sat there, bent over with my elbows on my knees. I tasted bile at the back of my throat. If Drew was telling the truth, those men—prominent businessmen on the island—had murdered one of their own after raping and killing a Vietnamese woman. They had covered up those atrocities for decades. The dead man had to be one of the MIAs whose family and the Army were still looking for. Could I believe what I'd just heard? After all I had no experience in war. Drew could have told me anything about their experience in Vietnam, and I lacked the background to cross examine him.

Half in and half out of the car, I thought about it. Drew Littlefield wasn't capable of making the story up. He had kept this secret for years. He wouldn't have told me the story now if Cutler hadn't died. Was his guilt wearing him down?

"Those smug bastards," I said to the asphalt driveway. Even as my tongue formed the words, I was ashamed of myself. What a hypocrite I was. Those same men had endured hell while I'd been dating and partying. They were young, trapped fighting a war half the world away, friends dying, and knowing their own country wasn't fully committed to their efforts. Freddie was right—I had no clue. *I might have committed the same kind of atrocities if I'd been in that war.* That didn't mean I could ignore what I'd just been told, but the realization of my ignorance tempered my disgust at what I'd heard.

I didn't want to sit in Drew Littlefield's driveway any longer. I swung my legs under the steering wheel and started the car. I drove back to Theo's cottage and threw myself onto the couch in the sunroom to try and make sense of what I'd learned.

Cutler Mead hadn't participated in the Vietnam murder, but he knew about it and kept quiet. He might even have stifled any inquiry. In return for his silence, once the squad members returned stateside Cutler demanded favors—shares of Scot Raybourn's company and venture capital from Tom Boxer. No wonder Raybourn and Boxer were happy Cutler was dead. While Drew Littlefield hadn't participated in the criminal acts, according to him, he had helped Cutler by greasing the political wheels for Cutler's business schemes. I suspected some of Drew's assistance crossed the lines of legal ethics, at a minimum. Perhaps were even indictable offenses.

The curious thing was that they had all kept quiet for so long. I would have expected someone to break the silence—get fed up with Cutler's demands. He must have put the fear of God in them. It made sense that Cutler's death was the result of someone reaching the breaking point. Who, though? Scot Raybourn's company was busy with lucrative Y2K contracts. Maybe someone was interested in buying his company, and he wanted those shares he'd signed over to Cutler. Tom Boxer's dismal investments with Cutler could have Boxer on the brink of losing his veterinary clinic. What about Drew? I couldn't imagine what would cause him to kill the man he said was his best friend, but even the best of friends could have a falling out. Suppose Drew had snapped and struck Cutler. What I was seeing as grief could be regret for his own loss of control. Thinking about Drew made me sit up. Now that he had exposed the group's misdeeds, he might be in danger if the others found out he'd blabbed.

That left Freddie. Where did he fit into the decades-long blackmail? I guessed Cutler liked to keep him around to remind the others of their history. The other men seemed to accord Freddie respect, likely earned during the War. Freddie hadn't struck me as an active participant in the blackmail. He'd ignored it and benefited, with free room and board from Cutler. Living on the premises, he had plenty of opportunities to do away with Cutler in less obvious ways. On the other hand, Freddie admitted that he had been "really crazy" after they had returned. Although he had gotten his act together, I knew that PTSD could recur. He could have struck out in the midst of one of his episodes. He might not even remember what he'd done.

I sighed. "Lord, what a mess," I said out loud to the sunroom. I needed someone to talk all this through.

"Theo?" I called. When there was no answer I prowled

through the cottage and the back yard. I picked up my cell phone and called, but Theo's phone went to voicemail. Maybe Theo had gone to the spa and turned off her phone while she got a massage. Deciding to give her an hour before trying again, I went into the guest bedroom to change. I'd worn a pair of Tahari slacks and a silk blouse for my visits around Sea Island— no sense in spooking the residents. Hard thinking required jeans, tee shirt and sneakers.

When I opened the door to my room, I saw a page covered in Theo's scribble stuck to the mirror.

"A—Sissy Mead left note when I was at the spa," it read. "Gone to meet her. T." At the bottom she'd added, "P.S. At Cutler's."

That was interesting. Sissy Mead back on Sea Island. Perhaps I'd said something at our luncheon that caused her to drive here. Or had Mike Bristol done something to stir her up? Probably neither one. If she was at Cutler's house, she was probably clearing out whatever she could get her hands on. Freddie owned the house now, but Sissy could be entitled to the contents, some of which might be valuable.

I mulled it over. What on earth did Theo think would be gained by talking to Cutler's widow? Maybe Theo thought she'd get more information out of Sissy than I had. While I doubted that a chat between those two would be anything more than a hiss fest, I was glad that Theo was willing to take Sissy on. I changed into my jeans and sneakers and went back out to the sunroom.

I sat down and began to organize what we had found out. Sissy Mead, Scot Raybourn, Drew Littlefield, and Freddie all had been in Atlanta when Cutler Mead was killed. But where had Tom Boxer been at the time of the murder? We needed to check his alibi. I trusted that Detective Bristol had that covered, but I needed to ask him.

Scot Raybourn, Tom Boxer and Sissy Mead all had motives. Raybourn and Boxer—hiding what happened in Vietnam. Mrs. Mead—fed up with Cutler's philandering and maybe hoping for financial gain. If so, Cutler's will must have been a disappointment. What motive might Drew Littlefield have had? He was clearly emotionally stirred up by his friend's death, but that didn't mean Drew was innocent. Was his part in Cutler's failed development near the golf course likely to cause him problems if it became known? The Bar Association would not look fondly on Drew's role, even less if Cutler was kicking back profits to Drew. The scandal would undoubtedly ruin Drew Littlefield. Men have killed for less.

Where did Freddie Somerset fit in? He knew about Vietnam, but wasn't a participant, according to Drew, who had no reason to lie about that. Freddie seemed capable of murder—more than capable—I thought—but what did he have to gain? I was convinced he was shocked to discover Cutler's bequest of the house to him.

I tossed my pen down and put my feet up on the couch. After the emotional drain of the morning with Drew I was tired. Dragging one of the lavender-colored pashminas from the back of the couch, I closed my eyes for a nap. I would talk over everything with Theo later.

When I awoke the sun was low. I listened for the sounds of Theo rustling about the kitchen. The house remained quiet. I reached for my cell phone and called Theo's number again. No answer. I stepped across the front yard and introduced myself to the neighbor Theo called "the nosy cat lady." Maybe she'd noticed what time Theo had left. Sure enough, the neighbor said Theo had pulled out of her driveway early afternoon. She couldn't help but notice because she heard the Mercedes' tires on the pea gravel in Theo's driveway, although the neighbor couldn't exactly pinpoint the time. Theo had been gone for hours.

I returned to the cottage and searched for the note that Sissy had left for Theo. I found it crumpled in the waste basket in Theo's room. The notepaper was nondescript and the message was printed, not cursive. It read:

"Mrs. Humphries,
I'd like to sit down and talk with you. It appears we have much in common. I'll be at Cutler's house this afternoon, if you'd care to stop by and share a glass of wine.
Sissy Mead."

Who leaves a written note for someone these days? Why hadn't Sissy phoned Theo and left a message? And finally, how did we know this note was written by Sissy? The block printing could have been done by anyone. The run-of-the-mill stationery didn't look like something Sissy would use. I gave Theo's cell phone another call. No answer.

There was definitely something wrong.

25

Theo in Trouble

I got in the car and retraced my route to Cutler Mead's Sea Island home—more accurately, Freddie Somerset's home. Several nights ago, I had gone around back to find Freddie. This time, I intended to go in the front door. If Theo were still here, either she and Sissy Mead were having a mutual girls' cry over a bottle of Chardonnay or there was trouble.

Theo's car wasn't in the driveway, nor was any other vehicle in view. I parked and jogged up the three steps to the porch. The double doors were dark oak on the bottom, but rippled glass from the waist up, admitting light, but managing to obscure the house's interior. I rang the doorbell, and the sound echoed through the house. I put my nose to the wavy glass panel and tried to make out if was someone inside. I pounded on one of the glass panels, but there was no movement, and no one approached. I pressed the thumb latch on the door handle. To my surprise, it released and I pushed the door open.

"Mrs. Mead?" I called, deliberately making my voice sound friendly. "It's Ann Audrey Pickering."

There was no answer, so I slipped into the house, undecided if it was better to thunder in like the cavalry or silently, like a cat burglar. I chose the quiet way, walking softly past the foyer to stand at an open great room. Unlike the Atlanta house, where—except for Cutler's study—Mrs. Mead or her decorator had stamped a feminine, or at least a neutral tone in most of the home, this place was clearly a male domain. Two enormous leather couches faced each other under a pecky cypress beamed ceiling. The floors were more dark wood, and the walls were hung with enough leaping fish to stir the heart of a marine biologist.

I didn't want Sissy or Freddie to find me wandering around. I called out again, "Hello. Anyone home? Mrs. Mead?" The house was silent, the temperature comfortably cool, but that meant little. This time of year, most people left their thermostats set low even when they weren't at home. I moved into a casual seating area at the rear of the house. From there a series of arched windows overlooked the pool area where I'd been with Freddie a few nights ago. The room was stunning, marred only by the intrusion of what looked to be Corinthian columns between each of the arched windows. Cutler or his architect clearly didn't understand when enough was enough. To my right was a charming breakfast nook overlooking the pool. On the table was an empty wine glass and a small plate with crumbs of what looked like brownies.

"Brownies," I said out loud. "Theo's kryptonite." Only one wine glass? Theo was supposed to be meeting Sissy.

I continued into a faux French Country kitchen, its dramatic marble island surrounded by bar stools. A hum caught my attention. It wasn't the SubZero refrigerator. The sound came from behind a locked door to the garage. Through a window in the door, I could see Theo's Mercedes, its engine running. Someone was slumped behind the wheel.

I turned the door knob, but it wouldn't budge. A Hobart mixer was plugged in to the center island. I pulled the cord away from the outlet and grabbed the thing in both hands. Bending into a squat, I heaved the 50-pound mixer over my head, then swung it downward against the door. A direct hit, but the door held. My forearms were numb from the impact, but I managed another wind-up and smashed it again. The doorframe gave way.

I clambered down the steps to the garage where the big Mercedes was pumping exhaust at full throttle. Through the windshield I could see Theo behind the wheel. I pulled at the door handle, but the car was locked.

"Theo," I pounded on the window. "Wake up and open the door."

I ran to the kitchen, found the keypad to open the garage door and hit the green button. The overhead gears screamed in protest, but the garage door jerked upwards, and I bent over to run under as it rose. Once outside, I flung my purse on the ground, dumping the contents. A knot of hair ties, a handful of Sharpie pens, used Kleenex, nickels and pennies, I pawed through them with both hands. At last I found the duplicate set of Theo's car keys she'd given me.

I opened the car and shut off the engine, but moving Theo was impossible. Alert and responsive, Theo was heavy, but now she was dead weight. Tugging at her limp body, I sensed someone behind me. I turned, both hands held like claws to rake whoever stood there.

"Get out of the way," Freddie said. "Let me shift her." He leaned into the car. When I didn't move he yelled. "Move, goddammit."

I slid away from the car, dizzy from inhaling exhaust fumes and the effort of trying to haul Theo.

Freddie heaved Theo out of the car. He was clearly stronger than his lanky frame implied.

"Grab her feet."

I clamped my hands around Theo's ankles, and we carried her into the fresh air, laying her down on the driveway. Freddie pressed his fingers against Theo's neck.

"Call 911," he ordered. "She's alive."

I wasn't about to let go of my friend. "You call. There's my cell phone." I pointed to the contents of my purse scattered on the ground.

Freddie looked at me across Theo's prone figure and reached for the phone. He dialed the emergency number, demanding an ambulance, and I heard him giving the address. When he hung up, I was sitting on the driveway with Theo's head in my lap. The hot concrete burned my thighs and rear end, but I was not going to move.

"Ambulance on the way," he said.

The EMTs were quick. There are only a few roads on St. Simons' and Sea Island, but island drivers always moved their cars to the shoulder at the sound of sirens. The EMTs were on the ground with Theo in minutes, and I got out of the way to let them work.

As they lifted Theo into the ambulance, I turned to Freddie, who was watching from the edge of the driveway.

"Thank you," I said to him. I was still queasy and foggy from the exhaust. "What made you come out here?"

"Heard the garage door go up" he said. "One reason I never oil the thing. Even if I don't see the silent alarm light up, I can hear that damn door screeching and know somebody's here."

"You must've heard it go up when Theo's car was driven inside."

"Nah. I just got here." He pointed to a car parked next to the guest house. "I was dropping a piece off at the gallery."

"Which gallery?"

Clearly offended by my question, Freddie stiffened, but he answered me. "Marie Kimpton's gallery on Frederica."

I wasn't thinking straight because of the fumes, but that could be checked. If Freddie had put Theo in the garage, he wouldn't have helped me drag her out of there. Would he?

I tailgated the ambulance to the local hospital where the EMTs disappeared through the emergency entrance. I followed inside, but got only a glimpse of Theo, her face covered by a plastic mask, an EMT forcibly squeezing oxygen into her lungs as she was rolled past. I took a seat on one of the hard plastic chairs, prepared to wait all night if I had to. I was barely settled when a doctor emerged though the double doors that led to the treatment rooms. He looked around and I stood up.

"We're sending her on to Atlanta by emergency air service," he said. "The Emory hospital has the best resources for this."

"Can I go with her?"

"Are you family?"

"No. We're friends."

"Sorry. Family only."

I didn't wait to watch for the helicopter to pick up Theo. I ran to my car and headed to the interstates. I could speed on I-16 to I-75 and lessen my chances of getting pulled over. With no stops for gas or bathroom breaks, I shaved almost an hour off the usual trip to Atlanta, slipping through the strangling traffic to park in the deck at Emory.

I found my way to the floor where Theo had been admitted, only to be met by a scrum of people with clipboards and nametags. "We need to contact her next of kin," they insisted.

"I'll find them," I said.

Theo never had children of her own, but George's adult children adored her, visiting several times a year. One of his sons lived in Texas, his daughter in Wisconsin. Both would come. Theo had a brother in New York, who traveled all the time. I would track him down. In the meantime, I was here.

"I'm her best friend," I kept repeating, only to have another person wearing a shapeless pastel smock ask me the same question about next of kin.

I waited. Finally a doctor appeared from the treatment room. He paused in the hallway near me, looking at his pager. He wore his crisp white coat over a neat bow tie. His salt and pepper hair was brushed long across his forehead. I took a chance that he was senior enough to ignore the rules about family only.

"How is she?" I asked.

He looked me over. "Are you the friend who found her?"

"Yes."

"We've put her in a hyperbaric oxygen chamber. She'll be on pure oxygen in there with the air pressure two to three times higher than normal. The pressure speeds up the replacement of carbon monoxide with oxygen in her blood."

It sounded like science fiction, but I was willing to believe anything if it would help Theo.

"That will help protect her heart and brain tissue," he continued. His brown eyes were kind. I was afraid to ask, but I couldn't help myself.

"What's her prognosis?"

"According to the EMTs she was still breathing when you got to her. That's good news. She couldn't have been exposed to the carbon monoxide too long. The bad news is that she was unconscious. That usually means more severe poisoning."

"I think she may have been drugged," I said, remembering those brownie crumbs. "She might have been unconscious before the exhaust got to her."

"Uh-huh," he said. "That's not unusual in these cases. We've done blood tests to identify drugs in her system."

"What do you mean—in these cases?"

"Suicides often take something to make them drowsy before they take the final steps."

I blinked in confusion, not sure I'd heard him right. "What? Theo did not try to commit suicide." By the time I'd forced out those words, I'd moved from confusion to fury. Was this a setup to make it look like Theo had tried to kill herself?

"I'm sorry. You should probably talk to the police about this. " He turned and started to walk away.

"Wait—doctor. Is she going to be ok?"

"We'll do some tests when she wakes up."

I focused on the blue-grey squares of the linoleum hallway. "What could happen—when she wakes up?"

"We'll just have to see. There can be long-term neurological complications," he said. "Has her family been contacted?"

"I'm working on that. I'm her best friend and—well, we've been friends for a long time."

"You should go home and get some rest. She's going to need you." He reached out and patted my arm before turning away.

26

Suicide?

I sat back down on the plastic chair. A familiar figure exited the elevator at the end of the hall, greeted the doctor in passing and made his way to stand in front of me.

"What are you doing here?" I asked.

"Official business," said Detective Bristol.

"You are NOT going to arrest Theo in the hospital." I stood up to confront him.

"Take it easy. The Glynn County Sheriff's Department passed along the information about Mrs. Humphries. They knew I'd be interested."

"You had them watching her." I'd suspected that Theo and I had been under surveillance. I'd noticed more Glynn County sheriff's vehicles than usual around the island. It hadn't bothered me, in fact, I welcomed it, since I knew there was nothing for them to report—until now.

"Sort of." Without waiting for an invitation, he sat down next to the chair where I'd been a moment ago, stretching out his long legs into the hall. From where I stood, I could see more silver in his dark hair.

Oh, what the hell. I returned to my seat, and we both stared at the opposite wall.

"What kind of official business?" I asked, after he made no attempt to open a conversation.

"Glynn County wanted me to ask you about your presence at the scene when the ambulance arrived."

"What about it?" I was on high alert at the question. What was Bristol implying?

"The EMT's reported two people were with Mrs. Humphries. Freddie Somerset, who lives there, and you. There is some confusion about what happened. Glynn County wants me to ask you." Bristol's voice was low, inviting me to confide.

"Ask me what, exactly?" I knew I was being unfair, but I was tired, angry at the doctor, and frightened for Theo. I was taking all that out on him.

He sighed. "Been a long day, has it?"

"She might not make it, Mike. Even if she does…."

At my use of his first name, he turned in his chair and looked at me. After a minute, he said, "She's in the best place she could be. This hospital handles complicated cases every day."

I clamped my jaws together to keep from crying in front of him. I blinked and looked away toward the elevator. "I was there because I couldn't contact Theo. She left me a note that she'd gone to meet Sissy Mead. When she hadn't come back, I got worried and went looking for her. You can ask the next-door-neighbor."

"Glynn County can do that, if it's necessary."

"There isn't anything else I can add." I knew he was just doing his job, but I was still angry that he had sought me out in this hospital corridor to ask these questions.

"Can you throw any light on why she did it?"

"Not you, too!" Now I was furious at him—and anyone who was crazy enough to think that about Theo. I spelled it out for him. "Theo did *not* try to commit suicide. This is a setup."

He crossed his arms over his chest and appeared deep in thought. He leaned back and spoke to the fluorescent lights over our heads.

"How did she react to your idea that her husband might have been murdered?"

I was caught flatfooted. Bristol knew Flynn and I suspected Theo's husband might have been murdered, maybe by Cutler. The detective assumed that I'd shared that notion with Theo. The truth was Flynn and I had agreed to keep our theory about George's death from Theo. Our silence was a clear indication we thought she wouldn't react well to the news. Flynn and I were anticipating that Theo would go ballistic, maybe seek out some form of revenge. We had not considered for a minute that the news would cause Theo to kill herself. But people who didn't know Theo like we did—the police, for example— might believe she would, and overlook other possibilities for how she'd gotten into that garage. Under the present circumstances, I decided to sidestep Bristol's question.

"I don't know. We've mostly been talking about Freddie." I kept talking to divert Bristol from asking further questions about what Theo knew about George's death. "I interviewed Freddie Somerset, after I found out Cutler had left him the house."

"Go on."

"Freddie didn't know about Cutler's will."

"You believe him?"

"I do. He was shocked—stunned, actually—when I told him."

"Anything else?"

"A surprise. Freddie Somerset is an up and coming artist. A sculptor. He carves beautiful animals out of wood. He has commissions for the next two years."

Bristol absorbed this news a minute, before he shrugged. "Back to Mrs. Humphries. Did you see her or talk to her this morning?"

"No," My brain began to stir. I'd been so overwhelmed with Theo's condition I hadn't given enough thought to how she'd gotten in this state. "Someone left a note for Theo that purported to be from Sissy Mead, asking Theo to meet her at Cutler's house. Maybe it *was* from Sissy. But the note was on drugstore-quality paper and written in block print. I was—I am, suspicious about whether Sissy actually sent it."

"Where's this note now?" Bristol asked, his voice quickening with interest.

I reached under my chair for my purse, opening it wide and combing through the mess. "I must have left it at Theo's." What an idiot, I thought. Why didn't I toss it in my purse when I left?

"There's no evidence of anybody else having been at the scene," he said, voicing what I feared. I remembered there was only one wine glass at the table.

"It's a setup," I said again. "Why did Theo go there? If she were going to do herself in, why not stay at her own home?"

"Maybe she didn't want you to find her."

"Then why did she leave me that note?" My voice was rising along with my panic that he wouldn't believe me.

Bristol drew in his feet and dropped his elbows to his knees. "One more thing to consider. Glynn County found a note from Theo in her car."

"I didn't see any note." I thought back, but all I could remember was Theo slumped over the wheel.

"You weren't looking for it. And I'm guessing the exhaust fumes were affecting you at the time."

I sat up straight and raised my chin. "What did it say, this note?"

"'C, I'm so sorry. I miss you so much,'" Bristol said, making air quotes.

"That's all? That doesn't sound like a suicide note. She could have been apologizing for a missed date. If Theo were writing a suicide note, it'd be a dissertation of everyone she loves. Trust me." I considered what he'd said. "Is it Theo's writing?" I asked.

"Appears to be." When I didn't respond, Bristol said, "the DA thinks he can use it to show she was overcome with remorse and couldn't bear the guilt."

"What do you think?"

"I think I'm not going to arrest a woman who's unconscious and…." He stopped.

"And may not be mentally or physically able to defend herself even if she wakes up." I finished for him. "That would make the Atlanta PD look bad, wouldn't it?" It was a cheap shot, but I was furious at the whole screwed up situation, and my inability to turn him around. I glared at Bristol and stood up.

"Has it occurred to Atlanta or Glynn County's finest that someone tried to murder Theo by drugging her and leaving her locked in that garage with the car running? Maybe the same person who killed Cutler? Maybe the same person who killed George Humphries?"

Bristol took his time rising to his feet. "It has occurred to some of us. It's also occurred to us that the deaths of two men she was close to might have pushed her to harm herself." He put both hands gently on top of my shoulders and spoke softly. "You have to consider it, Ann Audrey."

"It's impossible," I said. "You don't know her the way I do. And those notes don't make sense. Pay attention. Do your job and investigate. Stop accepting the obvious."

He dropped his hands. "Okay, Okay. But stop hanging around here. You need some rest. We can talk about this later." He turned and left me watching him walk away.

* * *

When I got home, I called Flynn to update him on Theo's condition. He insisted on coming over to talk about what happened.

"I still don't get it," Flynn said. He paced up and down in my living room. "What the heck did she think she was doing going over to Cutler's house to meet Sissy by herself?"

"I don't know." I poured myself a cup of coffee, staring out the floor-to-ceiling windows toward the Georgia mountains. They were fogged with murky gray smog, just like my brain at the moment. I rubbed my forehead.

"You got a headache?" asked Flynn

"It's probably leftover from the exhaust fumes in the garage." To say nothing of what I'd been through in the last 24 hours.

"I'll get you something." Flynn disappeared down the hall, and I heard him open the medicine cabinet. He emerged with a bottle of aspirin and a glass of water.

"Thanks." I sat down and took the pills. I propped my feet up on the coffee table and put my head back against the cushions. Flynn sat across from me in the oversized club chair and matched my foot position.

"We need to decide how to play this," I said. "Bristol thinks our theory about George's death tipped Theo over the edge. I didn't tell him that we kept that from Theo because we thought it'd be too much for her."

"Um, well, Audrey—we didn't exactly keep it from her," said Flynn. He stared into his coffee mug like he was searching for a hidden exit.

I recognized a look I'd been seeing since high school. It usually presaged a confession about some illicit encounter or Flynn's worry that he was about to be outed.

"Tell me," I said.

"She figured it out," Flynn said.

"How?"

"I called her yesterday just to see how she was doing, and she asked me what you and I thought about that squabble between George and Cutler."

"Flynn, no. You did not tell her we think Cutler killed her husband," I dropped my feet to the floor and sat up.

"Didn't have to," Flynn said. "She came out and asked me if it was a possibility. I had to say, yes."

I put both hands over my eyes and flopped back against the cushions. "Oh my God."

"I'm sorry, Audrey," Flynn said.

"It's not your fault," I said. "I'm always forgetting that instinct of hers. She was bound to guess it. But it feeds right into the DA's claim that Theo was unhinged enough to kill herself."

"Where were you when she left the cottage?" Flynn asked.

"Oh, that's right. I hadn't had a chance to tell you. I spent some quality time with Drew Littlefield and heard what happened to those guys in Vietnam." I laid it out for Flynn. He was a good listener. When I'd finished with Drew's tale, I closed my eyes. I would so love to go to sleep and make this all go away.

"Whew," Flynn whistled. "That sort of widens the field of suspects for Cutler's murder. What did Detective Bristol say when you told him about that?"

I shifted with unease. "Um…I didn't tell him."

"What? Why not?"

"I wanted to talk to Theo first," I said. "Before you lecture me on hiding important evidence from the police, hear me out."

Flynn sat tight lipped, but indicated I should continue.

"I don't want to be the one to name those guys as wartime murderers. I don't have any evidence, and they're going to close ranks and deny everything."

"Didn't Drew tell you that Cutler had hard evidence?"

"Drew would believe anything Cutler told him," I said. "It's even possible the evidence doesn't exist anymore. Cutler could have been blowing smoke for years. Anything's possible at this point. Who knows?"

"I don't believe it," said Flynn. "I think it's real. Cutler hid it somewhere that no one's found yet. But even if you could find it, would it help Theo? Audrey, we have to keep asking ourselves that."

27

Ann Audrey Rethinks the Scene

The days that followed blurred together. The hospital was as pleasant as such places can aspire to be, at least in the minds of their administrators and corporate type decorators, the walls painted in soporific colors, neutral tiled floors, nursing staff slipping in and out in rotating pastel scrubs. At the end of the hall past the central nurses station was a small lounge, giving a view from our top floor over the black-topped flat roofs of the enormous medical complex, in the distance the thick green canopy that surrounds the Emory University campus. Flynn and I sat there sometimes, bringing one another cups of hospital cafeteria coffee, but mostly we took turns sitting at Theo's bedside accompanied by the constant beep of her monitors. On the phone, I discouraged George's children from coming, telling them there was nothing they could do until Theo woke up. She was in ICU, her bed a clearing in a forest of poles hung with bags. At her head, liquid dripped through tubes into her veins. At her feet more tubing filled bags with yellow swill.

We passed the time by dissecting what we had found out in the wake of Cutler's murder. I kept returning to the same point: if the key to Cutler's murder was dropped decades ago in the muck of Vietnam, why did the killer target Theo now? Did Theo know something that endangered the killer? Or was there a second murderer—one who hadn't killed Cutler, but who'd made this attempt on Theo's life? We were missing something. One evening when I was alone with Theo, I began to wonder what the Atlanta police had found out while I'd been on Sea Island. Maybe Mike Bristol would have some ideas. The more I thought about Detective Bristol, the more I wanted to see him. Maybe I just needed a dose of his self-confidence after all these days of uncertainty in the hospital. I rose and went to Theo's bedside. I wrapped my hand around hers—warm, thank goodness—and squeezed.

"I'll be back, hon," I said.

I rubbed my hands together and pinched the tips of my

ears, aching from the arctic chill that the hospital inflicted on patients and visitors. I took the elevator down to the ground level, jogging the long serpentine route from the wing housing the ICU to the visitors' parking lot to warm up, I emerged into a sweltering twilight. Within seconds my numb hands were sweating. No sense turning the thermostat to a higher temp to save on the electric bill tonight. If I did, I'd be stuck to the sheets, peeling them off my back in order to turn over.

I got in my car, cranked the AC, and turned out of the hospital lot toward downtown. I decided to go through Lullwater Drive, a beautiful old residential neighborhood, beloved by Emory profs, mostly those senior enough to afford the substantial brick houses, and solidly upper middle-class families. It was one of my favorite drives in the springtime when azalea bushes two stories high bloomed pink and lavender in the deep front yards. No McMansions, thankfully, on Lullwater. The route would cut over to Ponce de Leon, the "Ponce" part of the name given heavy emphasis when spoken by locals, a wide boulevard designed by Frederick Olmstead of New York's Central Park fame, with landscaped parks set between the lanes.

At this hour, traffic was skimpy in the direction I drove, those commuters still on the road headed the other direction, out of town. I worked my way down Ponce through some of the City's grittier blocks, past the red neon art deco sign above the 24-hour Majestic Diner (*Open 24/7 since 1929)*, and the Clermont Lounge, Atlanta's first and longest continually operating strip club. Finally the road dove under a railroad crossing and City Hall East loomed up on my left. The massive building formerly housing the Sears store and warehouse had sat unused for decades before Mayor Maynard Jackson decided to buy it and fill it with assorted City departments, including a police station that moved in in 1992. Even with the City's presence, the place was half empty and downright spooky.

I parked the car and made my way to the lobby. I had taken a chance that Mike Bristol would be in, and I was in luck. The sergeant on duty handed me a visitor's badge and waved me through steel turnstiles toward the elevators. I slumped against the Formica panels until I remembered where I was. God knows what had been rubbed off in this elevator. I straightened up as the doors opened onto a broad hallway of gray walls and darker gray carpet. Bristol stood waiting, hands in his pants pockets, his jaw clamped shut. The muscles in his jaw moved as he ground his teeth at the sight of me.

"How is Mrs. Humphries?" he said as a greeting.

"About the same, as far as I can tell," I said. "The docs say she's holding her own."

"I'm glad." He looked relieved at this report, as if he'd expected bad news.

"Thank you for that." I was oddly warmed by his interest in Theo, the policeman's mask slipping aside for a brief minute.

"What brings you here?" Bristol asked, as he led me down the broad hall, fluorescent light fixtures humming overhead. We passed offices with doors open and closed and one big open area filled with desks, occupied and empty. Despite their number, the police officers headquartered here seemed to be rattling around in the huge box of a building.

"I wanted your help," I said. "I want to go over everything about what happened—both to Cutler and the attack on Theo."

He came to an abrupt halt in front of a door marked Lt. Bristol. He'd stopped so suddenly I bumped against him.

"Sorry," I said, trying to ignore the rush of heat I felt against him.

"No harm done," he said, showing me into his office. He closed the door, shutting out the sounds of one-sided telephone calls, male jibes, and passing footsteps. Pulling a greige, once teal, chair away from a metal file cabinet to alongside his desk, he motioned for me to sit down.

I had never been so near to him in such a small space. The intimacy of the room and my anxiety over whether I could persuade him to help made me nervous. He'd barely sat down when I launched into my spiel. "The attack on Theo doesn't make sense."

"You keep calling it an attack," he countered as he settled himself behind his desk. "We don't know yet that she didn't try to commit suicide."

"Go along with me for a minute," I said. "Let's assume it was an attack."

"Okay. I'll listen—just to hear what you have to say."

I remembered Flynn's advice that withholding information from the police could bite you in the ass. Flynn's words, not mine. I had to give up some information to get Bristol on board, but I didn't want to tell him everything Drew had revealed, since I had no proof. "I think Cutler was blackmailing at least two people—Scot Raybourn and Tommy Boxer. Maybe Drew Littlefield, too."

Bristol's dark blue eyes locked onto mine, watching me like a terrier at a woodchuck hole. I couldn't look away. The Atlanta police station's AC must not be as efficient as the hospital's, because I was downright sweaty. I plunged on. "See, I've been thinking for a while that this bad thing that Cutler was holding over the head of these guys was what led to his death. But what if it wasn't?" I paused to see if he'd say anything. I was strung so tight with the effort of trying to persuade him—to say nothing of the effect on me of his intense gaze—that I was sure he could hear my nerves humming. I told myself to get it under control and went on with my argument.

"The thing is—if this bad thing had been over their heads for so long, why kill Cutler now?" I asked. "I see only two possibilities: one, something has happened recently to make them fear exposure of this bad thing, or two, it's not the motive for Cutler's murder."

Bristol finally broke eye contact with me. "It's an interesting analysis. First things first: do you have any proof of blackmail?"

"Not really," I said, "it's just something I heard." Bristol's eyes narrowed in suspicion, but I wouldn't say more. I had only Drew's tale to support my blackmail theory, and I didn't think that would hold up without the gun and dog tags Cutler had hidden.

"You could be on the wrong track entirely," Bristol said.

His tone was neutral, not dismissive, and I was encouraged that maybe we were actually considering alternatives together. I propped my elbows on my knees and put my chin in my hand. "Were there fingerprints at the crime scene?"

"Lots of prints in the house and in the study. All could be explained by frequent visitors to Cutler's home."

That made sense. I was sure that all of the golfers and Freddie had been in that study often. If it was one of them, which wasn't a certainty. "What about those coffee cups in the study?" I asked.

"You'd have thought. But prints on both of them were smudged."

I wondered how to narrow down the list of suspects. "Do you know when he was killed?" I asked.

"Not precisely, but the ME thinks it wasn't more than an

hour before Mrs. Humphries says she found him, based on liver temp."

I was unhappy with Bristol's use of the phrase 'says she found him', but I didn't want to waste time confronting him about his language. I tried another tack. "What about alibis?"

"Looking at anybody in particular?" Bristol asked as he leaned back in his chair and linked his hands behind his head.

I tried not to look at his muscled torso, the buttons on his shirt straining when he pulled his arms back. I jerked my mind back to the task at hand and answered his question. "I'm interested in all of the golfing buddies—Raybourn, Littlefield, Boxer, Freddie Somerset."

"The veterinarian, Boxer, claims he wasn't here, but he doesn't have an alibi as such. No one on the island saw him, and you and I both know he could have driven to Atlanta and done it."

So Tommy Boxer was a possibility, and Bristol was aware of it. We were making progress. "What about the other three?" I asked.

"Well, Raybourn and Littlefield say they were together the whole time. They did have a business meeting mid-day, but after that they don't have anyone to corroborate what they were doing. They're basically alibiing each other, and I'm never satisfied with that."

I remembered the report of the meeting among the golfers and Freddie at the Seaside bar, and how Scot had tongue-lashed Drew for claiming he had nothing to do with the Vietnam affair. Drew was undoubtedly cowed by Scot and would say whatever Scot wanted him to. Bristol was suspicious, and my spirits rose on Theo's behalf. "But what about Freddie?" I asked.

"He was shopping,"

I was incredulous. "Freddie? Shopping? For what, pray tell."

"Art supplies, he says. He had some receipts, but the time stamps don't clear him. Don't know what else he might have been up to. It is a big town."

"And Mrs. Mead?" I was intrigued that Bristol hadn't mentioned her. I was convinced that she was hiding something.

"She's alibied for most of the time, with some kind of committee meetings. But dozens of people came and went. It's not clear exactly when the meeting broke up. She might've been able to slip away and not be noticed. It's not airtight."

So not a single one of Cutler's so-called buddies or his estranged-or-not wife was in the clear. There had to be something out there to place one of them in Cutler's Atlanta home the afternoon he was murdered. I was running out of ideas, and the lumpy padding in the chair was killing me. I wondered if Bristol would let me look at the police files to see if there was something that we hadn't considered. I was sure those files weren't usually available to the public, but, maybe if I asked nicely. "Detective, would it be okay if I looked at the crime scene photos?"

He tapped his fingers on the arm of his chair and appeared to consider the request. "Looking for anything in particular?"

"Not really," I said, admitting the truth. "I thought I might spot something."

He studied me. His hair curled over the edge of his shirt collar. He still needed a haircut. "Are you sure you want to see them?" he said. "I know you were there, but the crime scene guys get lots of close-ups. Those kinds of shots aren't pretty."

I grimaced, but didn't want to back out now. "Warning taken."

"They're in the incident room." He dragged his long legs

out from under his desk and scooted his chair back. "I'll set you up where you can look at them."

I followed him down the hall to an unoccupied office. He turned on the lights for me and disappeared. In a few minutes he returned and dumped a red bucket file of photographs onto the desk. I waited for him to leave the room before I started through them. I didn't want Bristol to witness my reaction to those pictures. I imagined that they were gruesome, and I was right. I skipped the grisliest ones where the police photographer dwelled with ghoulish interest on the hash that had once been Cutler Mead's head. Instead, I tried to make sense of the framed pictures, leather chairs, and side tables with coffee mugs that made up his masculine study. I had tried to memorize everything, and most of it I remembered seeing when I had come to pick up Theo at the scene.

The place was a personal shrine for Cutler. All those trophies and pictures of himself and buddies engaged in golf. His religion, Sissy had called it. But someone had violated the temple. I started back through the photos, trying to sort them into piles by subject. An inclusive shot of the setting. The body in situ. Then the body close up. The picture frames. The furniture. The coffee cups on the tables. The blood-soaked rug with the body. The rug after the body was removed, revealing the bloody golf trophy. Red smears imbedded in the dimples on the golf ball that sat on top of this memento of Cutler's victory. I flipped through the photos again, from the bottom of the stack. I went back to the inclusive shot of the entire scene. What was that on the floor near the end tables? What did it remind me of that I'd seen recently?

28

Confrontation

slipped away from the empty office where Bristol had parked me with the file, and took the elevator back down to the lobby. Unclipping my visitor's badge, I handed it to the officer on the front desk and left the police station. I found my car in the lot and headed home. I was conflicted about what I'd seen, and I wasn't ready to run it by Bristol, in case it was a crazy idea. Okay, I knew it was a crazy idea, but one that I needed to rule out. The only person who could clear this up was Sissy Mead. I would need to see her, but it would be tricky. An understatement. I didn't have any idea how she'd react to what I was going to say, but something told me not to call ahead and warn her I was coming.

My jeans and tee shirt wouldn't do for a visit to Sissy, so I took some pains to dress and do my makeup. I found her home address in the phone book. She had set herself up in an exclusive condo development tucked away off one of Buckhead's main thoroughfares. The place was an architectural embodiment of all I knew about Sissy—controlled, perfectly groomed and inaccessible. An iron gate protected a drive that circled a spraying geyser. Beyond the fountain, three arched windows, two stories high, showcased a marble lobby. Just as I was trying to figure out how to get by the gate, the goddess of blind luck took pity on me. A Jaguar driven by a woman with a bouffant hairdo dyed a hard black slowed to a stop alongside the intercom. The woman was oblivious as I nosed my car to her Jag's bumper. When the gate swung open, I drafted behind and glided under the raised arm, steering to the right to park around back and out of sight of the concierge loafing behind a tall desk in the glassed-in lobby.

My hands were shaking. I sat in the car and rehearsed what I knew and what I would say, centering myself. This might be my one shot to learn the truth about Cutler's death. My questions had to crack Sissy's elegant coating of Southern charm. Hiding underneath that patina might be something downright ugly.

The concierge looked up when I entered the lobby. I told him who I was visiting and signed in. "It's 302, isn't it?" I asked.

He gave me a questioning look. In response, I peered down my nose at him. The time I'd taken to dress and do my makeup, even throwing a Hermès bag—swag hard-won after years toiling for a big law firm—over my shoulder had been worth the effort. My disguise was apparently convincing.

"Not quite, ma'am," he said. "It's 316. To the right off the elevator."

"Oh, that's right. I remember. Thank you."

I headed toward the elevator, punched the button for the third floor, and, following the concierge's instructions, turned right toward 316 as I exited. Sissy opened her door at my knock.

Her expression was blank at first. I wondered if she remembered me. Then she gave me the well-practiced socialite's smile, the welcome not making it up to her eyes, and said, "Well, Miss Pickering. This is a surprise."

She didn't invite me in. Dressed in ivory silk, pants belted at the waist with a matching sash, the long-sleeved blouse tucked in and buttoned up to the collar, she stood her ground on a busy Aubusson tapestry rug.

"I hope you don't mind my dropping by," I said, walking forward so that Sissy was obliged to retreat and allow me inside.

"No, not at all," she said, leading the way into a robin's egg blue sitting room, furnished in delicate antiques. A huge mirror in a baroque frame reflected a formal dining room behind me where an old-fashioned swing door probably led to the kitchen. I wondered if a butler would appear to ask if we wanted tea.

"Thank you." I placed my purse on the seat of a dainty chair with spindly legs, but I remained standing. I wanted to keep open my options, in case I needed to beat a hasty retreat.

"Have you come to make a donation to the Azalea Ball? All of the tables are booked, but we'd be happy to accept a check." Sissy sank gracefully onto a pillow-laden settee, managing to sit and cross her ankles in one smooth movement. I was impressed, despite myself.

"Not exactly. I wanted to say that I regret the way our lunch ended."

"There's no need to apologize."

"I made you uncomfortable," I said. "My mother told me that was something a lady never did."

She looked down at her hands, graceful in her lap, her lavish diamond wedding ring, the center stone at least 3-carats, blinking from her left ring finger. "Mine said the same."

"Mama isn't always right."

Her head came up. Sissy had feline grey eyes, the pupils circled by a dark gold ring. I was being watched by a very alert, predatory cat.

We stared at each other. I let the silence draw out before saying, "Theo Humphries is in the ICU."

"I heard." She sat back against the sofa cushions.

"I couldn't figure out at first why someone would attack Theo," I said.

"Then you have very little imagination," Sissy said. "Oh, that's right, your husband isn't around these days for Theo Humphries to toy with."

I swallowed, surprised by her direct insult, but managed to keep going. "I think you put her there."

"My goodness." Sissy's eyebrows rose. "Is that what she said?"

"She's still unconscious."

"Ah." Sissy stretched her arm along the back of the settee. "I'd say your accusation is a bit premature. Why don't you wait and see what your friend says when she wakes up—if she wakes up."

"I don't need Theo to tell me what happened." Sissy was apparently not in the least dismayed by my accusation, and her unruffled poise made me uneasy. I gauged how many steps it'd take to reach the front door in case I needed to leave in a hurry.

"I don't know what you're talking about," Sissy said, her expression complacent, even bored.

"You left that note inviting Theo over to Cutler's house on

Sea Island. Merely a hint of wanting to be friends because of your mutual love for Cutler. "

"Don't be ridiculous. I would never pretend to be that woman's friend."

"Yes, it would be ridiculous for you and me to consider that kind of détente, but Theo is different. Theo is the kindest person I know. She tears up listening to a stranger's tale of woe on an airplane. Once she came in the door, all you had to do was convince her that you were hurting over Cutler, and she'd be sympathetic."

Sissy looked up at me and tilted her head. "So you believe Mother Theo came over to comfort me, is that it?" She rolled her eyes at my suggested scenario, but she hadn't budged since I'd started my tale. "There's not one iota of proof that I was there, and I'm told that note was printed on cheap paper. Not my style," Sissy said.

I had already figured that one out. "It was cleverly done—a double bluff—printed so your handwriting wouldn't be recognized, and you could claim that someone else sent it and signed your name."

Sissy didn't argue the point further. "Oh for heaven's sake," she said, waving one hand in dismissal.

"You told her to park in the garage," I said, "probably claimed that you were expecting movers who would block the driveway. You were planning to take some of the expensive furniture and art out of the house, weren't you?"

"Why not? It's mine. No reason to leave it down on St. Simons in all that heat and humidity. Lord knows what that clod Freddie Somerset is going to do with that house, but I'm not letting him put his filthy shoes on my furniture."

I went on like she had never spoken, working out in my

mind what must have happened to Theo as I paced back and forth. "When Theo arrived, you offered her something to drink and served brownies."

"I never eat brownies. Overrated calories."

"Did you know Theo wouldn't be able to pass them up?"

Sissy smiled. It was not a nice smile. "Everyone on Sea Island knows that Theo Humphries is a chocoholic. The Cloister Bar expressly stocks those little Godiva nibbles to put on the bar when she comes in for a drink."

"You laced those brownies with something."

"No."

I was stymied at her flat denial. I was positive Theo had been drugged with something in the brownies. I thought back on the scene at the house. The saucer with crumbs. The empty wine glass.

"Rohypnol. The date rape drug. You put it in Theo's wine glass to incapacitate her. Then you told her some weepy story about how much you'd loved Cutler, and she probably told you she'd once loved him, too."

I had a vision of Theo, reaching across the table to grasp Sissy's hand in sympathy—right before Theo blacked out.

"Love. That's a pretty word for what she had with Cutler," Sissy said. She straightened her shoulders, and as I moved back and forth across the Oriental rug in front of the settee, she moved slightly to keep her body in line with mine.

"You managed to get her into her car," I said. My heart was racing as my mind pictured the scene. "She could probably still walk with your help. You started the car with the garage door closed. You washed your own wine glass and put it away before you left her there to die."

Sissy was still as cool as a cucumber. "Why would I kill that slut?"

Was she deliberately goading me to slap her? My head was buzzing. I ground my teeth, but kept going. "Theo figured it out. You murdered your husband because he was finally going to divorce you. He may even have told you he was interested in marrying Theo." There, I'd named the shame that would undo most of the women in Sissy's circle. It was one thing to overlook a husband's discreet dalliances, but being tossed aside publicly would be worse than being accused of murder.

Sissy's calm didn't ripple. "Cutler would never have divorced me," she said. "We were a team."

Sissy hadn't admitted a single fact that would tie her to an attempt on Theo's life or Cutler's death. I'd seen something in the crime scene pictures that proved she was a liar. Now I was sure there was more to it, and I was determined to force her to admit what she'd done. "You were bound to him by golden handcuffs. That's what you told me at lunch. Because of Theo those gold bracelets were slipping off your arm. You'd lose the cushy lifestyle Cutler had given you."

Sissy uncrossed her ankles, gathering her feet under her. My stomach twisted at that small movement, thinking that I'd finally gotten beneath her skin. I waited for her to spring at me, but she merely shifted her position, resettling herself before she spoke. "Oh, please. It wouldn't have been me who'd lose their cushy lifestyle if Cutler and I divorced," she said, her voice amused.

"You mean you'd have stripped him of every dime." Sissy wouldn't be the first woman to stab a philandering husband in the wallet. "What an ingrate," I said. "You've been living in luxury, thanks to Cutler. He was the brains behind a lot of successful developments that funded your designer clothes and spa days." I didn't say that his successful methods were probably criminal.

For the first time my accusations appeared to have hit home. Sissy clinched her jaw, then said, "You still don't get it."

"Enlighten me, then." There was clearly more to Sissy than I had guessed—although I wasn't sure if she had more brains or just more chutzpah than I'd expected.

"I didn't give a damn about Cutler and his floozies."

"I don't believe you," I said.

She laughed. "You disappoint me. I thought you of all people would know to look behind the façade. You should have learned that from that scam artist you married."

Naturally Sissy would have known about my disastrous marriage, but I didn't get how that fit in to what she was up to. "I was slow to catch on to my husband's activities," I said, admitting the truth.

"You suspected long before you acted. You closed your eyes to him."

What was she trying to tell me? She had acted as if she were bothered by Cutler's cheating when we had lunch together at the Swan House. Was that all an act? Or was this an act? "So what have I closed my eyes to now?" I asked.

"You underestimated me, so did everyone, and that was fine by me. That left me free to work."

"Work at what?"

"Directing Cutler. The man was an idiot. He'd be nothing without me. I had to explain the deals to him, tell him who to cultivate and how to blackmail them so that they'd cooperate."

I was stunned by her bragging, but it made sense. Theo had told me the Chair of the Azalea Ball oversaw hundreds of volunteers, numerous events, multiple moving parts that ultimately resulted in tens of thousands of dollars. The same talents could run an even more profitable criminal enterprise—all while wearing high heels and lipstick.

"You knew about what happened to the squad in Vietnam."

"Of course I did," she said. "You don't think Cutler could have kept that from me. I figured out how we could use it to force Scot and Tommy to play along. When Scot tried to renege, I told Cutler to threaten him with exposure. He gave up 25% of his company for that misbehavior."

"What about Drew?"

"Cutler wanted to keep him out of it, but I suggested to Drew that he could be an accessory to murder. All he had to do was help get some developments through the zoning commission."

I was struggling to keep up with her, now that it was all pouring out. While my brain was sorting through the criminal acts she was detailing, my spine was tingling with fear, but I had to hear it all. "If you didn't care about Cutler's philandering, why did you kill him?" I asked the million-dollar question as matter-of-factly as I could manage, trying to match her blasé recounting.

She made a moue of distaste. "Theo Humphries."

"Cutler fell in love with her," I said. So Theo was right, after all—I should have known.

"I couldn't have cared less. In fact, it was good cover. With him carrying on his affairs, everyone felt sorry for Cutler's poor wife. It kept them from paying attention to what I was doing."

"Then, why?"

"Cutler felt guilty about George Humphries. I was worried the guilt would get the best of him and he'd tell her in some post-coital snuggle." Sissy's lip curled in distaste as she said it.

"You were afraid Cutler would confess he'd killed George." I stated it back to her to make sure I understood and get her to spell out her motive. "Wouldn't that be unlikely? Why would Cutler risk losing Theo by telling her he'd murdered her husband?"

"Cutler was weak," Sissy said with disdain. "I had to explain to him how to do it, how to slip the nicotine into the gin and tonic and leave it in the golf cart for George to drink. Cutler was a blubbering fool afterwards. It took days to get him under control." Sissy delivered these details as dispassionately as a college professor explaining a well-worn theory that was beyond challenge.

I swallowed in fear. I was talking to a psychopath in her own home. Why hadn't I told Mike Bristol where I was going? "And Theo?" I asked, hoping to keep Sissy talking, while I figured out how to get away from her.

"I couldn't take a chance that Cutler would tell her something, at least enough for her to put it together. She had to go."

I was staggered by Sissy's revelation and even more staggered by her nonchalance. We could have been discussing whether the Braves would win another pennant.

"You won't get away with it," I said. "They'll know you killed Cutler."

"They don't have a shred of proof," she said, preening with satisfaction.

"You were at his house that afternoon. Must have been a shock to find out Theo Humphries was asleep in the master bedroom."

"Not a shock. I knew she would be there—a ready-made fall guy—make that fall girl." Sissy laughed. "She'll be convicted. There's no evidence I was anywhere near that house when Cutler died."

"You're wrong about that. You gave yourself away," I enjoyed saying it, letting her know she wasn't away scot free. She'd forgotten that she'd had coffee with Cutler, and even though she'd wiped those coffee cups, in her hurry she'd left empty yellow packets at the scene, visible in those pictures.

"Oh, and how did I do that, exactly?"

"At the Swan House."

She frowned, then shook her head. "I don't know what you mean—but it doesn't matter. Cutler was a fool. I needed him to front the business or I'd have gotten rid of him years ago."

She eased her arm behind the cushions on the settee. When she pulled her arm out she had a pistol in her hand. The handle of the gun seemed too big for her hand, but she managed to keep her manicured fingertip on the trigger while pointing the barrel toward me. Mesmerized by the gun, I couldn't look away from how it followed me as I shifted my weight slightly. She moved one of the pillows under her elbow for support. I watched her get comfortable while I eased myself backward from her.

"Where'd you get that?" I asked, stalling for time.

"It's Scot Raybourn's. The gun Cutler took from him in Vietnam. I knew where it was hidden."

"So that's why you were talking to Scot in the bar at Sea Island last week."

"I wanted him to understand that Cutler's death changed nothing—except who they'd be answering to. I know what Scot and the others had done." No wonder Scot and his buddies were still searching for the proof that Cutler had held over their heads.

I heard the creak of the swing door that led into the kitchen and felt a faint breeze. I'd backed into something large. A man's dark arm, its hair bleached almost white from the sun, reached around my neck until the elbow was directly under my chin. The arm's flexion pulled up the short sleeve on the knit shirt, revealing a line of white skin. Squeezed between his forearm and muscular bicep, my carotid artery stopped carrying oxygen to my brain.

Golfer's tan, I thought, before I blacked out.

29

Scot and Sissy

cot Raybourn. I recognized him through blurred eyesight. He was arguing with Sissy, the two standing in the center of the room, their voices distant, muffled by the pounding in my head as blood began to flood my brain. I was on the floor, propped up against the wall, hands and feet tied and something stuffed in my mouth. The two of them were so intent on each other they hadn't realized I was awake. I thought it was best to keep it that way, so I gave up my undignified struggles and focused on what I could make out.

"I told you to wait in the kitchen." I recognized Sissy's voice.

"And I would have, until you pulled out my gun. I've wanted to get my hands on that weapon for a long time." Scot's voice was taut with anger.

"You dropped that chokehold too soon," Sissy said, ignoring his comment. She sat down again on the couch and leaned back to look up at him. He towered over her, but she seemed to be the one in control. Maybe it had something to do with the gun in her hand.

"I knew what I was doing," Scot said. "I wanted her out of the conversation, not dead."

"Don't you understand? She can't leave here and go to the police. Choke her again, and we can decide how to get rid of her body."

"Me? Why should I do your dirty work?" he said. "I'm only here to negotiate buying back the shares of my company."

"We are negotiating."

That seemed to give him pause, but he said, "No."

"Don't be such a baby. We've got to deal with her," Sissy said. I kept my eyes closed and my mouth slack so that they wouldn't know I was awake, but I was sure my ears were waving with the effort of hearing every nuance while the two of them decided my fate.

Scot shook his head. "She's not my problem."

"She is now. She knows, Scot."

"What d'you mean?"

"She's talked to Drew. He told me. Called me right after she left him. She knows you're a rapist and a murderer."

"Drew didn't see anything. Whatever he told her was guesswork."

Sissy shrugged. "Maybe so, but the accusation will ruin you. Take care of her, and I'll forget about what you did."

"There's nothing tying me to Vietnam except that gun. Give it to me, and I'll take care of her."

"I'm not a fool. Clean this up first."

He seemed to think about it, to my great unease. He turned away from Sissy and looked towards where I sat with my chin on my chest. Apparently satisfied that I was still out of commission, or he didn't care, he turned back to her.

"What about my company? You'll still hold those shares."

"Get rid of her, and we'll talk about that."

The two of them stared at each other. Sissy tightened her fingers around the pistol grip. My mouth was dry from fear as I watched Scot decide.

"Cutler was right. You are crazy," Scot said.

"Cutler shouldn't have said that. And you shouldn't either."

"Are you threatening me? After what I just overheard?" He laughed.

Sissy rose from the settee. She had to lift her chin to look him in the eyes, but the effect was icily regal, the oversized pistol a scepter in her hand. She trained it now on Scot.

"You didn't hear anything that can be proved," she said, "and I'll deny everything." Sissy waved her free hand toward me. "She won't be here."

Scot crossed his arms over his chest and cocked his head. I had to hand it to him. He wasn't cowed by the conniving lunatic.

"You going to shoot me, too? Then you'll have two bodies to dispose of."

"I hadn't planned to shoot her, but it'll be easier to use your gun, and tell the police that you did it. Miss Pickering came here to warn me that you'd killed Cutler and I could be in danger. You shot her to stop her from telling the police."

"That's nuts."

"It's your gun. Cutler told me the Army records personal firearms. Tommy or Drew might be able to identify it. It'll be enough to start an investigation."

He took a step back. "That's what you had planned all along. Did you invite me today to set me up?"

"I always have an alternative plan, Scot." She was smug as she explained how she would frame him. "I invited you here to ensure that your fingerprints were around the condo, on the glasses of iced tea and the plates of cheese straws. You could never pass up my cheese straws."

Scot gestured toward my side of the room. "Were you expecting her, too?"

"I knew I would see her again. I could tell she wasn't going to give up." Sissy gave a soft laugh. "It was serendipity you both showed up at the same time."

For a big man, he moved fast. With his open hand he slapped her hard enough to snap her head back, while his left hand grabbed her wrist and forced the gun upwards. The blow knocked her off her feet and backwards. He held her up by her wrist and twisted the gun away before dropping her back on the sofa. She lay there stunned, and he came toward me.

"Don't do this," I tried to say, through the gag.

"Turn over."

I stayed where I was, propped against the wall.

"Turn over, dammit."

I decided that maybe it would be better to not see the gun he had trained on my skull. I rolled over, and he straddled my legs. I closed my eyes and prayed. There was a tug and my hands were free, then my feet. He nudged my hip and I rolled over on my back, opened my eyes and looked up at him.

"Tie her up with these," he said, holding out the scarves that Sissy had used on me.

I spit out my gag and hurried to comply, fearful that Sissy would rouse. I tied her hands and ankles, looping the scarves so that her wrists and feet pulled against each other if she struggled.

I sat back and looked at Scot, still holding the gun on Sissy. I wondered if he wanted to murder her for all the years she'd tortured him.

"She's a dangerous bitch," he said.

"You've been called dangerous, yourself," I said.

"I'm not the same person I was back then."

I wondered what had happened to Scot Raybourn over the years. When we'd met, I hadn't felt threatened by him. I wouldn't call him a pussycat, but he wasn't menacing, sexually or otherwise. Given my own marital history, it was obvious that men could snooker me. But Scot hadn't set off the tiniest gut alarm. Maybe he had changed. Maybe he had been out of his mind in that war. I gave myself a mental shake. I couldn't begin to guess Scot's motives or what was in his head—then or now.

He dropped his gaze. "I've done everything I could think of to make up for what happened. Diagnosed with PTSD after I broke down bawling in front of the Wall. My knees are shot from running charity races for veterans. I've travelled back there and tried to apologize to complete strangers."

He waved one hand back and forth to brush away what he'd said. "I'm better off than most guys—don't always have the nightmares." He gave a huffing exhale. "I need to be free of it." He gestured toward Sissy. "Free of her."

"Here's your chance," I said. "Help me put her away."

He shook his head as he tucked the gun into the back waistband of his khakis. "I'm leaving."

"Are you just going to walk away?" I asked.

"Yep. I've got what I wanted. I'd appreciate your not mentioning that I was here."

"But what about Sissy?"

"She can't do anything to me now." He looked down at her, tied up and drowsing against the sofa cushions.

"You can't be sure of that," I said, trying to will him to stay around.

"She's not going to squawk about my past, if she can't produce any proof. That woman only plays the sure thing."

"She's not exactly rational. She's likely to say anything," I argued.

"All you have to do is say she's a raving lunatic. They'll believe you." Scot sounded more confident than I felt.

"What should I do with her *now*?" I asked him. "How am I going to explain this situation?" Would Mike Bristol and the Atlanta cops believe I'd managed to overcome and tie-up a pistol-carrying Sissy Mead by myself?

He shrugged. "You seem like a lady who can figure out what to do next."

I mulled it over. I couldn't stop him from leaving, even if he didn't have the gun. The Northside Drive bridge over the Chattahoochee River was 10 minutes away. We'd had lots of rain this summer, and the river was raging. If Scot tossed that gun into the river, there was little hope of retrieving it, even if Sissy or I could convince the Atlanta PD to look for it. I wouldn't forget what Scot had done all those years ago, but if he was tortured by his wartime history, maybe that meant some kind of justice. And he had saved my life, despite Sissy. *Prioritize*, I told myself. Nail Sissy for killing Cutler and George. I'd started this whole thing to save Theo. That was my task. A moralist might disagree, but I was a pragmatist.

Scot was watching me. He must have seen me make up my mind.

"If you've really got something that'll tie her to Cutler's murder, call the cops," he said.

"I've got something."

"Then you don't need me," he said, as the door into the kitchen swung shut behind him.

30

Ann Audrey Explains

In the wake of Scot's departure, I sat on Sissy's elegant rug and considered how to play this. Sissy was half conscious on the couch, moaning and squirming to free herself. I debated removing her gag, thinking it might appear a bit extreme. In the end, I decided to leave it in place so I wouldn't have to listen to her in case she woke up and started spewing invective.

My energy was drained from the emotional rollercoaster I had ridden for the last hour or so, but I still had to deal with the police. I gave myself a pep talk and made my plans. A few minutes to organize things, refine my story, and then, fingers crossed, to call the police. Detective Bristol answered the phone with his usual curt greeting. "Bristol."

"Mike," I said. "It's Ann Audrey."

I had no more gotten my name out, when he roared at me, "Where the hell are you?" I was so taken aback by his verbal assault I couldn't stutter an answer before he began again. "You walk out of the station without letting me know, and I can't find you anywhere. You haven't been to the hospital to see Mrs. Humphries. Even Flynn Reynolds doesn't know where you are."

Bristol was owed an apology for my not saying goodbye after looking at his files—I'd planned to soothe his feathers with some nice Southern girl's platitudes—the kind you use to mollify your date when you've kept him waiting too long while you fuss over your hair—but instead I was thoroughly on the defensive. It galled me that he had checked up on me at the hospital. There'd been no change in Theo's condition when I'd called the nurse's station before leaving my condo, and I'd planned to go directly to the hospital after meeting Sissy. And how the dickens had Bristol gotten ahold of Flynn? More important—*why* had he done it? All of this whirled around my brain as I struggled to answer his questions. I said the first thing that popped into my head. "Did the hospital say anything about Theo?"

"No change when I called them a while ago," Bristol said. "Now—where have you been?" he asked in a tone that brooked no nonsense.

"I'm at Sissy Mead's condo in Atlanta," I answered.

I could have sworn I heard Bristol mutter, "*Jesus Christ.*"

When there was nothing further from his side of the phone, I said, "I'm calling to report an assault." There—that ought to get him off his high horse.

"Are you okay?" His voice was thick with concern.

"I'm good," I said, "but I need some police assistance here."

"Just police—not an ambulance?" He was all business now. "Who's the assault victim?"

"Sissy Mead assaulted me," I said, matching his tone, "but I'm fine. She's okay, too. I just need an officer to take her into custody for that," I paused for dramatic effect, "and for killing her husband," I ended, trying not to sound too smug.

If I expected Bristol to congratulate me, I was mighty mistaken. His voice was steady, but I thought there was a simmering undertone of anger. "Right," he said, "assault, homicide... anything else to report?"

Damn the man, he was not going to make this easy. I was glad I'd taken the time to get my story straight. I gave him the address, and added, "No sirens. This is a quiet neighborhood, no need to freak people out. Tell the concierge at the desk you're there to see Mrs. Mead." I hung up and waited, but not long. He must have used his siren to blast his way up I-75 to Buckhead and Sissy's condo because he knocked at the door in less than twelve minutes.

I opened the door to Bristol and a pair of uniformed officers. Bristol and I stared at each other while the uniforms shifted their weight from one foot to another. I confess I was glad to see him. It didn't hurt that he looked good, his jacket straining at the shoulders like usual, his shirt smoothed neatly against his flat belly. For a moment I was distracted. I pulled my mind back into line and noticed that Bristol appeared to be cataloging every wrinkle on my blouse and pants, along with the mess my hair was in. I flushed because I looked like an unmade bed. To break his gaze, I pointed toward Sissy on the couch in the living room.

Bristol took a look at my captive and whistled. "Nice job hogtieing her," he said. "Where did you learn to do that?"

"Girl Scouts," I said. "I got a merit badge in tying knots when I was in the fifth grade."

He turned to the two officers who'd followed him in and pointed to Sissy.

"One of you untie that lady and escort her to the car. Keep the air conditioning running so she's comfortable. I'll let you know what to do with her when I'm through here."

Ignoring Bristol and glaring at me, Sissy allowed herself to be released from bondage. The taller of the two officers gently pulled her to her feet and waited for her to gain her balance. She acted a bit wobbly, and as he led her from the room, she leaned against him. I couldn't tell if she was feigning a need for assistance or if she really was that unstable on her feet. I'd removed her gag before the cops arrived. She'd stopped moaning and hadn't uttered a peep since. I guessed she was considering her options, one of which was to play the frail, delicate maiden. I didn't think Bristol would buy it, but I've learned not to underestimate men's stupidity around that helpless female ploy. I'd have to make sure he understood what Sissy was really capable of before he was alone with her in an interview room.

"You stay here," Bristol commanded me. He and the other officer prowled through Sissy's condo from room to room, until they'd checked out the entire floorplan. They returned to the living room, where I sat on the spindly-legged chair and waited for the inspection to finish.

Bristol dismissed the other cop and turned his attention to me. "Tell me what happened."

He seemed to be calmer, but I was still nervous that he might not believe that I had managed to knock Sissy out. Scot had disappeared, along with the gun Sissy had threatened us with, and trying to explain his part in this would distract Bristol from Sissy. I was determined that she was going to pay for everything she had done—and tried to do—to Theo, to say nothing of Cutler and George. I decided to ease into my story. "To begin with—I owe you an apology," I said. "I should have told you what I guessed when I looked at those files, but I had to know for sure."

"So you came here first." The muscle in his jaw was jumping as he clenched his teeth on the last word.

"I didn't realize how crazy she was," I said, trying to defend myself and embed Scot's suggestion to color the cops' perception of Sissy's version of the afternoon's events. She *was* crazy, that much I was sure of. I just didn't know what she was likely to say.

Bristol kept his eyes focused on me. "You said on the phone Mrs. Mead attacked you. What caused her to attack you?"

I cleared my throat, then mentally kicked myself for that show of nerves. "I came here to ask her whether she was at Cutler's house the afternoon he was killed. She denied it at first, but then when I kept pressing, she changed her tune. She lost her temper and started for me."

Bristol stood in his signature pose, hands on his hips, as he listened. "So you slugged her and managed to overcome her. You tied her up and called us. That it? Did it occur to you that she could have *killed* you?" He leaned over me, his voice rising as he asked. I decided it was a rhetorical question I wasn't intended to answer.

"It's all in here," I said. I dug in my purse and came out with a small silvery box. I handed it over.

"A tape recorder?" The machine was dwarfed in his hand.

"You mentioned that I recorded conversations with my husband for the FBI," I said. "That's true. I couldn't wire myself up for this interview, so I put this in my purse and had it running when I came through her door."

He turned the recorder over in his hands. "Is this going to give me a reason to arrest Mrs. Mead for murder—instead of you for assault?"

It irritated me that he asked that question. "It's on the *tape*," I said, with maybe a little more emphasis than necessary. "She admitted killing her husband. It wasn't the heat of an argument. She planned it and intended to frame Theo. She knew Theo would be there."

Sissy had spewed a flood of information on the tape. Before the cops had arrived, I had stopped the recording and backed up the tape, erasing anything after the point Sissy had confessed to Cutler and George's murder. There was nothing on the tape to show that Scot Raybourn had ever been here.

Bristol strode to the front door, opened it and motioned one of the officers to him for a brief discussion. "I'm sending Mrs. Mead to the station in a black and white," he said when he returned. "You need to make a statement downtown."

"I know," I said. I wasn't looking forward to more time in a police interview room. I was wiped out, and it would be hours before I could go home. "I need to call the hospital before we go, to check on Theo."

For the first time, Bristol looked sympathetic. "Good idea. Then you can ride downtown with me," he said. "I'll get someone to bring your car." He put his arm around my shoulders, and we moved toward the front door together. "On the way, you can explain how you figured out Mrs. Mead was the murderer."

31

Manuel's Tavern

After the face-off with Sissy I had been tired, but that was nothing compared to my exhaustion after hours at the police station. Bristol was all business. Now that he had his man—or woman—he was taking no chances the collar would slip. As the tape recording of my confrontation with Sissy played, his attitude changed from official to curious to hyper-alert to angry to relieved. As far as the tape went, it supported my statement that I'd bitch-slapped

Sissy after she'd admitted to killing Cutler. With the click of the player when the recording stopped, Bristol had completely abandoned any formality toward me. To my surprise—he was a man, after all—he showed no sign of resentment or sullen disappointment that I, not he, had broken the case. Instead he treated me with some respect as my statement was written, reviewed and signed, and the tape recorder entered into evidence, the chain of custody carefully laid out and documented.

I pushed back from the grimy table and stood up. "Am I finished?" I asked.

"For now," Bristol answered.

"Thank God." I opened the door and headed toward the exit.

Just as I reached the hallway junction, Bristol grabbed my arm. "Hold on a minute," he said.

From around the corner, a stiff-mouthed police matron was coming down the hall. She had a firm grip on Sissy Mead, still in her ivory pants and blouse, now accessorized with chrome plated handcuffs. It was a nice look. To avoid them seeing me, I stepped back into an open doorway, bumping into Bristol.

"Don't you want to gloat over the perp walk?" he asked.

"No. I don't ever want to lay eyes on her again."

His chest moved against me as we watched the procession, my hair curling as he exhaled or maybe that was my imagination. He didn't let go of my arm, so I stood pressed against him until Sissy and her escort were gone from view. Finally I pulled away.

"I'm glad that's done," I said. "I need to stop by the hospital to see Theo."

"Give them a call," he said. "If there's no change in her condition, come with me. You need a drink."

I didn't argue. I used the phone in his office to call the nurse's station, and, luckily got one of the aides who told me Theo was resting comfortably, but there was no change. First thing in the morning, after I'd had a good night's sleep, I'd be at the hospital. Bristol and I took the elevator down to the police garage and found my car. He held out his hand, and I gave him the keys, grateful I didn't have to negotiate downtown Atlanta streets as tired as I was. He slid behind the wheel and pushed the seat back to accommodate his legs. He took the car out of the garage and turned east down Ponce. We didn't go far.

On the edge of a run-down neighborhood, Manuel's Tavern has been a favorite cop spot since it opened, referred to as Zone 7 by a police force with only six official zones. The patina of beer rings on the oak tables could have been carbon-dated to 1956. The place was dark and quiet, intentionally so. Manuel Maloof, a first generation Lebanese American and the bar's founder, banned live music and juke boxes in favor of conversation. By virtue of its location, you'd expect a mostly blue collar clientele. Instead, due to the owner's liberal (by Georgia standards) philosophy, the place is frequented by local and national Democratic pols—both Bill Clinton and Al Gore were here during the last election—laborers, bankers, Catholic church hierarchy, cops, journalists, and, notably, since its founding, occasional homosexual couples who were left unbothered to enjoy their beer at the bar.

We went in through the rear entrance, a narrow hall funneling us toward the long, golden oak bar, hunkered over by a half-dozen drinkers on backless stools. A collage of Atlanta and American history rivaling any museum-quality folk art was mounted behind the bar. Franklin Roosevelt and Maloof's hero, Jack Kennedy, stared out from their frames at patrons, alongside pennants from sports teams, local authors' books, black and white historical photos, and hundreds of beer cans from around the world, brought back to Maloof by customers.

Bristol swung to his right into the adjoining dining room. He nodded to a quartet of uniforms sitting over burgers at a four top and chose a table against the far wall. The foursome gave me the once over, but there were no knowing smirks, just curiosity, so I relaxed. Bristol offered me a chair beneath a faded white and blue sign reading "Atlanta Police Homicide Task Force." The special task force working the Atlanta Missing and Murdered Children cases was stationed just around the corner in the 1980's. When the unit relocated, their sign ended up at Manuel's, alongside other police memorabilia.

"What'll you have?" Bristol asked.

I had to think about it. Beer was the obvious choice, since Manuel's only started serving hard liquor in the late 70's, but I needed a spine stiffener.

"Maker's Mark. Straight up, with an ice water chaser."

"Whatever the lady wants," he said, heading to the bar to give the order.

"Kathy'll bring it," he said, reseating himself. "I'm hungry. When's the last time you ate?"

"I can't remember."

"Okay, then. Burger or dog? Or meatloaf?"

"Burger," I said. I wasn't about to mouth one of Manuel's foot longs in front of the cop audience across the room.

He dropped the inquisition, and we waited for Kathy to bring our drinks. She was a hefty fifty plus with a dirty blond pageboy and straight cut bangs that didn't hide the roadmap that was her forehead. Around her eyes, deep-set crow's feet from smiling showed she had a rich sense of humor, despite, or maybe because of, years behind Manuel's bar. Kathy gave the full wattage of her smile to Bristol and carefully set down a full pour of Johnnie Walker Black without spilling a drop.

"Honey, how's your day been?" she asked, not looking at me. I may as well have been a crumpled napkin she'd have to clear up later.

"Pretty good, Kath," he answered. "Wound up a tough one today, thanks to this lady." He pointed to me.

"That right?" she said, still ignoring me. "Well, how 'bout something to eat?"

Bristol cut his eyes in my direction, asking permission to order. I nodded him to go ahead.

"Two burgers, Kath. Everything. And fries."

"You got it," she said. "Give us a minute."

"She likes you," I said, when Kathy sashayed toward the kitchen.

"Kathy likes cops, in general. Her husband was one. Manuel hired her when Bill was killed working off-duty security. Liquor store holdup."

"That's awful."

"Yeah. She mothers everyone in the force."

I didn't think Kathy's attitude toward Bristol was particularly motherly, but I kept my mouth shut. When the food came, we both tore into it like ravenous dogs.

"I meant to thank you," I said, chewing my last French fry.

"For what?"

"For the way you handled this case. You could have put Theo in jail and refused to look any further."

"You should thank yourself, not me. You kept finding things that kept the case open—Scot Raybourn's grudge about his company, the fraud Cutler tried to pull on George Humphries, that squabble among the golfers. Most of that I might have uncovered, but it would have been easy to limit the investigation to Theo Humphries."

"Why didn't you?"

"You were so passionate about her, so convinced that she was incapable of killing anyone. That's pretty common, of course. I've had countless parents and wives who were sure their dearest could not have murdered someone. But you weren't content just to say it. You got out and turned over one rock after another. I couldn't ignore that." He gave a soft laugh. "And when you came to me with the theory that Mrs. Humphries' husband had been murdered, you were so torn up about that, I realized I wanted you to be right about your friend. You'd changed my thinking." He reached across the table and put his hand on my wrist, circling it between his thumb and index finger. I hoped he couldn't feel my pulse jumping into high gear.

"You're an unusual woman, Ann Audrey. Unpredictable."

My heart was pounding in my throat as I tried to think of what to say. "Detective…"

"Mike," he said.

"Okay—Mike," I said. "I may be a tad unusual. I've had a weird life, the last few years."

He turned my hand over and lightly massaged the base of my wrist and thumb, continuing up into the palm of my hand, all the while watching me with those navy blue eyes. When I tried to speak, my mouth was dry.

"I don't know…"

"Yes, you do," he said.

I pulled my hand away from his grasp. "I'd like to go home now."

He broke his gaze and looked down. "Are you sure?"

I felt I owed him the truth. "To be honest—no."

"Good."

When we reached my car, I hesitated. He came around me and opened the passenger side door.

"Do you want me to drive you home?" he asked. "I can get a black and white to pick me up."

"No. I can drive myself home, after we get back to the station." I didn't trust myself with him at my front door.

He nodded, and I sat down in the passenger seat. He slid behind the wheel and put the key in the ignition.

"Put your seat belt on."

I fumbled for the strap in the dark and felt him reach across me, pull the strap out and click it home. Leaning into me, he took my chin in his hand and tilted my mouth toward him. I closed my eyes and enjoyed the soft warmth of his kiss, his tongue lightly circling my lips before pushing into my mouth. I reached around his neck to wind my fingers into the hair that curled around his collar.

A yellow gleam of light spilled across the hood of the car, as the back door of Manuel's was thrown open.

"I don't give a shit what you say, man. Fifty bucks says the Falcons will take the Saints this year."

"You ain't got fifty, you pork whacker."

"Put it up. I'll get it."

"Shut the fuck up and go home. Shift starts at 6."

We broke apart as the trash talking duo moved away from the bar and toward their own cars.

"Mmmm," Bristol said. "Want to reconsider that drive home?"

"No," I said as I tried to get my breathing under control. Those few minutes had taught me he was gentle and experienced. A deadly combination, if you weren't ready for it, and I didn't think I was. Quite yet. He had stirred up feelings that had been dormant for years, ever since I'd discovered what Charlie was really like. I hadn't expected to feel that level of desire again. It was good to be wrong about that. But I wanted to have time to think this over, not just fall into bed with the first man who'd gotten my pulse racing. I wasn't like Theo, wasn't casual about sex. And Mike Bristol was obviously used to seducing, and probably, casually dropping women. That wasn't what I wanted, despite what my body was trying to tell me.

"As you wish," he said. "But this isn't ending here."

32

Rehabilitation

T he sun streamed over my shoulder into Theo's room, flashing off her glasses as she sat propped up in her bed after a long session of PT. She was alert and restless, peppering me with questions about what had happened during the many weeks before she woke up and finally left the hospital for this rehab center. The media interest had mostly died down in the interim, Sissy's fancy lawyer having negotiated a plea that would keep her locked up and avoiding a trial and the possibility of a death sentence. All fine with me, as there would be no need for any testimony on my part or any awkward questions about my role in Sissy's undoing. Flynn and I developed a schedule for visiting Theo, and together we moved her into her present location, where she'd stay until the doctors and therapists thought she could safely go back home.

The upscale red brick facility was situated in a neighborhood near Emory University. Inviting gardens and walking paths visible from the window wound through the grounds. Theo's room was crammed with accoutrements for her comfort—lush pashmina throws, framed photos and a small oriental rug under the table in the corner, safely out of foot traffic. Cards, bouquets, and plants bearing Get Well messages smothered every horizontal surface. I surveyed the offerings Theo pointed out.

"That potted azalea is from Tom Boxer," said Theo. "And look at that, from Freddie Somerset." She pointed to a palm-sized rabbit, his back leg raised in an attempt to scratch behind one long ear. Carved from beach driftwood, the faded grey and brown bunny was amazingly realistic. An elaborate floral arrangement occupied pride of place on the table next to the couch. I leaned over to read the card.

"Is this from...my Lord, these are from Scot Raybourn," I said.

"I know. Aren't they gorgeous," Theo enthused.

I made a mental note to call Scot and make it clear that it would be a good idea for him to keep Theo at arm's length. He was a handsome man, full of life and troubled by demons—just her type. I shuddered to think of the complications if she decided to direct her considerable charms in his direction. I preferred never to see Scot again, hard enough to achieve in a small coastal community and impossible if he and Theo became an item.

Flynn pushed open the door with his shoulder. He balanced three Styrofoam cups in his hands.

"If there was ever proof that I loved you two, this is it. I can't believe I'm drinking coffee from a vending machine."

Flynn placed the coffee carefully on the tray in front of Theo, then pulled a chair to the other side of her bed so that he could look across at me.

"Ugh, this is nasty," he said, taking a sip.

"It's better than the swill we drank in the hospital," I said. "Thank goodness we're out of there."

"We?" said Theo.

"Audrey might have just as well checked in and gotten her own room," said Flynn, "she was there night and day."

"I know," said Theo. "I mean, I didn't know at the time, but I do now. Thank you Annie, for staying with me. And you too, Flynn. I know you were there, too."

"It was no big deal," I said. "I'd have rather been with you than hanging out with the cops."

"Even if one of said cops is the handsome Mike Bristol?" asked Flynn. "How is Beau Blue Eyes?"

Theo sat up. "Ooo, tell."

"There's nothing to tell," I said. "The case is over. Forget about him." I was trying not to think about him myself. Since that moment of weakness in the parking lot at Manuel's Tavern, the memory of Mike Bristol's kiss popped into my mind at the most inconvenient times. He'd called me and left voicemails that I'd ignored since that episode. I hadn't heard from him in a while, and I'd been occupied attending PT sessions with Theo to keep up her spirits. Flynn's question brought the memory back in sharp focus.

To divert Theo and myself from Mike Bristol, I asked her, "Are you feeling well enough to talk about what happened to you?"

I stared a warning at Flynn as I asked the question. The two of us had so far shielded Theo from the full details of Sissy's confession, other than to let her know the police had arrested Sissy for Cutler's murder. We agreed that she was entitled to know what we had found out about Cutler and George's murder, but we had to tread carefully. The doctors had cautioned us that unnecessary stress would hinder Theo's recovery.

"I can't remember anything after driving to Cutler's," Theo said.

"Don't worry about it," said Flynn. "Just keep getting better."

"I'm trying. Dr. Sinclair says I have to continue physical therapy to strengthen my arm." Theo screwed up her face with distaste.

"That's right, you do. How're you going to pull on your panty hose with only one good hand?" Flynn said. He glanced over at me, both of us giddy with relief now that Theo was out of the woods and recovering.

Theo opened and closed her hands, spreading the fingers wide. "At least I can move everything. That's better than a few weeks ago."

"The doctors say you'll get it all back," I said. "If you do the exercises."

Theo lifted her coffee carefully with both hands, before returning to Flynn's question. "I hate having a blank place in my memory."

Flynn and I both said, "It's okay," our voices cancelling each other out. Theo didn't seem to hear us. She was talking more to herself than us.

"I think I remember a note from Sissy that said she wanted to talk. She said she'd meet me at Cutler's," Theo said.

I rushed to encourage her. "You're right. She did leave you a note. I saw it, in fact."

"I guess I should've figured something was wrong to begin with," Theo continued.

Flynn rolled his eyes at this evidence of Theo's unsuspecting nature. Before he could say something we'd regret, I shook my head to shush him.

"What made you decide to meet her?" I asked.

For a moment Theo didn't answer. With a sigh she put her coffee cup down. "Because of George. Once I guessed that he'd probably been killed..." Theo trailed off.

"You thought Sissy had done it?"

"No." Theo shook her head. "That never occurred to me. But I thought she might know something about it."

"You were right about that," I said. I summarized the whole thing to Theo.

"Oh, my God," said Theo. "Will they be able to convict her?"

"I got her confession on tape when I confronted her," I said. "Her lawyer realized that she was good and truly caught. She'll plead guilty. The interesting thing is, since she's been in custody, she won't stop talking—she wants everyone to acknowledge how clever she is. I think she confessed to me because she was sick of hiding her formidable skills behind Cutler."

"Formidable skills as a criminal mastermind, you mean?" asked Flynn.

"Well, yes." I said.

"But why did she try to kill *me*?" asked Theo.

"She was afraid Cutler would tell you the truth," I said.

Theo squirmed around in the pillows. "I thought it was because she hated me for sleeping with Cutler."

"She says not," I said.

"Hmmpf." Theo looked away and waggled her fingers.

"You should be complimented."

"How do you figure that?" Theo asked.

"Sissy was afraid that Cutler would confide in you because he'd fallen in love with you," I said.

At that, Theo sat up and leaned forward. "I told you he wasn't losing interest, didn't I?"

Flynn laughed. "Baby girl, you sure did. I'll never doubt your man-instincts again."

"Make sure you don't," Theo said. She sat back on the pillows with an air of satisfaction.

"Let's change the subject," said Flynn. "Audrey, how did you figure out it was Sissy, instead of one of the other guys? Scot Raybourn and Tom Boxer both had good reason to want Cutler Mead dead."

"For a long time I thought one of them had done it, but I couldn't figure out why. There didn't seem to be any crisis that would have triggered their killing him after all this time. There's no evidence he was threatening to go public with what they'd done," I said.

"What had they done?" Theo asked.

I shot Flynn a look of appeal. We hadn't had an opportunity to share the tale of what had happened in Vietnam with Theo, what with her disappearance and then her loss of consciousness. It didn't seem like a good idea now. This visit was meant to cheer Theo up, not make her miserable.

"Just more of the same stuff," Flynn said, stomping firmly on my slipup.

"Oh, that," Theo said. "And don't forget, it was Sissy who pointed to them in the first place. She was trying to send you off on a false trail."

"Good point," said Flynn. "But, Annie, what made you think she killed him?"

"The sweetener."

"What?" Theo and Flynn said together.

For a second or two, I enjoyed their expressions. Flynn frowning and Theo's eyes stretched wide open.

"Oh, come on, Audrey. Tell," said Flynn, sounding like his sixth grade self.

"Okay, okay," I said. "When I had lunch with Sissy at the Swan House, she made a point of asking the waiter for Splenda sweetener for her tea. It comes in little yellow envelopes. The restaurant only had the pink or blue kind."

Flynn and Theo looked puzzled, so I explained, "Splenda's a new brand. It only came out in the US this year, and lots of places don't have it yet. Sissy likes it so much she carries it in her purse. I noticed empty yellow packets on the floor of the crime scene, in Cutler's Atlanta house. Theo doesn't drink coffee in the afternoon, and she told me Cutler drank his black. Sissy had to run out of there in a hurry, to get back to the committee meeting that was her alibi, and she overlooked them."

"My God," Flynn said. "You went to see a madwoman because of her sweetener addiction?"

"It was a workable theory," I said.

"Pretty circumstantial," Flynn said, giving me a critical look.

"A bit more than that," I said. "I noticed at the Swan House lunch that after Sissy used one of those little yellow envelopes, she'd fold it lengthwise and then twist it. I think it was a nervous habit. She didn't even realize she was doing it. Those twists were on the floor in Cutler's study."

Theo clapped her hands. "Great work, Annie."

"You should have called me," Flynn said. "I would have come with you."

"You're absolutely right," I said. "I'll never go to a suspected murderer's condo alone, from now on."

I swung my feet off the couch to the floor and stood up, leaning over the bed to give Theo a hug. "I'll see you tomorrow, hon."

"Bring chocolate."

Flynn followed me into the hall. When Theo's door was closed, he reached out and grabbed my arm.

"That woman could have killed you."

"I know. She wanted to. I got lucky." I had spent a lot of time thinking about that as I sat at Theo's bedside. I'd had a narrow escape, and sometimes I woke up in the middle of the night in a sweat, dreaming that Sissy had fired that gun and Scot Raybourn hadn't been there.

"What did Bristol say about this whole incident?"

I winced. "It would be an understatement to say Mike wasn't thrilled."

"Mike? He's *Mike*, now?" Flynn took a step back and raised both arms out to his side with his hands palms up.

"Don't be so dramatic. I told him he could call me Ann Audrey, and after all this, it seemed a bit formal to keep saying 'Detective Bristol.'"

"I'll give you a pass for now, but I'll be paying attention."

"You do that." If my brief experiment—one kiss didn't justify calling it anything more—with Bristol was already over, I didn't want to give Flynn any ammunition. He'd be lecturing me about my fear of relationships, and more. I didn't need that.

"You're still not telling me something," Flynn said. "Not

just about Mike Bristol. What are you going to do about what those guys did in Vietnam?"

"Nothing." I'd pretty much made that decision when I'd let Scot walk out of Sissy's condo with his gun, probably now at the bottom of the Chattahoochee River. I had some regrets—those guys had done unforgiveable things in Vietnam—but I'd nailed Cutler's and George Humphries's killer and saved Theo. That was my mission, and I'd have to live with my actions.

"Are you kidding?"

"There's no proof, Flynn. I'm through battling dragons. Theo's safe, and I'm going back to my quiet life in my nice, cool, air-conditioned condo."

"Believe that if you can—everybody in Georgia knows you solved this case. Mike Bristol even thanked you publicly for your assistance. Your days of seclusion are gone. There're people out there you could help."

We hugged each other goodbye in the lobby of the rehab center, and I went out to my parked car to drive home. Theo would be leaving this place soon, and I'd help her get settled. By then fall would be almost upon us. My favorite time of the year, less humidity giving Atlantans pure blue skies, the spread of green that I saw from my windows turning gradually into red and orange as the season spread from the north Georgia mountains down to the leafy canopy in the city. Change was coming. I was ready for it.

THANK YOU

I'm very grateful that you spent time reading about Ann Audrey and her two best friends, Theo and Flynn. The best way to introduce other readers to the Ann Audrey mysteries is through honest reader reviews. If you enjoyed this story, please leave a review. And, keep reading for a preview of the next mystery in the Ann Audrey series, *Death with Sweet Tea,* available in May 2022.

DEATH with SWEET TEA

The Second Ann Audrey Mystery

At Flynn's request, Ann Audrey looks into a family's suspicion and uncovers a murderer—but her snooping may trigger the murderer to strike again...

The four of us sat over salads and iced tea while I counted the ways Flynn could be made to pay me back for the loss of this hour and a half from my life, never to be recovered. He had prevailed upon me to have lunch with his so-called aunts, really his distant cousins. The ladies advertised the worst of every stereotype of Southern women, incessant chatting, raucous hoots of laughter, frequent shrieks of denial—"He didn't really say that!"—all warbled in an ear-quivering south Georgia accent. I opened my eyes wide and raised both eyebrows at Flynn to signal my torture.

"They're nervous," Flynn whispered, pretending to pick some lint from my cardigan to disguise why he was leaning so close to my ear.

"How can you tell?" I said. Like him, I kept my voice to a murmur so that the sisters couldn't hear what I was saying.

Maribelle, the older sister, was lean, her dry complexion a labyrinth of wrinkles, eyes deeply set and tired with the kind of weariness that a long-time illness causes. Her thin grey hair was cut in a neat pageboy. The younger sister, Druyce, was plump, hair professionally colored a golden blonde that emphasized her bright pink lipstick, ever so slightly bleeding outside her lip line.

"We shouldn't keep telling family tales in public," said Maribelle.

"I don't know why," said Druyce. "Flynn's family, isn't he?"

"Second cousin, I think," said Flynn. "On Momma's side."

"That's right," nodded Maribelle, with authority. "But let's not bore Ann Audrey. She's wondering why you dragged her to lunch with a couple of old ladies."

"No, no," I said, as etiquette demanded. "It isn't every day that I get treated to lunch at my favorite restaurant. I'm happy to enjoy the food and the company." The rhythm of this get-together was familiar. I had sat through many such meetings when I practiced law, waiting out the new client until they could bring themselves to talk about the real reason for the consultation. While I waited, I enjoyed the view.

We sat in Canoe Restaurant's lower room, where a wall of windows exposes a lawn sloping down to the western bank of the Chattahoochee River. At this time of year, the brilliant azaleas and forsythia were dormant, but pervasive English ivy and holly bushes kept the view green and lush. Beyond the foliage, the river was running high. If the rain continued, the yard and Canoe's patio might be under water, and not for the first time. The spring inundation was one of the hazards of a riverside establishment.

I turned away from the view of the roiling water to see four light brown eyes watching me.

"We actually do have something to ask you," said Maribelle.

"Okay," I said. "Go ahead, but remember, I'm not practicing

law anymore, if that's where this is going." I was forever telling friends that I couldn't advise them on how to get their nephew out of the Atlanta jail, sue their neighbour because his dog barked at all hours, or, god forbid, help them file for divorce.

"It's not legal advice, exactly," said Druyce.

That was a mercy. Maybe this was something that required only a sympathetic ear over an extended meal. "What, then?" I asked.

Maribelle touched my arm to regain my attention. "It's about Junior," she said, and then fell silent.

"Your nephew, Richard Mendenhall, Jr.," Flynn prompted her.

"Yes."

"And his father, Richard Sr., would be your brother?" I asked, trying to clarify the family tree.

"He was, yes," said Maribelle. "Richard Senior died a long time ago, but we've called our nephew Richard, 'Junior.' so long, we just kept saying it."

I wasn't surprised they had followed that tradition. Every Southern family has its share of "Juniors," "Treys," and "Trips," nicknames borne since toddlerhood by middle-aged men whose progenitors have been in the grave for decades.

"Junior married a woman a few years ago," said Druyce with a snort. "Trash."

"Druyce," Maribelle said, her voice warning her sister to hush. "We went to the wedding. You could just tell what she was, the way she acted at the reception."

What social solecism had their nephew's bride committed? Maybe gotten drunk in front of too many Southern Baptists or danced a bit too provocatively with a man who was not the bridegroom. Maribelle was not forthcoming, and I was left speculating on what the wedding high jinks had to do with this luncheon party.

"We thought, well, you know, it was none of our business, really," Druyce said, waggling her head.

"That's right," Maribelle said. "None of our business."

The sisters sat with their hands clasped in their laps, seemingly unable to go on. I turned to Flynn for enlightenment.

"Richard Jr. passed away a few years ago," Flynn said.

"Is there a problem about his estate?" I asked. "I'm not sure how much I can help, but I could read the will and explain to you what I think it intends."

"No, no. That's not it," Maribelle said. "Flynn told us all about how you figured out who really killed that real estate developer last summer."

I had injected myself into that murder investigation only because the police thought my old friend, Theo Humphries, had killed the man with whom she was having an affair. I gave Flynn a quelling glare.

He shrugged. "Well, you did solve the case. I wasn't exaggerating."

Glancing around the restaurant to assure herself that no one was standing nearby, Druyce leaned forward and said, "We want your help. We think Junior was murdered by his wife."

I couldn't stop myself. I had to ask. "What makes you think so?"

"Because she's done it again," said Maribelle.

**_Death with Sweet Tea,_ the second
in the Ann Aubrey series, available in May 2022.**

ACKNOWLEDGEMENTS

I'm grateful to members of two writing groups with very different styles who helped me write, revise, and finish this story. Rixey Jones and Greer Tirrell, fellow Atlantans and founding members of HHWG, heard and critiqued my earliest attempts to write a mystery about Ann Audrey and her friends. The group encouraged me and pounced on my mistakes about Southern food, speech, manners, and mores. Their friendly shredding always led to a better scene. Thank y'all. A thousand miles away, my northern Michigan writers group of Aaron Stander, Peter Marabell, and Marietta Hamady were pushy, picky, and demanded a publishable manuscript. They set a regular schedule and rarely canceled, even in the direst days of a Michigan winter; the group's high standards and consistency gave me the structure that I needed. Many thanks for your gentle edits, your support, and for hanging with me to the finish line. To my editor Susanne Dunlap, who nudged me to reveal more of the inner Ann Audrey and tighten the plot, brava, and bushels of gratitude for all your hard work.

AUTHOR'S NOTE

This book takes place in the late 1990s, and some of the settings, in particular on Sea Island and St. Simons, are long gone. Readers familiar with Sea Island only after it was redeveloped in the first decade of the twenty-first century may not recognize my descriptions of the old Cloister Hotel or the casual Beach Club that sat across the street. Southern Soul didn't open until 2006. I fudged the timeline to establish it in the late 1990s, as I couldn't imagine St. Simons without that bastion of barbecue. In Atlanta, the dreary and cavernous former Sears building that once housed a division of the Atlanta Police Department is now the bustling Ponce City Market.

If you have memories of special places in Atlanta and Sea Island during the late 1990s and early aughts, I'd love to know about them, along with your comments about Ann Audrey, Theo, and Flynn. Please email me at winnie@winniesimpson.com. I look forward to hearing from you.

ABOUT THE AUTHOR

Following her mother's lead, Mississippi native Winnie Simpson was an avid murder mystery reader beginning in the third grade, starting with Nancy Drew and moving through the classics of British, American, and international crime. Winnie studied music at Duke University, later receiving an MFA in music at SUNY Buffalo, where she worked as an arts administrator before throwing it all over in order to make a decent living. After finishing law school at Emory University, she became a partner in a large firm in Atlanta, where her practice focused mainly on securities litigation. Retiring early, Winnie relocated to northern Michigan, where she lives in a renovated nineteenth-century building that served as an asylum for the state of Michigan, an address considered appropriate by her friends. For more than a decade, she has taken writing classes and participated in writing groups. She is fond of opera, hiking, cycling, and Duke basketball, most seasons. Winnie is currently working on the second book in the Ann Audrey series, *Death with Sweet Tea*. Follow her at winniesimpson.com.

CPSIA information can be obtained
at www.ICGtesting.com
Printed in the USA
FSHW020750270521
81774FS